**"STRONG AND FAST-PACED . . .
EXCELLENT!"** —*Booklist*

Dr. Evelyn Sutcliffe has a brilliant career at a
prestigious New York hospital, and so had her
best friend, Dr. Shelley Reinish. But now
Shelley is suddenly, mysteriously dead and the
authorities are labeling it suicide. Evelyn
doesn't believe them—Shelley had too much to
live for as a successful doctor/writer/wife—she
is sure Shelley was murdered! But why? Who
would want her dead? Little by little, clues
to something being nightmarishly wrong pile up,
but each point Evelyn in a different direction,
blurring the reality in a maze of dangerous
distortions and contradictions. But most chilling
of all is Evelyn's realization that a mysterious
enemy is after *her* life, too . . . closing in on
her in a terrifying game of cat and mouse . . .
wherein she, the hunter, has become the hunted
at every turn. . . .

**"Captures all the tension, frenzy and energy
of a medical emergency room in crisis."**
—*Bookazine*

**A Troll Book Club
Alternate Selection**

BLOOD RUN

A Medical Suspense Novel

by

Leah Ruth Robinson

AN ONYX BOOK

NEW AMERICAN LIBRARY

A DIVISION OF PENGUIN BOOKS USA INC.

PUBLISHER'S NOTE

NAL BOOKS ARE AVAILABLE AT QUANTITY DISCOUNTS
WHEN USED TO PROMOTE PRODUCTS OR SERVICES.
FOR INFORMATION PLEASE WRITE TO PREMIUM MARKETING DIVISION.
NEW AMERICAN LIBRARY. 1633 BROADWAY.
NEW YORK. NEW YORK 10019.

Blood Run previously appeared in an NAL Books edition published by New American Library and published simultaneously in Canada by The New American Library of Canada Limited (now Penguin Books Canada Limited).

ONYX TRADEMARK REG. U.S. PAT. OFF. AND FOREIGN COUNTRIES
REGISTERED TRADEMARK—MARCA REGISTRADA
HECHO EN DRESDEN. TN. USA

SIGNET, SIGNET CLASSIC, MENTOR, ONYX, PLUME, MERIDIAN and NAL BOOKS are published by New American Library, a division of Penguin Books USA Inc.,
1633 Broadway, New York, New York 10019

First Onyx Printing, August, 1989

1 2 3 4 5 6 7 8 9

PRINTED IN THE UNITED STATES OF AMERICA

CHAPTER

1

The phone next to the bed went off like cannon fire and blasted me out of a dead sleep. As usual, my feet hit the floor before I even got the receiver up to my ear, and my mind came up through several layers of sleep almost instantly.

"Evelyn Sutcliffe," I said.

"Yo Sutcliffe!"

I held the phone away from my ear a little. "Yeah," I sighed wearily. It was dark in the room. "What day is it?"

"It is Monday, and it is eight P.M. It is snowing like shit outside and I need you. Both Steinbergs are stuck in Queens and can't get in, and His Doctorship Hollander has just fallen on the floor and fractured his friggin' forearm. We think both the radius and ulna, but we're waiting for the X rays. You know how it is: 'My ladyship asked for, the nurse cursed in the pantry, and everything in extremity.' "

"Well, that's quainter than saying 'Situation normal, all fucked up,' " I said. I was fully awake now, although a little sluggish around the edges. I sat back down on the edge of the bed. "It's still Monday? I don't know, I was on call last night and it was a zoo . . ." I ran a hand through my hair and looked at Phil, who was beginning to stir beside me.

" 'Madam, I beseech you follow straight,' " Dr. Alex

7

McCabe intoned, dropping his voice an octave to lend it theatricality. Then, in his normal pleasant tenor, "One of the Steinbergs promises to swap with you as soon as it stops snowing. When that'll be, I don't know. However, we've had three codes since I came on at six, and with Hollander out of it, the next patient who codes is dead."

Phil was rubbing his beard up against the small of my bare back. I sighed. "All right," I said finally.

"Evelyn, I kiss you!" McCabe made a kissing sound. "You are a scholar and a gentlewoman. Hollander's in the plaster room waiting for the Hispanic ortho guy, what's-his-face."

"Hernandez."

"Right. *Wait a minute, don't throw that out!* Just a second."

I heard the phone on the other end bang against the wall. Bracing the receiver between my shoulder and ear, I turned on the light and started squinting around for my cigarettes.

"What's up?" Phil murmured, his mouth moving up my spine.

"Aah, Alex McCabe says the Steinbergs are snowed in in Queens and can't get in and Jay Hollander fractured his forearm, they think both bones."

Phil lay back on his pillow. "Ohjeez, how'd he do that?"

McCabe came back on the line. "This is a plot to drive me crazy," he said. "I've been waiting for this guy to piss all afternoon and the premed's going by with the bedpan—"

"Alex, you can tell me when I get there. How did Jay fracture his arm?"

"The snow—floor's wet. Listen, do me a favor. I haven't eaten in *days.* You got anything you can make me a real fast sandwich?"

"I dunno, I'll look. You want it with or without mold?"

"Preferably without. Don't give me any of those stranger-than-science experiments you've got going in tinfoil behind the beer bottles. *Just a second, I don't want him going to X Ray yet, he isn't blooded!* Listen, I don't think Jay had any patients when he fell down, but you should go see him when you get here in case he has to sign out to you, O.K.? See you. And thanks for the sandwich."

I heard the phone slam down at the other end. "He slipped on the floor," I told Phil.

"Who's casting him?"

"Hernandez."

"You going over?"

"Yeah, looks like it." I lit a cigarette. They could probably do without me twenty, maybe twenty-five minutes, but not more.

It used to be when I got calls like that I figured they could do without me five, maybe *ten* minutes. That was when I was a fresh-faced intern. Either fresh-faced or semihysterical or both. Nowadays I was a jaded resident, more than halfway through my second year in the emergency room. If I was in the hospital on duty when they called me, I dropped whatever I was doing and went; if I was off duty at home, I smoked a cigarette and then went.

I got off the bed and into a pair of tan corduroy Levi's and a blue Brooks Brothers button-down.

Phil was not in such a hurry to get dressed. He was standing at the window, stark naked, holding the curtain aside. He pushed the casement window open and snow and cold air gusted into the room.

"You flashing the neighbors, or what? And shut the window, it's cold."

"Will you look at this? We got a fucking blizzard here!"

"Yeah, and a psychiatrist in his birthday suit hanging out the window gawking at it. You wanna put some clothes on?" I sat back down on the bed and started to lace up my running shoes, all the while admiring Phil's body. I never got tired of looking at him. He was short and slender, with pale freckled skin from his mother's Irish ancestry and straight blond hair from his father's north Italian side.

Beyond him I could see a wall of swirling white.

"Phil, for Chrissake," I laughed. "Shut the bloody window!" I watched him affect great exasperation as he pulled the window to. "Be nice if you were here when I got back," I said before I could catch myself.

Damn. I hadn't wanted that to slip out. I finished tying both shoes, but stayed hunched over the bed, holding my breath a little.

"I don't know," he said. Loud pause.

Slowly I untied one of my shoelaces and retied it.

"I should go upstairs," he said. "Actually, I should go upstairs and call Beth."

I felt my throat close down, and I swallowed. Screw you. Screw Beth. No, let's amend that: *don't* screw Beth. Screwing Beth is the whole problem here. I had an overwhelming desire to crawl back into bed and pull the covers over my head, to sink back into sleep, down and down and down into blissful unconsciousness.

"Sure," I said, not looking at him. I got up and pulled on my white coat, took my stethoscope off the dresser, and stuffed the bell end of it into the front pocket of my Levi's. "They're five hours ahead in London, Phil. It's one o'clock in the morning there. She's probably asleep." I took a deep breath. "You always want to call Beth after we go to bed, you know that? 'I have to call Beth. I have to call Beth.' You're a goddamned psychiatrist and you have to call Beth. I have to go."

"That's not fair," Phil protested. He had his jeans on by this time, but not his shirt, and his biceps flattened as he crossed his arms over his chest.

"Yeah, well, you don't have to tell me every five minutes that you have to call Beth. You don't call her, so why do you have to tell me that you're going to call her?"

"O.K.," Phil said after another lengthy pause. I could almost hear the click of his mind as he went into his psychiatrist's mode. "O.K." was the friendly, tell-me-more byword that he used with difficult patients in the emergency room.

"Fine, Phil, it's O.K." I went into the bathroom to brush my teeth. As I jammed the brush into my mouth I examined my face in the mirror. I looked puffy-eyed from just having gotten up, and my face was gray from winter and the fatigue of too many nights on call. Terrific. I was thirty-four years old and the lines came up around my mouth and under my eyes when I didn't get enough sleep—which was a perpetual state of affairs in the medical business. I thought for the umpteenth time how much better I had looked in my previous life as lecturer in English. At twenty-six I had landed a good job teaching at an Ivy League women's college, had been respected by the faculty and students alike, and had been halfway through my doctoral dissertation when I got the godawful idea I wanted to be a doctor after all. I say "after all" because my parents had pushed me toward it from a very young age. Like many of my physician colleagues, I was the child of a doctor and a nurse, and all doctors and nurses want their kids to grow up to be doctors. Or so it seems. My parents had taken the evasive tack of repeating at every given opportunity, "No, of course we want you to choose your own profession . . . *We just want you to keep your options open.*" To keep my options open I had taken a double major in college in biology and English. And had gone on to graduate school to do Ph.D. work in English literature. Had done really well at it, in fact.

And in the middle of doing really well at it I had realized that something was missing.

I wondered briefly what kind of life I would be

leading now if I had finished my dissertation on Shakespeare, if I had become not Evelyn Sutcliffe, M.D., Resident in Emergency Medicine, but Evelyn Sutcliffe, Ph.D., Assistant Professor of English Literature. For one thing, my years as assistant professor somewhere would be coming to a close by now, and I would be looking for a job as a full professor with tenure and a chair. A chair was almost impossible to come by in my field—you had to wait for someone to die or retire. To say nothing of all the people you had to compete with for the chair. . . .

I'm tired, I thought. My mind is wandering.

I wondered where I would be ten years from now, if I would still be at University as an attending physician in emergency medicine, perhaps an associate professor at the University College of Physicians and Surgeons, or if I would pack my bags and leave New York and go to another hospital in another city.

And I wondered if I really wanted to marry Phil, which on some days I thought I wanted to do. Or if I had chosen Phil precisely because he had another lover and didn't seem particularly interested in marrying either of us, which is what I thought on other days.

On my next birthday I would turn thirty-five.

On Phil's next birthday he would turn thirty-three.

I poked at my light brown hair—recently cut short during a moment of wild inspiration. It was sticking out every which way, certainly wild and certainly *not* inspiring. My hazel eyes looked back at me with annoyance. Fine, Phil, it's *O.K.* Go call Beth. Who cares?

I rinsed my mouth and bared my teeth for inspection, catching a glimpse of my father's face in mine: my birthfather and namesake, Lieutenant Evan Farley Sutcliffe, the dashing World War II fighter-bomber pilot who had bequeathed me his strong square jaw and fine marvelous teeth. And then had run his car into a bridge support during a thunderstorm and killed himself before I was born.

He had been driving home to London the night he was killed; he and my mother, an American volunteer nurse with His Majesty's Armed Forces during World War II, had settled there after the war.

I thought about the picture of the pilot that my mother kept in the lingerie drawer of her dresser. I always thought of him as "the pilot" because that's what my mother called him whenever she talked to me about him. I also thought of him as "the pilot" because I thought of the man my mother had married shortly after my birth as my "real" father: Dr. Sandy Berman, pediatrician, who always pretended he didn't know my mother kept a picture of the pilot in the dresser drawer underneath her stockings and lace panties.

I wondered briefly, examining my teeth in the mirror, if there was a connection between the picture of the pilot under my mother's underwear and the picture of Beth on Phil's dresser. I always imagined Beth asleep—as the picture on Phil's dresser depicted her—with her honey-colored shoulder-length hair fanning out over the pillow.

Phil poked his head into the bathroom. "O.K.," he said. "I won't call her tonight, I'll call her tomorrow. Can I have a hug?"

"No." I ran some hot water in the basin.

"You're jealous."

"No shit, Sherlock."

He sat down on the edge of the bathtub and watched me throw hot water on my face. "Ev, you knew I was involved with Beth when you got involved with me."

"That's not the point."

"O.K., what is the point?"

Stop saying "O.K.," I thought. "You know what the point is. This isn't the first time we've talked about it. I'm just really sick of . . ." Sick of what? Of Beth?

Beth was in New York only four days a month; I had Phil pretty much to myself the rest of the time. Of Phil's constantly calling Beth? Of his and my constantly discussing his calling Beth? "Forget it. Just forget it. Let's talk about something else. What do you think about Shelley's book?"

"Shelley's book. O.K., what about it?"

Shelley Reinish was one of the surgical residents at the hospital. She was writing a book about surgeons and I was working on the manuscript with her as a kind of editorial consultant. Shelley didn't actually need much help with the writing; she was a good, natural writer, clear and articulate. But she did seem to need someone to *tell* her that she was a good, natural writer, clear and articulate. So that's what I did. Occasionally I made suggestions about how to iron out lumpish grammar, but mostly I just functioned as a one-woman rah-rah squad. "Well, what do you think of it? *The Wonderful World of Surgery*, by Dr. Shelley Reinish, our very own talented hotshot surgeon here at University Hospital. Soon to be a major motion picture and all that." I heard myself being sharp and reached for a towel.

"Ev, this is stupid. Let's back up a little. You're angry, ostensibly about my calling Beth, but I'm not sure that's what you're really angry about."

"Why not? Why can't I just be angry about your calling Beth? Anger is a simple human emotion, what's to analyze? Why don't we talk about how come you're so provocative all the time? How about why you have to tell me all the time you're going to call her? Do I have to know that?"

Phil got the look of a cat avoiding eye contact while he thought about that. I threw my towel over the shower-curtain rail.

"Yeah?" I demanded.

"Minor detail," he conceded.

We both laughed. I said, slowly and in my best

imitation of Phil's shrink voice, "Would you like to talk about that a bit? Why you're so provocative all the time? I think there may be something here, something we may want to take a look at."

"I'm sorry, but we'll have to finish now. The hour's up."

More laughter. I rummaged around in my makeup kit for my eye-shadow compact. After a moment Phil said, "Shelley's not really calling it *The Wonderful World of Surgery,* is she?"

"I don't know what she's calling it. Sometimes she calls it *Surgery Talks, Nobody Walks,* but I think she's kidding. Though Tony Firenze acts like that's the real title—you know he threw a pair of surgical scissors at her the other day?"

Phil stopped laughing. "When was this?"

"Well, not exactly the other day. Last Monday. A week ago." I paused in mid-stroke with my mascara wand to look at him. He was suddenly uncharacteristically still. "Why? What's the matter?"

He shook his head. "Can't tell you. Patient confidentiality."

"Oh, right." I kept forgetting that Shelley was one of Phil's patients; he was not only her colleague on rounds, he was also her psychotherapist. I went back to my mascara artistry.

"Why did Firenze throw the scissors at her?"

"He's upset because Shelley writes down everything she hears in surgery." I finished with my makeup and snapped the case shut. "Come in the kitchen with me, I have to make McCabe a sandwich. Firenze says he doesn't mind talking into a tape recorder when Shelley's doing formal interviews for the book, but he's damned if his off-the-cuff remarks in surgery are going to wind up in print." I went into the kitchen and opened the refrigerator and took out two hard-boiled eggs.

"How old are those eggs?"

"Gimme a break, I cooked them day before yesterday. I'm one step ahead of you. Look, I write the date on them. See? It says 'Sat—26.' "

"Today is the fourth."

"O.K., so I cooked them *last* Saturday. They're still good. We used to eat Easter eggs for a month after Easter when I was a kid."

"You had Easter eggs? You're Jewish."

"We did all the holidays." I busied myself making egg salad with some mayonnaise and a piece of celery.

"You didn't write the date on the celery too, did you? Never mind, I don't want to know. So Firenze doesn't want to be quoted out of context."

"Yeah, well, everybody knows Shelley has a mind like a steel trap and that she can write down a conversation verbatim. I told you about that time Attenborough and I had that discussion in surgery about life-support systems for the hopelessly ill and afterward Shelley came around to see me with a transcript of the conversation. 'Ev,' she says, 'I want to put that conversation you had with Attenborough in my book. Will you check it for accuracy, please?' Jesus Christ. Would I check it for accuracy. I looked at it and said, 'Shelley, are you wired for sound, or what?' "

"Yes, I know," Phil said dryly. "This is at least the sixth time you've told me this story, Ev. So Firenze threw the scissors . . . ?"

"That's it. Firenze was talking to Hollander in surgery, and he turned around, and there was Shelley with her *I-heard-that* look on her face, and Firenze just lost his temper. You know Firenze. He's always yelling and throwing things."

Phil scratched his beard. It was a copper-colored beard, neatly trimmed, and I liked the way its color offset the blond of his hair. "Well," he said, "I suppose we should be grateful he always throws high enough over your head he never actually hits you. Who relayed this small gem?"

"What?"

"Who told you about it?"

"Jay Hollander."

"Ah. Just want to keep the footnotes straight. Speaking of Hollander, you should hop it. I'm sure they'll dope him for the plastering, and you want to sign out from him before he nods out."

"Yeah." I made two sandwiches out of the egg salad and some rye bread. I saw Phil looking at the rye bread. "I bought the bread Friday morning," I explained defensively.

"Did I say anything? I did not. Can I have my hug now?"

"Sure." I put my arms around him and tilted my head down to kiss him. I was six feet tall with my shoes on and Phil was five-feet-nine in his bare feet.

"I love you," I murmured, brushing my lips against his ear and waiting for him to tense up at the forbidden phrase.

"I love you too," Phil said at length, surprising me. "But I just need my freedom right now, O.K.?"

"O.K." I felt peaceful suddenly. Things were beginning to look up a bit.

Later that night I would remember this moment of tranquillity and it would seem very far away.

CHAPTER

2

University Hospital sits on a bluff overlooking Manhattan's Harlem Valley in New York City. When the hospital was built in the late nineteenth century, its wrought-iron balconies offered a pastoral view of Harlem's cowfields, trees, and farmhouses. Today the same balconies overlook one of the most embattled, bombed-out neighborhoods in New York City. "The Valley," as it is called, is a junkie fiefdom where drugs are bought and sold, addicts overdose hourly, and drug-runners shoot, knife, and batter one another daily.

When the police arrive at the scene to pick up the pieces, they bring the survivors to the emergency room at University.

I have heard that the original population in the neighborhood was fairly well-to-do, and that wealthy patients arrived at the hospital in horse-drawn carriages, disembarking beneath well-kept sycamore trees on the hospital's lawns. Now most of University's patients are indigent, transient, or on welfare. Half are black and a third are Spanish-speaking. The hospital no longer renders elitist care to those who can afford it; instead, it provides a kind of combination social-work/health-care-service for those who can afford no better. The poor, who cannot pay for private physicians, come to University for routine care. Drunks, who in suburbia might be locked up overnight to sleep it off, are brought to University's emergency room to dry out. Criminals wounded in action come in with their police escorts.

"What's wrong with this guy?" I asked the police one night when two strapping representatives of New York's Finest brought in a disheveled young man who was obviously experiencing some difficulty standing up by himself.

"Well, Doc, it's like this," one officer explained while the other nodded somberly. "The guy was going up and down Broadway licking car fenders."

"Licking car fenders?"

"Yeah, you know, with his tongue."

"Ah. Right. With his tongue." I looked at the man's ratty clothing and filthy, matted hair; he was listing slightly to the left and examining the ambulance squawkbox. "O.K.," I sighed. I was getting callous; I had stopped wondering why I had never seen patients like this on *Dr. Kildare*. "Take him over to Psych and tell the nurse."

The night Jay Hollander fell and broke his arm, we did not have a fender-licker in the ER, but we did have a fair representation of the usual types of patients awaiting treatment:

A middle-aged woman suffering from a seizure disorder and alcoholism. She knew she was not supposed to drink alcohol while taking her medication, so she'd *stopped* taking it for a two-day drinking spree. She drank five bottles of gin, suffered four seizures, and was brought to the emergency room by relatives.

Three homeless "bagmen" with vague, unspecified complaints. Their biggest complaint, although they didn't exactly say so, was that they had nowhere to go to weather the snowstorm. During bad weather the homeless always turn up in the city's hospital emergency rooms.

A college student who had been struck by a car.

Several patients complaining of chest pain. When it

snows, the number of heart-attack victims in the emergency room increases. Besides the obvious candidates for heart attack who shovel snow against their doctors' orders, we usually see a few people who have never had heart trouble before or for whom the added effort required merely to *walk* through heavy snow causes chest pain and other heart-attack symptoms.

Two crazies. The first crazy was lying on his stretcher peacefully enough, carrying on a thoughtful-sounding monologue about sex, moonlight, and the FBI. The second crazy had drunk a bottle of Kwell shampoo earlier, and was now busy vomiting it up rather noisily in the men's room next to the nurses' station. One of the nurses gave him something to bring up the shampoo. "If you liked the shampoo so much, you'll really go for this," she commented dryly as she offered the old man a small paper cup of ipecac. He quaffed it in one enthusiastic gulp.

Three "orthos"—patients with fractures or suspected fractures—who required the attention of an orthopedist. Two had fractured their right forearms, the third his lower left leg. All three said they had slipped in the snow.

A very disoriented little old lady from the nursing home across the street from the hospital, who had inhaled part of her dinner instead of swallowing it.

Madame, a favorite patient of the staff. An older woman who had come to the States as a war bride in the forties, Madame was a neighborhood matriarch of sorts. She lived in an old brownstone across the street from the firehouse, where her husband had been fire chief up until his death about a year before. In tolerable weather—and some intolerable—Madame could be found perched on her lawn chair on the sidewalk in front of her building, ready to dispense old-time Parisian practicality. She was eccentric and she was funny and everyone loved her. She was not very well, and it frustrated us no end that we couldn't figure out exactly what was wrong with her.

A teenager shot in the leg by a plainclothes detective who happened by while the kid was waving a sawed-off shotgun around a liquor store. The detective was well-known in the ER as a good cop but something of a cowboy. When he brought the kid in, the charge nurse said, "We don't have enough work to do here, you gotta go out and *make* work for us?" The detective affected great offense. "Hey, honey," he said, "if you would go out on a date with me like I keep asking you, I wouldn't have to shoot people to get to see you."

And last but not least, Dr. James J. Hollander, who had fallen on the floor and fractured his forearm. When I got to the plaster room, Jay was sitting on the edge of the stretcher looking sullen and exasperated. In front of him, Dr. Manuel Hernandez was unwrapping packets of plaster gauze and dropping them into a bucket of water in the sink. Jay was naked to the waist and held his arm out stiffly in front of himself. A premed student from the nearby women's college stood next to Jay, holding his arm in midair with one hand in his armpit and the other clamped tightly around his wrist.

"Atta way to go, J.J.," I said flippantly. "You gonna arm-wrestle this woman here or you just holding your ring out to be kissed?"

Jay tilted his head to look at me over his shoulder. He had a mountaineer's jawline and the high cheekbones of a male model, and I was, as usual, done in by the magnificence of his profile. He broke into a grin when he saw it was me. "Nothin' like the sympathy of a kind-hearted woman when a man is down," he said.

"Hold still, Jay," Manny complained. He began to wrap Jay's arm in Webril, the gauze padding that goes under the cast. Jay watched his arm disappear under the white strips of Webril and sighed with mock resignation. Suddenly I realized how tired he looked; his beautiful brown eyes were bloodshot and his face was drawn.

"You want to sign out to me, Jay?" I asked.

"Yeah, guess I should. The only one I have is Madame. I sent for her chart—not like anybody has to read it, though, huh?"

I shook my head wryly. "Nothing definitive?"

"I can't figure it. Same vague stuff. She's lost weight. Her abdomen is distended. Firm, nontender liver edge but no spleen. Extremities O.K., heart O.K., lungs clear, vitals O.K." Jay shifted restlessly, arching his back and tilting his head from side to side to stretch his neck muscles. Jay was known throughout the hospital for not being able to sit still. He also had a hot reputation among the nurses as a pleasing and energetic lover, although it was beyond me how all the nurses knew this to be a fact when not one of them would admit outright to having bedded him.

"Hold *still*, Jay!" Hernandez barked. "Hold the fingers, like this," he said to the premed, showing her how to hold Hollander's fingers, as if she were a gentleman about to kiss a lady's hand. The premed braced her arms against her ribs, the better to support Jay's arm. Manny dipped his hand into the bucket and fished out the plaster gauze, then deftly wrapped the dripping strips around Jay's arm.

"What's Madame's chief complaint?" I asked.

Hollander watched Manny's long brown fingers sweep over the quick-drying plaster, smoothing the new cast, like a potter's hands at the wheel. "I'm not sure. I sort of get the idea that she came in because it was snowing. She didn't feel well, not sick enough to come over, but maybe afraid if she got worse she might not be able to get herself over here because of the weather."

"You blood her?"

"Yeah, but I broke the tubes when I fell. You'll have to do it again."

"O.K., I will. Anything else?"

Jay shook his head and took his eyes away from mine. He looked defeated.

Manny gave the cast a final slap. "Let go," he said to the premed, and she stepped back. Manny took Jay's newly casted hand in both his own and began to press down, arching Jay's wrist downward.

"Jesus, Manny!" Jay screamed.

"This just takes a second, hang on." Manny continued to press.

Jay sucked his breath in and let it out again. I could see his eyes start to roll up. "He's going out, Manny, let's get his head down," I cried.

"Just hold him up a second."

I put my arms around Jay and let his head sag onto my neck. I could smell his shampoo, which somehow made me feel embarrassingly intimate with him. I was getting overheated and I didn't like it. I could feel a flush start to creep up my neck.

"O.K., Ev, let's get his head down. *Yo! Jay!"* Manny carefully held on to the casted arm while I leaned Jay forward until his head was between his knees. The premed hovered nervously, in the way.

Suddenly there was a muffled pounding from the ambulance bay, which was directly next to the plaster room, and some shouting started. I exchanged a puzzled look with Hernandez over Hollander's back.

"What the hell is that?"

"I don't know. . . . Sounds like someone banging on the door."

Patients arriving at the hospital on their own were not allowed to come into the ER through the ambulance bay. Ambulances announced their arrivals in the bay with a series of siren bleeps.

No one ever banged on the door.

"How you doing, Jay? Ready to sit up?"

More thumps and shouts from the ambulance bay. Then a loud bang as the door was thrown open against the wall behind it. A rush of snowy air swept into the corridor.

"Get me a doctor!" a man's voice cried, joined by that of a nurse, who shrilled, *"I need a doctor here stat!"*

"Help Dr. Hernandez," I said to the premed as I ran out of the plaster room.

I collided head-on with Dr. Shelley Reinish.

Dr. Reinish was upside down, thrown over the shoulder of a bearish-looking man with snow in his beard and panic in his eyes, and she was unconscious.

CHAPTER

3

"I can't wake her up. Her pulse is funny and her lips are blue and she's freezing cold. She had the *windows* open when I came home, and there was snow on the floor—"

"Where was she, on the floor? You're her husband, right?"

"Yes. No. I'm her husband, I've met you guys before. She was on the couch."

We all bumped through the swinging doors into the ER in a heap and the man heaved Shelley onto a stretcher in OR One. Her arms and legs flopped and her head sagged. Leaning over her, I peered into her face. Her skin was the color of a wet slate sidewalk and her eyes had rolled up into their sockets as if she'd fainted at the sight of God.

I slapped Shelley across the jaw. Her head rolled lifelessly.

Is she dead?

"Is she breathing?"

"Not much. I think we'd better bag her."

Alex McCabe, the chief resident in the ER, a tall black man, was shining his penlight into Shelley's eyes. His loosely curled Afro brushed against my mouth as he bent over. Hands came out of nowhere with a plastic airway, white tape, and an ambu-bag. I saw they belonged to Whizkid, a medical student, who was as usual one step ahead of everybody else.

"Pupils fixed and dilated," McCabe said.

I felt the electric tide of adrenaline surge out from my chest into my arms.

Whizkid began to pump the ambu-bag. The ambu-bag looks like an inflatable football. By squeezing it and unsqueezing it, you inflate and deflate the patient's lungs. I made a fist and twisted my knuckles as forcefully as I could into Shelley's breastbone, a maneuver guaranteed to get a response out of anyone who isn't seriously comatose.

Nothing.

I reached for my stethoscope.

I was beginning to find it difficult to breathe. My heart was swelling larger and larger, a banging sledgehammer that crushed my lungs against my rib cage. For a minute I felt underwater. Time elongated, people around me swam at a leisurely pace, and the sound of a generator throbbed inside my head. I was coasting through the deep the way you do after a dive when you let your momentum carry you. And then I burst out of the water and flew up and up and up and into gear: my head cleared, and the clarity—as always—amazed me. I jammed my stethoscope into my ears.

McCabe turned to Shelley's husband. "O.K., she was on the couch. What, like she was asleep?"

"No, uh, maybe like she sat down and passed out. I mean, her feet were on the floor."

"You think she took anything? Valium? She keep anything like that around the house?"

"No. I'm pretty sure she doesn't take anything like that. She takes a lot of aspirin."

"Aspirin?"

"Yeah."

"What for?"

"I don't know, headaches, pain in the back, what d'*you* take aspirin for?"

McCabe paused, then dropped it. "She's not diabetic or anything?"

Shelley's husband shook his head. He stared at his wife with wide, horrified eyes.

"Has she got *any* medical condition?"

More head-shaking. Then, with sudden realization: "She may be pregnant."

The medical staff froze momentarily.

"How pregnant?" McCabe asked softly.

"I don't know. She missed her last period. She's about three weeks overdue." Shelley's husband ran a hand across his forehead and into his hair, grabbing at the black curls as if he were about to pull them out. He drew a long breath.

"Rabbi," said one of the nurses sharply, "would you like to sit down?"

He shook his head.

My eyes moved to the muscular bearded man in the three-piece pin-striped suit who had thrown an unconscious woman over his shoulder, run down two flights of stairs to the street, and charged through knee-high snow half a block to the hospital. I knew he was a rabbi; I had met him on a number of occasions before. He simply did not fit my mental stereotype of a skinny, pale-faced scholar sitting in a room full of dusty books.

The rapid *lub-dub-dub-dub* of Shelley's heart in my ears snapped my attention back. The beat was weak and hurried, and the normal *lub-dub* of Shelley's heart had become lost in a cacophony of "extra" heart sounds which are heard only when the heart is in trouble.

Big trouble.

Shelley's heart was in failure.

I cleared my throat. "Can I get an electrocardiogram and a BP, please?" My mouth was beginning to taste like I had been gargling with pennies and nickels. "Alex, I'm getting gallop and rales."

McCabe stopped talking to the rabbi and took my stethoscope out of my ears and jammed it into his own. He looked at me while he listened, and I watched his hazelnut-brown face anxiously. "I want Cardiology, stat!" he ordered, pulling the stethoscope off again. "Get a neuro consult down here, also stat! See if Dr. Madding is on the premises. Beeper 240. And page me Respiratory, also stat!"

My eyes fell on the Band-Aids on Shelley's left arm at precisely the same instant that the nurse's freckled hand darted forward and tore them aside.

There were fresh needle punctures underneath. One at the crook of Shelley's elbow and the other on the back of her hand. Oh-my-God, *she shot herself up with something.* I reached across Shelley's chest and yanked her arm up in front of my face where I could see it better.

"Dr. McCabe, you'd better look at this," the nurse said quietly.

Alex looked. There was a split second of silence; his face worked with the implications as his mind zoomed into focus.

"Helen, get us an amp of Narcan," I said. "And what's taking so long with the BP?"

"Blood pressure is sixty."

Ominously low.

"O.K., let's get a drip going. Give me a bag of D5-W."

"Twenty-cc syringe. . . . Large IV needle, please. . . . Blood tubes, give me two green-tops and two purple-tops."

"Let's get her clothes off."

"I'm gonna take a blood gas. Can we get some ice, please?"

"Sutcliffe, you wanna tube her for urine?"

"Yeah, soon as I blood her."

Shelley's husband didn't know what the tracks were. He had never, he swore in a quavering voice, seen her shoot up with anything. All she ever took, the rabbi insisted, was aspirin. In fact, he had just purchased a very large bottle of aspirin the week before.

I tore the paper wrapper off a large IV needle with my teeth as the nurse wound a piece of rubber tubing around Shelley's right arm for me. The blood pressure was so low I thought the vein would never stand up, and I prodded at it with my thumb until it bulged enough for me to get the needle in. A gush of maroon bloodied my hand while I fumbled for the syringe with my other hand and teeth.

Shelley was wearing OR scrubs—lots of doctors wear them at home like lounging pajamas—and the Jamaican orderly began slicing them off now with a pair of scissors. As the blue material fell away from Shelley's thighs, a videotape started rolling in my head: I went swimming with Shelley once and saw her naked in the locker room. I saw her again now as I had seen her then: tiny, with amazingly white skin; the kind that is called peaches and cream. Strands of fire-colored hair coming undone from the bun on top of her head. Close-set eyes peering at me from behind implausibly turquoise contact lenses, a hue I was convinced did not occur anywhere in the natural world. Stretching to the utmost top of her height to push something back onto the top shelf of her locker, hopping little hops to elongate the stretch. The top shelf of the locker had been about level with my chin. Mutt and Jeff, I had thought at the time. We're like Mutt and Jeff. The orderly was slicing through my reverie along with Shelley's scrubs; I had the distinct feeling of moving sideways out of my body and back again. The scrub shirt came off in pieces. Shelley wasn't wearing any underwear. I saw her hopping the little hops to push whatever it was toward the back of the locker shelf. What the hell was she putting in there, and why couldn't I think of it now? Her arms were stretching up and up and up, she was naked, she was hopping. I pulled my sweater over my head and reached out a long arm to help her. I was naked now too, and taller than anyone else in the locker room, awkward in my nakedness but proud of my tallness, reaching out an arm that got longer and longer as I thought about it—and I got taller and taller as I watched. I was reaching to help Shelley. I was going to help her.

Help her do what?

I could see now that I was in a nightmare. Everything was falling irrationally into place. I was focusing on things that made no sense and missing details I knew were important. My hands, smeared with blood, sticky with it—Shelley's blood—were pulling more blood from her veins. I unclicked the syringe from the needle in Shelley's hand and hooked the needle up to the IV line from a bag of dextrose hanging on the rack over my head. Other hands passed me the tubes, and I injected each tube with the blood, stabbing the needle through the color-coded rubber stoppers. My hands were steady. They seemed steadier than usual.

They were very, very steady.

And covered with blood.

I felt larger than life. The Narcan I had ordered arrived and everyone stepped back while I injected it. Narcan reverses the effects of morphine and heroin and it works so fast that people getting it have been known to bolt upright and take swings at the medical staff. It also works as a diagnostic test: if the patient revives, you know they took morphine or heroin. If they don't revive, that's not what they took.

Shelley did not revive.

McCabe groaned.

"You have to tell me what's going on," Rabbi Reinish said.

"We don't know yet," I said.

McCabe was holding Shelley's right knees up in the air, smacking around with his neuro hammer on the lower edge of her kneecap. He laid the leg down and traced a sweeping pattern on the sole of her foot.

I watched for the telltale curving of the toes, but nothing happened.

"It's bad, though, isn't it?"

"Yes," I said. I hated myself for telling him.

"Did she have a stroke?"

"I don't know. Maybe."

He peered at me. He had eyes the color of midnight in a coal furnace, and I couldn't see where the irises stopped and the pupils started. I looked away helplessly. I could lie to him. That would save him, maybe only for a little while, and it would cost me. Lying takes energy. Or I could tell him the truth. That would cost him and save me.

"But you don't really think she had a stroke."

"I don't know. Maybe. A stroke is one possibility."

"You think she took something."

I hesitated. "Yes."

"So she could have had a stroke secondary to whatever she took."

I heard the hint of medical phraseology and looked at him in surprise.

"I was a medic in the Army," he said.

I knew that but I'd forgotten it in the heat of the moment. "It could be a stroke secondary to whatever she took," I said. "It could be a number of things. We'll know better when we hear from the lab. In the meantime we're trying to find out exactly what it did to her, whatever she took, how bad it is."

His eyes held mine for a moment. "Thank you," he said levelly. "I don't want to get in the way. But I want to know."

Paul Roussy, the intern, ran into the room, stuffing the last bit of a tuna-fish sandwich into his mouth. He looked at Shelley and began to choke.

"Somebody page Dr. Madding?" the clerk shouted out from the nurses' station.

"I did. Tell him to get his ass down here!" McCabe

31

bellowed back. He reached for the funduscope on the wall.

"Oh-my-*God!*" Roussy cried, his mouth finally free of sandwich.

McCabe turned off the lights and bent over Shelley, his cheek next to hers. He aimed the tiny light beam of the funduscope into her eyes. We all stood quietly in the dark and waited.

"Dr. Madding wants to know what you want!"

"I am going to personally kill that man," McCabe said, turning the lights back on. "Sutcliffe, get on the phone and tell His Shitfaced Doctorship Madding what we want. *What line is Madding on?"*

"Two."

I yanked the phone off the wall and spoke to Madding. I don't remember what I said; rapid-fire medicalese no doubt. I was breathing deeply and rhythmically, as if I had just run up four flights of stairs.

Madding said, *"Dr. Reinish? From *our* house staff? Why didn't you say so?"*

Then he hung up on me.

I stood there looking at the phone on the wall. I was suffering zoom-focus at the moment. I read the numbers on the buttons for the different telephone lines. 1811. 1812. 1813. I read the red button that said *Hold*.

I was afraid.

I was afraid Shelley was going to die.

This is it, I thought.

"What do we know?" Roussy asked. He had a soft Texas voice but it was so soft now I could hardly hear him. For a second I thought maybe I hadn't heard him, I had merely read his mind.

"She's very depressed," Alex sighed. "No reflexes. No signs of trauma, and I don't think she's got any brain-stem or cranial-nerve injury, but that's hard to rule out without being able to compare right and left reflex response."

I looked at the data-base-video-readout machine,

familiar to thousands of television viewers the world over. It was going blip-blip-blip just as it did on afternoon soap operas. The med student faithfully squeezed and unsqueezed the ambu-bag, adding its whoosh-plop-whoosh to the blip-blip-blip.

"But what happened?"

"Her husband came home and found her unconscious on the couch and carried her over here," I said. I didn't like what I was seeing on the data-base video readout, and I leaned over the back of the nurse to look at the paper readout from the electrocardiograph. The machine was turning out reams of paper under its spiderlike needle and I ran several feet of it through nervous fingers.

"Tachycardia with inverted T-waves," the nurse said.

There was a freeze-frame like you see when you watch sports on TV. I thought: Now the announcer's voice will come on and tell us what's happening. Then they'll roll the film again and Shelley will sit up and thank us very much and go home. And we'll eat peanuts and drink beer and play the tape over and over again and say to one another: *This is where Shelley sat up and went home and was all better.*

"Think we should give her anything?" Alex asked me.

"Like what? You mean for the heart?" I thought about this a minute. "I don't know, Alex. She's very depressed. We have the drips going and we're bagging her, I'd just as soon wait for the lab results."

McCabe glanced at Roussy; Roussy nodded.

I reached out and took Shelley's hand in mine. It was cold, blue, and sweaty. My entire head emptied out of its usual stream of consciousness; for a very long moment I did not think anything. I looked at Shelley's hand.

The data-base machine ran two blips together in rapid succession, skipped a beat, and blipped again.

Then the line on the screen began a series of wide, irregular sweeps as Shelley's heart stopped functioning.

"She's fibrillating!" I cried. My own heart flew up against my collarbone.

"Paddles," McCabe ordered.

The nurse manning the crash cart handed over the paddles. McCabe planted one of the paddles squarely over Shelley's breastbone and the other underneath her left breast near her armpit, exactly where I had slid my stethoscope fifteen minutes ago. *Fifteen minutes ago*. It seemed like years. The long white coiled cords, which resembled the cords on home telephones, snaked back under McCabe's arms to the defibrillator on the crash cart. "Four hundred volts," he said. "Stand back." He shifted his feet so he was clear of Shelley and her stretcher and depressed both paddle buttons with his thumbs. Shelley's chest and shoulders arched rigidly off the stretcher and thudded down again. The line on the data-base machine bounced, spiked, bounced again, and went into a pattern that was more or less normal, if rapid.

Everyone in the room stared at the video screen. McCabe stood with his shoulders back, paddles in his upraised hands like a percussionist with cymbals waiting for his cue. The blip-blip-blip continued steadily.

McCabe relaxed his arms somewhat.

But I could see that the tops of the spikes of the cardiac rhythm as it rolled across the screen were not as tall as they should be.

"*Blood gas on Reinish!*" the clerk shouted out.

McCabe put the paddles down. He was beginning to sweat, his hazelnut skin glistening. "*What is it?*" he shrieked.

The clerk shouted out the five-part test result.

Roussy gasped.

The acid-base balance of the blood must maintain itself within very narrow limits, or the body systems begin to break down and the delicate mechanism that sustains life starts to go haywire. If the pH, the acid-base balance, dips below a certain level, the patient goes into shock and dies.

Shelley's pH had just tipped over the cliff.

"Give me some bicarb," I said. I began sucking my tongue against the bottom of my mouth to try to get some saliva going. Nobody else said anything. The nurse handed me the syringe and I injected it into Shelley's IV line just as the data-base-video-readout machine began another series of wide, erratic sweeps. *Blip-blip-blip.*

"*Shit!*" McCabe roared. "She's fibrillating again! Give me the paddles!"

We all stood back as McCabe planted the paddles on Shelley's breastbone and ribs. Her rib cage flew up into the air and fell back again. There was a corresponding jump on the data-base video, but her heart failed to return to rhythm.

A young woman arrived from Respiratory, took stock of the situation in less than a second, and shouldered Whizkid aside.

McCabe shocked Shelley again.

"Give me some lidocaine," I said.

"Whizkid, do chest compressions. Sutcliffe, make sure you get a good femoral pulse from his compressions. *Call a code.*"

Oh, Jesus, I thought. *This is it.*

Whizkid got up on a footstool, ran a finger along Shelley's ribs to find his hand position, and started external cardiac compressions. He was counting in his head and I couldn't hear him, but I began to reel off the mnemonic count in my own brain: *one-one-thousand, two-one-thousand, three-one-thousand.* I pushed my fingers into Shelley's groin. Every time Whizkid rocked forward I felt the blood go out through Shelley's arteries. *One-one-thousand, two-one-thousand.* Pulse. Pulse.

"Quit a second and see if we have anything," McCabe said.

Whizkid leaned back.

Shelley's pulse disappeared from beneath my fingertips. I shook my head.

"Stand back." McCabe shocked her again.

Nothing.

"Lidocaine."

"Lidocaine on board."

"Stand back."

"Bicarb."

"On board."

"Stand back."

Each time Alex told us to stand back, we stood back. Whizkid got down off his stool, the woman from Respiratory put the ambu-bag down, I took my hand away. It reminded me of a square dance we used to do in seventh grade in gym class. We had held hands, charging into the middle of the circle and then dancing out again, until we pulled at one another's outstretched arms.

Stand back. Stand back. *Stand back.* In and out, in and out.

Whizkid got down off his stool, I leaned back.

"Stand back."

"Alex . . ." I said finally.

"Give me some more bicarb."

"Alex, it's forty-five minutes."

"I know it, goddammit!"

"Listen to me." I took the paddles out of his hands.

"Oh, God," he said.

Everyone turned to look at Rabbi Reinish. He had been sitting on a stool, but as we turned he was rising to his feet and slowly moving his right hand toward his left armpit. I watched him as if through a penny-arcade viewer that had got stuck; everything that was happening was happening in jerks and repeating itself. We turned. Rabbi Reinish raised his right hand. We turned. He raised his hand. We turned. He raised his hand toward the collar of his shirt, popping the top button from its threads as he pulled at it to get air.

Then there was a cry. It was like no cry I had ever heard before and it was not English; it was Hebrew. It swelled up and out of his throat like the roar of a bear, reverberating off the walls, swirling around our heads, piercing our ears.

Dr. Shelley Reinish was dead.

CHAPTER

4

The snow came halfway to my knees. My running shoes had soaked through after the first half-block, my corduroy pants were becoming damp, and I had no hat. If McCabe hadn't forced his ski jacket on me I would be plowing around the southeast corner of the hospital without an overcoat as well, my white lab coat flying behind me like Batman's cape. As it was, I turned onto Morningside Drive straight into a northerly wind that was whipping needles and tiny bullets of snow directly at me—and I didn't care. It is very likely that had I come around the corner wearing nothing but my lab coat imitating Batman, I still wouldn't have cared. My heart was swelling in my chest like one of those automobile safety balloons that inflate on impact, I was gasping in the snow-filled air as if the earth's supply of oxygen would deplete itself within the next five minutes, and I couldn't tell if I felt hot or cold. I presumed cold. That seemed rational, given the circumstances of being outside in a blizzard. But I wasn't really sure.

This is a New York City Government Record and should be Accurately completed. From University Hospital, New York, *February 4, 1985. To Chief Medical Examiner of the City of New York: Statement and particulars of the death of* Shelley Lynn Davidsohn Reinish, M.D.

It was a nightmare. I was filling out paperwork on a nightmare. Dear Medical Examiner, last night I dreamed Shelley died, but then I woke up, thank God.

I wished. Oh, how I wished.

   Residence New York City. *Age 29 years 3 months 22 days. Color* wh. *Occupation* physician. *Single, Married or Widowed* married. *Place of Birth* New York City. *Father's Name* Otto Davidsohn, *Father's Birthplace* Berlin, Germany. *Mother's Name* Sylvia Kahn Davidsohn. *Mother's Birthplace* Newark, N.J. *How long in United States* since birth. *How long in New York City* 9 years.

I had met Shelley's parents once. I had met Shelley's father and mother the same day I had met her husband, Steve, for the first time; Phil and I had gone to the New York Philharmonic at Lincoln Center to see a performance of *Carmina Burana,* and we had bumped into the Reinish party in the bar downstairs afterward, and had joined them for a drink.

I stopped for a moment under the awning of the Jefferson Pavilion to listen to the silence made by the roaring of the wind. The Jefferson Pavilion was at the back of the hospital and faced Morningside Park, and below that, Harlem Valley. It was a building of laboratories and completely deserted at this time of night, a circumstance that added to the eeriness of standing in a snowstorm in front of it. I breathed two more minutes' worth of the last five minutes of oxygen left on earth and looked out over Morningside Park toward the Valley. I could barely make out the buildings on the other side of the park through the swirling whiteness.

Shelley's parents were art dealers, and they had been entertaining a Japanese art dealer the night we all saw *Carmina Burana.* I remembered the art dealer had risen and bowed majestically when Phil and I were introduced to him. Shelley's father, an old-style German aristocrat, had risen and bowed as well, clicking his heels ever so slightly.

I imagined myself going to Shelley's parents now to tell them she had died. I imagined her father and the Japanese art dealer bowing to greet me, and their gracious bowing postures crumpling when I told them the news.

Admitted 4th *day of* February *19* 85 *at* 9:15 *o'clock* P.M. *By (state whether by ambulance or friends)* Rabbi Stephen Reinish, husband. *From (state whether from a public place, a precinct or a residence and give the street and number)* 1240 Amsterdam Avenue, New York City, residence of the deceased and her husband. *Examined by* Evelyn F. Sutcliffe *M.D.*

Whenever it snowed, Paul Roussy would say, "I always get jealous if someplace else gets more snow than where I am." It usually made me smile. I remembered it now, but without smiling. I could hear a shovel scraping on a sidewalk. Somewhere I listened to it for a while and tried not to think.

Symptoms, subjective and objective: Clinical, X-Ray and Laboratory Findings. (state whether from Natural disease, poisoning or injuries. If the latter, the location, extent, number and character of injuries, whether in shock, conscious or unconscious) Patient admitted to hospital in advanced state of shock, unconscious and unresponsive. Death due to acute respiratory depression and cardiovascular collapse. No X rays taken. Lab findings revealed a serum salicylate of 85 mg and SGOT 924 units. Copy of lab report attached. Diagnosis pending autopsy: cardiopulmonary failure due to advanced salicylate poisoning.

Is this English? Does anybody talk like this? Think that was the wording Steve Reinish would use when he called his in-laws to tell them Shelley was dead? "The facts, ma'am. Just the facts." Acetyl salicylate is plain over-the-counter aspirin. A blood-serum salicylate level of fifty milligrams in an adult would indicate severe poisoning. A blood-serum level of fifty to seventy milligrams in an adult would be found in a dead person following suicide by aspirin overdose. You want facts? How are those for facts? Is there anywhere on this form where they ask me maybe how I feel about filling out a statement on the death of a colleague?

> *Injuries said to have been received (State when, where, how, by what means or persons received; in falls, the distance and location of the fall; in burns and scalds, the circumstances; in highway deaths the line of street car, bus or railroad, the type of conveyance whether truck, taxi, private car, etc.; in weapons, the character, firearms, penetrating and cutting instruments, blunt instruments, etc.* ALWAYS GIVE SUCH INFORMATION AS WILL LEAD TO THE ACCURATE KNOWLEDGE OF THE CASE AND FACILITATE JUDICIAL INQUIRY AND JUSTICE) No injuries.
> *(State name, date, place, character and results of any operation or amputation performed)* None.
> *Death took place on the* 4th *day of* February *19* 85 *at* 10:25 *o'clock* P.M. *Remarks: (State here any important facts not embodied in the above statements)* Deceased was a house staff physician at this hospital and personally known to all hospital personnel present at her death.

I had written that, then crossed it out with a single line so it could still be read clearly. I was damned if I would write under *Remarks:* "None."

House Surgeon Physician Evelyn F. Sutcliffe *M.D.*

I slogged up the steps to the door of the Jefferson Pavilion, angled my face into a corner made by the door and its jamb, and tried to light a cigarette. My hands were freezing. You're going to get frostbite, I thought. So what? Shelley's dead. I lit five matches and they all blew out. I resorted to a trick Shelley had told me Israeli soldiers used in the Sinai: I broke the head off one match, stuck it up the cigarette, and lit the entire incendiary device with a second match. I understand they have very high winds in the Sinai. I almost set my hair on fire. Probably why soldiers, Israeli and otherwise, keep their hair so short, so they don't set it on fire lighting cigarettes in high winds.

It was beginning to dawn on me that maybe I wasn't all there. *Not All There* is a bona-fide medical diagnosis; you see it on charts all the time. Mental Status: *Not All There.* Everything that had happened this evening was jumbled in my head into one single moment without a continuum of time. In med school when I used to smoke dope at end-of-semester parties I had the sensation that there was no continuum of time, but the other way around: time elongated into one very long moment. What I was feeling here was exactly the opposite, and I wondered if there was a drug that produced this sensation, and if there was, whether anyone would want to take it recreationally. Here, smoke this, it will take your entire evening and encapsulate it into one single moment, and you will be totally confused and Out to Lunch for the rest of the night. *Out to Lunch* is another bona-fide medical diagnosis. You don't see it much on charts, though.

Do you know where you are? I am at University Hospital, standing under the awning of the Jefferson Pavilion. What day is it? Monday, February 4, 1985. Who is the President? Ronald Reagan. I had had a patient the week before who knew where she was and what day it was, but when I asked her who the President was, she told me "Eisenhower." I wrote in the chart, "Patient is oriented X2 but states President is Eisenhower."

Mental status: *Not All There.*

Let's see if I can put this all together: Shelley died. The rabbi is screaming and Alex McCabe is crying on my shoulder but I can't cry so I don't. I say I will pronounce, because I can see Alex can't do it. Then I go around to Admitting and borrow their new ward clerk who's never been in the hospital before tonight. I have to get someone who doesn't know Shelley or her husband to go in and get this information out of Shelley's husband, what her father's name and birthplace are and so forth, because there's no one else who can deal with doing that. After that I go up to the lab to get the lab results and find out the SMAC machine—the blood-analysis computer—is down. I sit there for a while smelling the old blood smell; it always smells like they're defrosting about seventeen rump roasts in the blood lab, and the smell gets in your nose and sticks. I look at the long black counters and they remind me of dissecting worms in eighth grade. God, I hated those worms. I read the signs on the wall: "PLEASE LOG IN AT COMPUTER ROOM" and "SMAC MACHINE IS DOWN PLEASE SEE MR. CHRISTOPHER."

I can see Ramesh Christopher, the technician, from where I'm sitting. He's doing Shelley's lab work by hand. I've specifically asked for a serum salicylate. The computer will do about sixty tests automatically, but that would take Christopher all night, so you have to be specific, you pick maybe ten tests out of the sixty and you say, "Do these." The whole time I'm sitting there I keep thinking: *If you were Shelley and you decided to kill yourself by injecting yourself with something, would you cover up the injection sites with Band-Aids?* So I ask for the serum salicylate on the off-chance that she didn't shoot up with anything, she swallowed something, and Reinish said she took all this aspirin. So then Christopher gives me a serum salicylate of 85 mg. I sit there at least another five minutes with my head on one of those black lab counters thinking: *Now what are those injection marks all about if she took an*

OD of aspirin? That is when I start to lose it, I begin feeling like I'm not totally inside of myself, part of me is outside watching me think all this with my head on the lab counter.

I get up and go downstairs and fill out the form for the medical examiner. Just as I'm finishing this, Paul Roussy sits down and says, "Shelley used to pray before she went into surgery, did you know that?" I didn't know it and I don't think I can talk about it right now, so I shake my head, which Roussy takes to mean that I want to hear all about it, and he launches into the whole thing, when I really don't. About then, I start breathing like there's only five minutes of oxygen left on the earth.

Roussy says, "You need some air," and takes me out to the ambulance bay. So I have some air and he tells me all about it, but hearing this makes it seem like there's *less* air: "When she was scrubbing she used to hold her hands up in front of her face, like this" —Paul holds his hand up in front of his eyes, looks at his palm, turns his hand over and looks at the back of it, then turns it and looks at the palm again—"always with this turn-it-over-twice-and-look-at-it motion. She did it real quick. I asked her about it once and she got embarrassed. I said—sort of teasing her, you know— 'Shelley, what the hell is that you do with your hands and that mumbo-jumbo under your breath at the scrub sinks?' She said, 'Oh that—that's the prayer for not screwing up.' She was trying to laugh it off, I guess, because she was embarrassed that I'd noticed. But I wanted to know what it was she was saying, and I pestered her until she told me. I've never forgotten it." He takes a deep breath. " 'And let the pleasantness of the Lord our God be upon us, and establish Thou the work of our hands; the work of our hands establish Thou it.' "

This is when I say I'm going for a walk around the block. Paul says I can't walk around the block without a coat. I say I can if I want. He drags me back into the ER. I'm yelling by this time that I'm going for a walk around the block. McCabe takes one look at me and puts his coat on me. He's stopped crying and he knows I'm going around the block because I can't cry. He puts my arms into the sleeves of his coat like I'm five years old, but he has enough sense to know I have to walk around alone.

So that is how I got to the Jefferson Pavilion. I was standing there smoking my third cigarette lit by Shelley's Israeli-soldier trick when McCabe came around the corner in Roussy's coat.

"You O.K.?" he asked, putting his arms around me.

"Yeah," I said.

I lied.

CHAPTER

5

It was half-past three in the morning. McCabe was sitting in a chair in the nurses' station telling Roussy about his grandmother. I'm not sure how he got on this topic; he suddenly launched into it out of the clear blue sky, winding up to the pitch with all the concentration and excitement of a rookie about to throw his first shut-out. I thought: He doesn't want to talk about Shelley, he can't talk about her. Talk about something else. Grandmother. Roussy meanwhile was eating a sweet roll and drinking a cup of coffee which I knew from experience he had dumped three packets of sugar into; Roussy was a growing boy and needed his nourishment. I was sitting at the opposite end of the nurses' station about twenty feet away from the two men, the phone cradled between my shoulder and ear, waiting for the ward clerk at Sinai Hospital to find a certain Dr. Albert Le Doux for me. I had one of Dr. Le Doux's patients parked on a stretcher in front of me and I was hopping mad about it.

Actually I was not quite hopping yet. I was played out, overwrought, and sick at heart, and I was feeling belligerent. On my mad dash in the snow I had somehow managed to fall headlong into the middle of a John Wayne movie, and I wasn't going to put up with this kind of shit from anybody. *This kind of shit* being a slur against humanity on Le Doux's part, a violent flaunting of the Hippocratic oath in general and an assault on the health of poor Mrs. Gravehouse in particular. Mrs. Gravehouse was the patient parked on the stretcher in front of me about whom I was prepared to become hopping mad. No, *determined* to become hopping mad. Shells could be exploding to either side of me as I clambered over the hills of Iwo Jima, soldiers and pieces of blasted soldiers could be flying in all directions, but I—champion of the rights of patients and Mrs. Gravehouse—would slog on.

The facts of the matter—although I had passed the facts with maudlin alacrity miles back—were actually fairly commonplace, not very complicated, and certainly would not have lent themselves to fodder for hysteria on any other night.

A patient had been released from one hospital, her condition had worsened precipitously, and she had landed the very same day in a second hospital. Mine. To be fair, I had once or twice released a patient from University, only to get a cranky phone call five or six hours later from a physician elsewhere complaining about my medical judgment in releasing said patient. Why, he/she had the patient at St. Somebody Hospital and the patient was seizing/hemorrhaging/in cardiogenic shock, pick one. However, being fair was not on my agenda at the moment. McCabe's voice wafted across to me. There was a kind of trembling desperation to it, and the topic, at least obliquely, was death. "So my grandmother calls my father and she says she's going to get into bed and she's going to stay there, she isn't going to get up to go to the bathroom, she isn't going to get up to cook or feed herself, she isn't getting up for anything, period. Naturally my dad goes to fetch her, he says she can come stay with him and my mother for a few days until she feels better. She says feeling better isn't the problem, she doesn't want

47

to feel better, she wants to die. He says 'Yes, Mother,' and puts her in the car and drives back to Cambridge with her."

I smiled hollowly and shifted the phone to my other ear. I pictured McCabe's father, a regal light-complexioned black man in a conservative camel-hair coat who spoke in carefully measured, sonorous tones, escorting the feisty little Jamaican lady to his dark blue Mercedes. McCabe had told me this story the week before, when it happened. The image had been funnier then, painted at the time by McCabe in amusing pastels as a standoff between his dad and the senior Mrs. McCabe, in this corner, Ladies and Gentlemen, Stuffed-Shirt Exasperation, and in that corner, Feisty Rambunctiousness. Now he was reworking the portrait in somber grays and blacks, underscoring the line about dying, obliterating with wide frantic sweeps of the brush anything that might once have been funny about the story, and all this in a shaky attempt to not talk about that other death, the one we had here this evening. O.K., we won't talk about Shelley, we'll talk about my grandmother, *who just happened to say something about wanting to die last week.*

"Dr. Le Doux." The voice was impatient.

"Dr. Le Doux, this is Dr. Sutcliffe at University. I have a patient of yours here, Esther Gravehouse?"

"Yes?"

"She's in pulmonary failure."

"Yes?"

I sighed, just loud enough for him to hear, but only if he were paying attention, and I suspected he wasn't. He sounded bored as all get-out and I pictured him with his eyelids languidly at half-mast. I said, "I understand you released Mrs. Gravehouse from Sinai this afternoon."

"Yes?"

I paused. I wanted to say: You fucking asshole, you release a woman in pulmonary failure? I didn't say this. I said, as levelly as possible, "I am sending this patient back to you."

He said, "We have no female beds," and hung up on me.

"So my grandmother gets to my mother's house and immediately she starts in on my mother, wants to know why my mother doesn't do wash on Mondays. My mother's maid does wash when she comes on Thursdays, right? This isn't—"

"Excuse me a second, Alex," I said. "I need to borrow Roussy for a minute." I also needed to stop hearing this story; I couldn't bear it any longer.

"Sure, what for?"

"I want you to get on the phone and call Sinai Admitting, and find out if they have any female beds. Tell them you're Dr. Le Doux."

"Dr. Le Doux?"

"Right."

Roussy obligingly called Sinai Admitting. He identified himself with impressive panache as Dr. Le Doux, and got the information I wanted. "They have five female beds," he told me when he got off the phone.

"Thank you," I said. I called Le Doux back. I said, "Le Doux, you son of a bitch, you have five female beds, and I am sending Mrs. Gravehouse back to you." Then I hung up on him.

And then a strange thing happened. I had thrown the phone receiver down, and I was in the act of withdrawing my arm, leaning back against the chair and starting to put my feet up on the countertop, when I simply got stuck. My field of vision suddenly cropped itself: produced of its own accord a photographer's cutting board, arranged its own picture, and neatly guillotined its surplus edges. The effect of this telescoping was to produce a sense of profound alienation in me; everything that was left in my range of sight suddenly felt as if I had never seen it before.

The phone. The countertop. My stethoscope, lying next to the phone. Hell, my fake malachite cigarette lighter, a gift from my brother Alan. *Not us,* they seemed to say. *We don't know you.* Some part of me started to argue with the phone; what idiocy was this, I wondered, why, I used this phone dozens of times a day. There were eight phones in the nurses' station but I liked *this* one, I always used *this* one when given the choice. Now the phone seemed, well, foreign somehow. *Martian* even. I noticed for the first time—surely I must have known this, but at the moment I had no command of the memory—what color it was. Red. All the phones in the nurses' station were red.

I looked at the countertop; it was white, with a wood-tone trim. But wasn't it white with wood-tone trim ten minutes ago, yesterday, last week? I raised my eyes to the nurses' medicine cabinet with its huge glass-paneled front. It was locked. Of course it's locked, it's supposed to be locked, if you want something you have to get the charge nurse to open it for you. Yes, but it's *locked.* The voice inside my head, that voice that served as *other* in the internal dialogue, the devil's advocate, was lugubriously insistent, whispering, insidious. It began to dawn on me that this internal voice was not the voice I usually heard in my head, it wasn't the 'right' voice, it was some other voice that didn't belong to me. Actually, now that I thought about it, *I* didn't seem to belong to me at the moment. And to top it all off, I was about to laugh—but not my own laugh, I could see that right away.

I'm losing my marbles, I thought. *Whose laugh do you suppose it's going to be if it isn't yours?*

No, not my laugh.

An accident was about to happen. A seventeen-car pileup. I remembered driving on the New York Thruway one time, when I saw a car about three lengths ahead go into a sideways slide across four lanes of traffic. *Hit the brakes.* Now in the ER I was trying to get a grip on this laugh, the one that wasn't mine, the one that I was about to have the accident with. I could see McCabe and Roussy somehow through all this—their bodies and faces were rolling into laughter as well, rolling the way detonated buildings collapse on film in slow motion, a horrifying sight. My mouth was sliding sideways across four lanes of traffic into a wildly triumphant leer—*no no no not my mouth*—and I hit that laugh broadside, mixed now with the laughter from McCabe and Roussy that I quickly perceived wasn't their own either.

And then I was suddenly on the other side of the laugh. The far end of the field. The opposite shore.

McCabe was shrieking, "Brava! Brava!" and sobbing with laughter. Roussy had his Texas football player's arms wrapped around himself and was rolling from side to side in his chair, absolutely convulsed, crying alternately, "Bravissimo!" and, "What did Le Doux *say?* 'Le Doux, you son of a bitch, you have five female beds!' What did he *say?*"

This was the only time all evening anyone in the ER laughed. There was a terrible edge to it. It was at once a great relief and a horrendously black piece of humor, an out-of-sync moment that abruptly rotated the pain of Shelley's death 360 degrees, tumbling us into that point in time that occurs in the middle of any disaster, when you realize, stupidly at first and then more philosophically, that Life Goes On. You find something that might be funny, play it out so it becomes funny, laugh over it as if it were funnier than it is, and then feel guilty about laughing at anything at all. In the middle of a gasp, ready to launch into a fresh peal, I suddenly stopped laughing. I felt guilty. *Shelley's dead and you're laughing.* Then I felt relieved in a very poignant way, relieved to be alive, relieved to wiggle my toes inside my wet running shoes and experience the soggy discomfort of having wet feet in cold shoes on a cold winter's night, relieved to be able to move in one fluid movement from the counter I was sitting on across the expanse of the nurses' station, relieved to see with my eyes, hear with my ears, smell with my nose, and taste with my mouth. Then guilty again. Then relieved, then confused. My internal emotional milieu snapped this way and that like a flag beaten about its pole in five different directions by a brutal wind. Snap. Bang. Clunk. Whoosh.

Time to get up and do something, I thought.

This same thought seemed to occur to McCabe and Roussy. They both stopped laughing, the laughter trailing off into chuckles and then silence. "Ha," Roussy drawled, as a kind of afterthought. McCabe cleared his throat. The two men got out of their chairs, chose suitable displacement activities, and went about fussing over whatever it was. I went over to look at Mrs. Gravehouse. She was sleeping, wheezing great wheezes and wuffling peacefully like a horse in a warm barn at night, and I decided I would keep her overnight and send her back to Dr. Le Doux in the morning. Hell, there wasn't much of the night left. I had her propped up on piles of pillows to keep the upper lung fields clear of fluids. As I rearranged the pillows she woke up and smiled at me as if I were her favorite granddaughter. "You a sweetheart, honey," she wheezed.

I was regaining my familiarity with the world; I had reentered the stratosphere. Next I looked in on my overdose patient. The charge nurse, Kathy Haughey, was slapping him on the chest, calling, "Mr. Andrews, wake up, sir. I need you to drink this." When she saw me she said dryly, "You ever figure out what this guy took?"

"I don't know," I said. "Everything I mentioned, he agreed. Amphetamines? Yeah. Valium? Yeah. 'Ludes? Yeah. He doesn't know what he took either, I'm not gonna worry about it. You giving him the charcoal now?"

Kathy nodded, propping the groggy Mr. Andrews into a sitting position. I opened his eyes and shone my penlight briefly into each of them. This small act seemed to center me. *Do you know where you are? What day it is? Who's the President?* "He'll be O.K." I grinned. I would be O.K. too. While I held the patient's head up—yet another self-affirming gesture for me—Kathy fed him the mudlike charcoal mixture through a straw. "Drink it through the straw, I don't want you to taste it, it's vile stuff," she told him matter-of-factly. "That's it, get it all down, you're doing great, you're *excellent,* you're my *best* patient today." I thought: the guy's so out of it, he doesn't know what he's drinking. I wouldn't drink that stuff. Gawd. Yuck.

Kathy put the empty charcoal container down and offered Mr. Andrews a shotglass-size paper cup of sorbitol. "This is sweet," she said. "Drink it all down, excellent, *excellent.*"

"Ever think of coaching football?" I asked.

"They couldn't handle me. Besides, who wants to hang out with naked guys in a locker room when you can hang out with naked patients in a hospital?"

"I don't know, these guys here are a little out of it, don't you think?"

"Yeah, better for me, I'm a *married lady.*" Kathy put her hands on her hips and struck a pose of indignation.

"Don't know how your husband lets you work here, all these naked guys and all."

"Aah, he hangs out with the same naked guys." Kathy's husband was a medic, one of the best I knew, in fact.

I smiled and began moving away from her; I was still a little giddy and over-oxygenated from the laughter with McCabe and Roussy, and at the same time the banter was beginning to sour on me. I felt myself sliding back into halfheartedness. The most incisive thing I probably thought all night came into my mind at that moment: *Let go. Just let go. Grieve.*

But I grabbed myself back from that cliff just before I pitched myself over it. I preferred to sneer in my beer like John Wayne and call Le Doux a son of a bitch and hang up on him. I would rather stay in that place I had got to with the laughter with McCabe and Roussy, perched on the razor-sharp edge of hysteria and slicing myself to shreds on it, than fall apart with grief. And that's how I thought of it: *falling apart with* grief.

I knew that had I died, leaving Shelley behind, she would have planted her two feet on the floor in the middle of the emergency room, weeping and wailing and carrying on until she had done justice to me. After that she would have washed her face, resterilized her implausibly turquoise contact lenses, fixed her equally implausible bright blue eye makeup (Shelley had been fond of blue mascara even), and gotten back down to the business of seeing patients. Shelley had been too dedicated to her patients to fall apart more than briefly. But she would have fallen apart. Just for a little while. And she would have had no problem doing it, either. She would have cried without shame.

Now, why couldn't I do that?

Because John Wayne wouldn't. It was as simple as that.

I went out the back of the ER and around the corner past the plaster room to Holding. At the end of the corridor Helen Yannis and Gary Seligman, two of the nurses, were sitting quietly over mugs of tea in front of a desk that had one of those metal-shaded lamps on it that cast all the light down and none up. Everything was in shadow except what was on the desktop right under the lamp, and the light was eerie. Their voices were low, and their backs were to me. I slid noiselessly into one of the examining cubicles, sat

down carefully on a plastic chair, and looked at Jay
Hollander. He was sleeping with his head thrown back
and his mouth open. Very undignified. He'd probably
shoot me if he knew I'd snuck in to watch him sleep
like this.

Maybe not. Hard to tell; Hollander and I had been
carrying on a flirtation for months now. I had simply
never taken him seriously. I considered his approach
so outrageous, so blatant, so hilariously unsophisti-
cated, I couldn't *possibly* take him seriously. He nuzzled my neck in front of the nurses. He called my
beeper and said things like, "For a good time, call
. . ." (whatever extension he could be reached at). He
left me chocolate bars in my mailbox, rolled up his
sleeves and offered me the opportunity to feel his
biceps—quite admirable, he lifted weights—and went
around telling everyone I was the best diagnostician in
the ER. He also insisted to anyone who would listen
that I had better legs than Bobbi Kaplowitz (Dr.
Kaplowitz was our local Farrah Fawcett stand-in). Once
he feigned fainting at my feet, rolling over on his
back, all four limbs akimbo. He claimed to like older
women (he was almost twenty-six; I was thirty-four).
Yet never once did he ever offend me; every leer was
followed by a wink, and I knew instinctively that he
would have withdrawn every touch with profuse apology had I ever made the slightest show of complaint
about it. The truth of the matter was this: he never
really struck a chord with me. I laughed at him.

I was not, however, laughing now. I was actually
wondering what he would do if I leaned over and
woke him up with a kiss like Sleeping Beauty. I was
surprised to find myself wondering that; so surprised,
in fact, that I didn't take my thoughts any more seriously than I usually took his flirting with me. I wrote it
off to shell shock—the classical *situational reaction,* as
shell shock was called in the current psychiatric litera-

ture. But the thought stayed in my mind, undissipated by my fancy psychobabble terminology: *what if I leaned over and kissed him right now?* Then I wondered what Phil would say if I went to bed with Jay. Huh, I thought, a decidedly less safe thought than simply thinking about kissing Sleeping Beauty. You sure you want to consider that one? I pondered it delicately, lighting a cigarette furtively in the half-darkened cubicle, cupping my palm soldier-style around the red-glowing coal of the tip. Lots of soldier imagery tonight, I thought wryly. And what would Jay say? Here you are, taking advantage of the poor guy while he's unconscious, stealing all this intimacy from him without even consulting him, having wildly graphic fantasies—actually, I was not having wildly graphic fantasies, my mind balked at that just now—I was having *mildly* graphic fantasies, I was imagining kissing him. *That's all.* Oh. Sorry. Wouldn't want to make any false accusations. Forgive me if I seem to press you, Madame Prime Minister, but could you tell us your thoughts on this matter, please—just imagining for a moment, purely hypothetically—if the gentleman in question were to, shall we say, express some interest in your motives, how do you see yourself responding to that?

As if he had overheard my thoughts, the gentleman in question stirred in his sleep and tried to turn over, but the weight of the cast across his chest pinned him. He shifted his legs elaborately instead.

I bolted upright in my chair.

"What?" Jay asked very distinctly.

I sat very still. Down at the end of the corridor, a chair grated on the floor. Shit, I thought. I tried to look nonchalant, smoked my cigarette, holding it the normal way between my first and middle fingers. Jay opened his eyes, didn't see anything because he was still asleep, and shut them again. Gary Seligman, however, was *not* asleep. He was standing at the edge of the cubicle looking at me, a sly smile playing about his mouth. I did a Lauren Bacall: I tilted my chin down, took a long dramatic drag, and blew the smoke out languidly, all the while holding Gary's gaze. Gary is very responsive to camp. He gave a small smiling snort and went away again.

After a moment I put my cigarette out and went away myself. Leave Jay in peace, I thought. Don't give him any strange ideas.

I probably should have thought: Don't give *yourself* any strange ideas.

But I didn't think that. I wandered into the utility room, which was actually a corridor between the ER and the doctors' lounge, and leaned on the counter for a moment. I really didn't have anything to do. I turned on the radio that the orderlies kept for listening to ball games and sat down on a stool. By resting my chin on the counter with my ear flush against the speaker, I could keep the volume low enough not to wake anyone. I wondered where Phil was. I had been calling him every half-hour since Shelley died, and had gotten no answer. Where the hell could he go on a night like this? I found the news station I wanted ("You give us twenty-two minutes; we give you the world"), and the weather came on, broadcast in a breathless, confidential voice over the *rackaracka* of teletypewriters in the background. I suspected that teletypewriters in radio news stations had long since been replaced by computers that delivered the news silently across video screens, but why begrudge the stations the romantic urgency of the *rackaracka?* Especially during a blizzard, which was a bona-fide media event. Seventeen inches of snow had already been logged in at Central Park, the announcer confided with measured hysteria, and five to ten inches more were expected. New Jersey commuters who had left their jobs in Manhattan as early as four P.M. were sleeping in their cars because they could not cross the George Washington Bridge to get home. People on their way to Long Island were spending the night in armories in Queens.

I took my head off the counter long enough to call Phil's beeper. He didn't answer that either. I couldn't imagine where he was. It was very unlike him to go out without turning on his answering machine; he was compulsive about answering the phone when it rang, even when we were in bed together, which drove me crazy, and he wouldn't think of going out without turning on the machine.

I could hear McCabe snoring in the doctors' lounge. He had a very distinctive snore, which would absolutely appall him were he to be informed of it; knowing this, the rest of the medical staff kept a conspiracy and never mentioned it. Roussy you could razz about snoring; McCabe you couldn't. McCabe was just too damned dignified. I considered going to bed in one of the examining rooms. Fleetingly, I entertained the fatuous notion of going back to Hollander's cubicle and lying down on the other stretcher, but I could never get away with something like that; the whole hospital would know about it the next morning. With some regret I turned off the radio and opted for the examining rooms. I lay down fully clothed, shoes and all, and pulled a rough hospital blanket over me. As soon as I lay down, I thought about the picture of Beth on Phil's dresser: Beth sleeping with her hair fanning out on the pillow; Beth in some kind of spaghetti-strap negligee, half-covered by sheets that looked cool and crisp from the laundry.

I arranged the rough hospital blanket over my blood-spattered corduroys and turned on my side.

Most of the time it didn't really bother me that Phil had another lover. Beth worked as a production assistant for a major news network and she was rarely in New York more than four or five days a month. The rest of the time she lived in London. She and Phil were old friends and had been lovers on and off for nearly ten years. In London she had another lover, named Nicko. Phil didn't seem to have any problems about Beth sleeping with Nicko and Beth didn't seem to have any problems about Phil sleeping with me and I figured it was only fair that I seem not to have any problems about Phil sleeping with Beth.

But some of the time I did have problems about it. Sometimes Beth would fly in from London and Phil would go over to her sister's apartment on the East Side and stay there for a few days. I would wander listlessly around the hospital thinking that he was going to come home and tell me that he didn't want to sleep with me anymore, he was going to marry Beth or something. Sometimes after Beth flew away again and Phil came home, I would watch him for a few days, dwelling on his smallest gestures and hanging on his every word, trying to see if I thought he might be thinking about telling me that he didn't want to sleep with me anymore.

Sometimes I fantasized about flying to London and going to bed with Nicko. I had never even met Nicko.

I wondered if Beth were in New York right now and Phil had decided not to tell me for some reason, and if he were with her and if that was the reason I hadn't been able to get ahold of him all evening.

I thought about Phil in bed. He routinely went into a kind of trance when we were together; he was one of those men for whom the exercise of lovemaking was not so much an athletic event as an act of emotional divination. For a minute I ached very deeply for him. I wanted to crawl into his arms, feel his mouth snuffling against my jaw, run my hands over the silky smooth skin of his back. I wondered how Beth was in bed, and if Phil liked sleeping with her better than he liked sleeping with me because he was bigger than she was, whereas I was taller than he was. I thought vaguely: Hollander is six-feet-four. Hollander was one of the few doctors in the hospital who was taller than I was, although some of the others, McCabe for one, were the same height. I had got to Roussy, who was the same height as Phil, only stockier, when I fell asleep.

I jolted out of sleep with a gasp. Throwing b
hospital blanket, I hit the floor with my feet
For a minute I sat there in a daze, list
air going in and out of my lungs and my
against my breastbone.
I turned on the light and looked
Five-thirty A.M.
I turned the light off again
sat there waiting to calm do
I began to recall the fi
I had just finished m
and had landed a s
was the Fourth of
air conditionin
medical floo
breathless
vous as
just s

A needle-holder maybe.

And then I saw Shelley's hair fly loose from her
Gibson Girl bun; I saw it cascade to her shoulders and
waft into the air, blown by a strong malevolent wind
that threw open the heavy metal door to the OR. I
saw the brightness in her eyes warp from intelligence
to despair. I saw her hands reach into the open surgical incision and come into view again holding not a
needle-holder but a large bottle of aspirin. I heard her
scream. Her hands rose up and up into the wind and
the patient rose up off the OR table, following her
hands into the air. The top came loose from the aspirin bottle and aspirin tablets were tumbling from the
large gaping wound in the patient's chest, tumbling
everywhere. Shelley was scooping them up in her gloved
bloody hands and shoveling them into her mouth.

ack the

ening to the
heart thonking

at my watch.

and I lit a cigarette and
wn.

st time I went on the wards.
second year of medical school
mmer clerkship at University. It
July weekend and it was hot. The
was malfunctioning on two of the
s, where I had been assigned, and I was
and sweaty. Breathless and sweaty and ner-
ell. There's no boot camp in medicine; they
nd you to the front.

ou go to the laundress with some forms they give
ou and the laundress gives you your whites.

You go to the Barnes and Noble bookstore on Fifth Avenue at Eighteenth Street and buy your Littmann stethoscope.

You show up on the wards in your new whites with your new stethoscope and you pretend to be a doctor.

You think to yourself: Somebody waved a magic wand and now I'm a *doctor?*

Who are they kidding?

You notice the intern they assign you to wears his stethoscope around his neck; you very hastily take yours out of your pocket and hang it around your neck as nonchalantly as possible and hope no one noticed you had it in your pocket.

When the resident comes in, you notice she has her stethoscope in her pocket and you very hastily take yours off your neck and put it back in your pocket as nonchalantly as possible and hope no one noticed you had it around your neck.

You don't know how your beeper works and you're afraid to ask anyone.

They send you to the lab and you don't know where it is, but you're afraid to ask so you get lost and are gone forty-five minutes and are deeply mortified for the next two hours.

The nurses look at you with scorn and you lock yourself in the bathroom and cry.

You pray.

You cringe.

You have rescue fantasies. You've had rescue fantasies since you started medical school; rescue fantasies that you personally are going to rescue every single patient in the world. Now you have rescue fantasies that someone will rescue *you*. You judge all the interns, residents, and attendings not on their ability to teach you anything but on their ability to exhibit positive motherly or fatherly characteristics in the way they relate to you.

You regress.

You panic.

You forget everything you've learned so far in medical school. Immediately. Totally.

And in the middle of the afternoon when there's a code and you have to go and it's your first time, you personally exhibit all the signs and symptoms of impending cardiac arrest.

I was in the intensive-care unit when they called the code. I had gone up there during a break to see a patient I had taken up the day before; the nurse told me matter-of-factly that the patient had died and went back to whatever she was doing. I was standing there trying to feel whatever it was I thought I was going to feel about my first patient dying. I didn't understand that a self-protective device I didn't know I possessed had already kicked those feelings down the basement steps. I thought: I know I'm going to feel something.

But I wasn't feeling it. I was puzzled, and then disturbed.

The phone behind the ICU desk rang.

I watched the nurse pick it up.

I thought: He died. Feel it.

I thought: What's the matter with me?

The nurse said, "Code on three."

I thought: Where am I?

Then I thought: Three.

There was a flurry of activity behind me. I stood in my self-induced daze, and a line from a song I had learned as a kid for Passover came ludicrously to mind: *Who knows three? I know three. Three patriarchs, two tablets of the Covenant, one is our God in heaven and on the earth.*

Three. My floor. I'm on three. *God Almighty, there's a code on my floor.*

I found myself running through the corridors with two nurses from the ICU, the three of us hauling a crash cart at breakneck speed. Taking corners like cars in a Hollywood car chase. My heart was pounding. *I'm going to have a heart attack. Right now. Here.* We caromed off the far wall of a particularly ill-negotiated turn: *BAM!* We hardly lost speed for the bounce. At the next corner the same thing happened: *BAM!* Maybe it is Hollywood, I thought. I looked at the two nurses tearing along beside me: a slight Filipino woman who looked to be no more than fifteen years old and whose name I couldn't pronounce; what was it again? Anunzionata? Anunzionata Something and Gary Seligman. A former Navy officer with the unlikely moniker of Submarine Gary. They were established and experienced medical personnel, old hands at this crash-cart chase through the hospital corridors, and I wanted to run like they did, look like they did; I wanted to *be* them: I wanted to soak them up through osmosis into myself, incorporate their knowing deadpan professionalism into my being, eat their livers for their courage. I looked at their faces: Anunzionata the doll warrior;

Gary the medical God of War. Gary took a hand off the cart during an open stretch and swept a hairy forearm through the sweat on his brow; loping beside him, I swept my own forearm across my brow. He saw me do it and winked at me as he ran. It was a wink of encouragement, a wink that said: *We're in this together.*

I'm one of them, I thought. *I'm going to be a doctor.*

Two interns and a resident were in the room when we made our clattering entrée. The interns were doing CPR on a man who looked to be fifty-five or sixty; his head was pulled back, his face partly covered by the mouthpiece of the ambu-bag.

I took in the faces of the interns and the resident; I didn't know any of them. I took in the panicked face of the patient in the other bed. Jesus, I thought, pulling the curtain between the two beds. A guy in the next bed, and nobody pulls the curtain; what's the matter with these people? I took in Gary, fussing at the crash cart. I took in Anunzionata's face as she assessed her surroundings and placed herself next to Gary, her posture At the Ready.

I took in myself, my posture *not* At the Ready. I put my hands in my pockets and stood up straighter. I removed my hands from my pockets and clasped my forearms behind my back: *at ease, gentlemen.* Too military. I waved my arms next to my body. Anunzionata crossed her arms over her chest, relaxing somewhat. I crossed mine, trying to relax too. *I'm going to jump out of my fucking skin.*

I had no idea what I was supposed to be doing. I was hoping someone might notice me and tell me what I was supposed to be doing, but then if they did that I probably wouldn't know how to do it anyway, so what was the point?

One of the interns was running EKG tape through his fingers. "I've got complexes but no pulse," he said.

I thought: Electrical-mechanical dissociation. The

heart's electrical system is working but its muscle isn't. Give the guy some calcium.

"Let's have some calcium," the resident said to Gary. "Who are you?"

I jumped. *They're going to ask me to do something and I'm not going to know how to do it.* "Evelyn Sutcliffe," I said. My voice squeaked. I uncrossed my arms, didn't know what to do with them, and crossed them again. I knew the resident was asking for name and not rank; he could tell by looking at me that I was the medical student—I was wearing the distinctive ID badge issued by the College of Physicians and Surgeons with "CLINICAL CLERK" stamped on it in large letters like a "STUDENT DRIVER" bumper sticker.

"Do compressions," the resident said. "Tom, get down and let her do it."

I was already climbing up onto the low stool to do it, thanking God to the high heavens that I knew how to do chest compressions. I clasped my hands together, found my position on the patient's sternum, and began the rhythmic compressions. I counted out loud while I compressed: "One-one-thousand, two-one-thousand, three-one-thousand." *I'm doing something.* I relaxed a little. Not much, but a little. To my right, one of the interns worked the ambu-bag, forcing air in and out of the patient's lungs. *I'm doing something here.*

Then I realized the intern was not paying attention to my count; he was squeezing the bag on my down-stroke instead of on my up-stroke. Consequently, most of the air was going into the patient's stomach.

I unrelaxed. In fact, I panicked. It was not my place to correct an intern. I began to talk to the resident in my head in the desperate hope he might notice the patient's belly distending, filling up with air: *the patient's distended, the patient's distended.*

I wondered if I would ever get to the point in medicine where I would be able to open my mouth when I thought something.

The resident leaned over the patient and his name tag bobbed before my eyes. It read "W. Hamden, M.D." *Dr. Hamden, the patient's distended.* I looked at the top of his head, which was balding, and tried to blitz him with ESP: THE PATIENT IS DISTENDED.

Jesus Christ, I thought.

"Stop a second," Hamden said.

I nearly shrieked with relief.

"There's no pulse," Hamden noted. He nodded to me, and I started the compressions again. I thought: The patient's probably in tamponade. The sac around the heart, called the pericardium, can fill up with blood or fluid and the patient's heart gets stuck in there and can't beat.

"Think he's in tamponade?" the intern with the ambu-bag asked laconically. "You wanna stick a needle in him?"

Work the goddamn bag! I screamed at him in my mind.

Hamden considered this. "Nah," he said. "That never works. You don't know where you're going; it's a guess whether you're in the pericardium or the left ventricle or even one of the major vessels. You could hit anything with that needle; you don't know."

I thought: I'm going a hundred miles an hour, and these guys are going five miles an hour, and *the patient is going to die.*

Another resident had come into the room, a tall thin man with glasses too big for his face who looked bored already. "Aw, c'mon, Hamden," he said. "You see if it clots."

"Yeah, and if it does, you've hit the ventricle, which isn't what you wanted."

"So watch the EKG and see if you get a stress reading."

"Great," Hamden said without enthusiasm. He wiped the sweat out of his eyes with the flat of his wrist. "Christ, it's hot in here."

The intern with the ambu-bag clicked his tongue derisively. "This is more fun than being an astronaut," he muttered.

A short woman with red hair, wearing street clothes and no white coat, had come into the room.

Thank God, I thought. An attending. I looked at her closely. My eyeballs jumped out of my head and landed on her shoulders. I thought: *Do something*. My eyes jumped to her face: she had an intelligent, no-nonsense expression. My eyes jumped to Hamden. He was briefing her, deferring to her. I thought: Maybe she's a teaching fellow. I sucked my eyes back into my head and willed her to look at me.

The patient is distended. The patient is in cardiac tamponade. Help!

"You're standing on the IV line, Hamden," she said dryly.

Hamden moved his feet.

I read her name tag, which was clipped to the waistband of her flowered-print skirt: "S. Reinish, M.D." The skirt billowed in the breeze that came in through the open window and I thought immediately and incongruously: The Princess of Wales.

Reinish looked at the patient and then at the intern with the ambu-bag. "He looks a little distended," she said.

My knees went weak with relief.

Next to me, the intern made a small effort to coordinate the bag with my compressions. "Is it too late to go into law?" he joked.

"I'm beginning to think you should," Reinish snapped. "Is there a patient in the next bed?"

"Yes," I said. It was the first thing I'd said since I'd told them my name, and everyone looked at me.

"Then you watch your mouth, Doctor," Reinish said in a low voice to the intern. "It does nothing to inspire confidence in the patients, you making jokes about going into law. Do you understand me?"

The intern lowered his eyes and said nothing.

I wanted to cheer.

"And pay attention! You're bagging on the downstroke; no wonder the patient's distended. Step out." She pointed at the other intern. "Get on the bag." She turned to Hamden. "Do you want me to do this, Bill?" She turned to Submarine Gary, manning the crash cart. "Give me a red-top tube; the purple-tops have sodium citrate, and we want to see if it clots." She turned to me. "Stop."

I was mesmerized by her. I took my hands off the patient's chest. She can't be more than five feet tall, I thought, dressed like a Laura Ashley ad in a flowered-print skirt, and here she is commanding like a member of the British aristocracy. A line came to me from somewhere: *The lady sways her house.*

Reinish took a long needle with a red line attached to it, felt with tiny delicate fingers along the patient's ribs, and gently pushed the needle through the chest wall. She drew off a quantity of thin-looking reddish fluid.

It did not clot, even after two minutes.

She had hit the pericardium on the first try.

I pledged undying allegiance to her in my mind.

We had resumed CPR. There were no more scurrilous remarks from the assembled company, and the patient ceased to distend.

Eventually we got something resembling normal sinus rhythm on the EKG, I got something resembling normal sinus rhythm on my internal monitoring of my own heartbeat, and Submarine Gary and I wheeled the patient off to the intensive care unit. A nurse from the floor trailed behind us with Anunzionata, the two of them pulling the crash cart the way you lead a thoroughbred after a good race.

"Who was that masked woman?" I asked Gary. "A teaching fellow?"

He turned and gave me a wide grin. "Dr. Reinish,"

he said. "She sure acts like a fellow, doesn't she? When I met her the first time I thought she was the dean of the medical faculty. She's a first-year surgical resident."

I almost dropped the patient's IV bag. "You're shitting me."

"No shit, Sherlock."

"What's her first name?"

"Shelley. She'll tell you to call her that, too. She doesn't stand on ceremony." He backed through a set of swinging doors, pulling the stretcher through. "She's good. She's *very* good. One of the best."

One of the best.

Gary's words rang through my head as I sat on the edge of the bed and smoked my cigarette.

I felt numb, incapable of feeling anything.

It was profoundly upsetting. There was a buzz going on in my chest which I took to be the buzz of some feelings somewhere trying to get out, but I didn't seem to know how to *let* them get out.

I heard Phil's voice in my head, saying, "See if you can make that conscious." Phil's voice took up a duet with Gary's voice:

One of the best.

See if you can make that conscious.

One of the best.

I realized a man was standing in the doorway to the examining room.

In the dark, I couldn't see who he was. A middle-of-the-night terror lit itself like a brushfire in my chest, flaring out across my shoulders and into my arms. I leapt to my feet and stumbled over the metal chair that was next to the bed.

"I have to talk to you," the man said, moving toward me.

"*Who is it?*"

He stopped. Backlit by the dim light from the corridor, he was a ghostly apparition. "What do you mean, who is it? It's me. Tony."

For some reason I did not relax, even though it was one of the doctors and not some demented or malevolent patient sneaking up on me in the middle of the night. The terror subsided, but a watchfulness remained in me, mixed with annoyance. "Well, I can't see you in the dark," I snapped. "Turn on the light."

"No. Just sit down."

"Is this some kind of joke, Firenze? I've had a hard evening here and I'm not in the mood to talk to you in the dark. If you don't mind." I made a move toward the wall where the light switch was.

I should have listened to the tone of his voice. Dr. Anthony Firenze was famous for his bad temper and ferocious outbursts, an old-style surgeon despite his youth, who got his way in the OR by bullying people and throwing things. Like the scissors he had thrown at Shelley for threatening to publish his off-the-cuff remarks.

Like me, whom he now threw up against the wall.

"Hey!" I protested. I wasn't hurt, but the force of his toss seemed a little beyond Firenze's usual arm-waving aggressiveness. He got me in a viselike grip around both biceps, leaning his weight against me so that my shoulders were pressed flat against the wall.

"I want you to tell me what she wrote," he said in a low voice.

His face was about two inches away from mine; my eyes crossed trying to focus on him. "You are assaulting my person," I pointed out to him, "And you're AOB." Alcohol On Breath. To myself, I thought: Why are you putting up with this? How come you're just standing there letting him squash you up against the wall? Why don't you kick him? "C'mon, Tony," I tried to cajole him. "This is a little melodramatic, even for you. Let go."

He let go of one of my arms and grabbed me by the face, digging his thumb and fingers into my jaw.

"That hurts, Tony! Get off me!"

"You listen to me, Sutcliffe. I know you've read the whole goddamn manuscript, and you tell me right now what she wrote about me!"

I levered my free arm up between us, trying to jam my elbow into his ribs. He swung me around by the arm he was still hanging on to and my back slammed up against the doorframe.

"She's *dead,* you asshole! *Or don't you know that?*"

"What the hell is going on here?" Gary Seligman demanded. His shoulder was suddenly between mine and Firenze's.

"You keep out of this, you faggot," Firenze said.

I stiffened.

"Aw, Jesus," Gary said, not batting an eye at the epithet. "What is your problem exactly?"

"He's drunk."

"I smell that." Gary pushed Tony away with the long-suffering air of an eternally rational male soothing his eternally irrational counterpart. Gary had done three tours of duty on a submarine in the Navy and was used to spontaneous outbursts between people who had been cooped up too long with each other. It made him a very fine nurse. "What are you doing here anyway, Tony?" Gary wanted to know. "You're not on tonight, are you?"

"I'm tired," I announced suddenly. "He's drunk, he threw me up against the wall and assaulted me, someone should punch him in the face. I'm going to go get myself a cup of coffee." I turned on my heel and stomped out of the room. "Thank you for intervening," I said to Gary over my shoulder as I left.

I was simply too tired to be mad.

Or so I told myself. The real problem was probably this: I was humiliated that I had stood around passively while Tony Firenze bullied me, and I was humiliated to have been "rescued" by Gary Seligman. I should have stood up to Tony myself, told him just once in my life what I really thought of him. *Grow up, Tony. I'm sick and tired of giving in to your goddamned temper tantrums all the time.*

I went around the corner through the utilities room to the doctors' lounge, moving quietly so as not to wake McCabe, who was still snoring in there. *And I'm sick of all this macho bullshit! Who do you think you are, pushing me around like that?*

Forget it, I told myself. Just forget it.

I poured a cup of coffee for myself and went back out to the nurses' station. My hand shook.

"Did he leave?" I asked Gary, who was shuffling through some test results back from the lab.

"I pointed him in the right direction," he said. "What was that all about?"

"I don't want to talk about it." In fact, I didn't even want to think about it; I just wanted to put the entire incident out of my mind.

CHAPTER

7

"All major roadways in the five boroughs are passable, with at least two lanes open. However, roads are still slick and authorities ask motorists not to drive unless absolutely necessary. Two of the biggest trouble spots so far: Brooklyn-Queens Expressway closed from Humboldt Street to the Kosciuszko Bridge; the New England Thruway is snowed under . . ."

The radio announcer droned on. "You driving anywhere today?" I asked Paul Roussy.

He shook his head, not any more awake than I was. Possibly less awake; Roussy was a self-proclaimed night owl, whereas I was always going around telling people I was a morning person. Although at the moment I definitely did not feel like a morning person; in fact, I was dubious about the *person* part. "So we gotta listen to this?" I wanted to know.

Roussy turned unfocused eyes on me and drifted off into the next hemisphere.

I leaned over and slapped his cheek lightly. "Wake-up call. You got a big cup of coffee between your two fat fists there. Drink."

" . . . on the subways, the Double-L is out of service from Myrtle Avenue to Canarsie; N out of service from Fifty-ninth Street to Coney Island-Stillwell; D out of service from Prospect Park to Stillwell Avenue; A out of service . . ."

Paul and I were sitting on stools in the utility room, waiting to talk to the detectives. It was, by my watch, 7:03 A.M. Tuesday.

". . . in some areas of the tri-state area some less-traveled roadways are still very treacherous, as in Connecticut." A female voice replaced the male one with a woman-in-the-street report. "Yesterday's storm dumped between ten and twenty-four inches . . ."

"They like the word 'dump,' " I said.

Roussy rested his coffee cup against his chin and breathed the steam. He was beginning to look slightly more alert. "You're a thrill in the morning, Ev," he said.

"What? Try putting your teeth in."

" . . . and the Long Island Expressway just out of the Midtown Tunnel, a crew of sanitation snow plows and highway police are clearing the road of abandoned vehicles in snow. The cars are being towed by the Traffic Department tow trucks to areas just off the highway, so if you left your car anywhere on the Long Island Expressway, just look to the side streets near the area where you left it."

"You leave your car on the LIE, Paul?"

"Yeah, I just wanted to park it someplace artistic, you know? Then I walked here. It's only about eight miles and the snow was only up to my knees, piece of cake. In fact, I went out on my supper break, drove the car to the LIE, abandoned it, and walked back here, and it only took me a half-hour."

Paul didn't own a car.

I raised my eyebrows and gave a low whistle of appreciation. "Not bad, Paul. That's at least four sentences and it's only seven o'clock in the morning, I'd say that's a major therapeutic advancement there. Last time I was on all night with you, you could only get out *two* sentences at seven o'clock."

He lifted his shoulders in an elaborately modest shrug the way our illustrious mayor does. We were just rolling into a comradely chuckle when Alex McCabe came out of the doctors' lounge. We cut it off immediately.

"O.K., Sutcliffe," McCabe said. "You next."

My heart started to go the way it had the time I appeared before the grand jury to testify that a certain police officer examined by me in the ER did indeed have cuts and bruises consistent with defense wounds. Alex patted me on the shoulder as he passed me. "By the way," he said, "do you know where Phil Carchiollo is? I've been calling him and beeping him and I can't get an answer."

"How the hell should I know?" I snapped.

McCabe shot me a look he reserved for expressing private amusement. "Well," he said, "if you find him, call him in. They want to talk to him." Alex tossed his head toward the doctors' lounge, still moving, walking backward. Then he turned and went around the corner into the ER.

Detectives John Kelly and Richard Ost were sitting at the kitchen table in the doctors' lounge, drinking coffee from Styrofoam cups, and smoking cigarettes. When I came in, both officers pretended to get up: leaning forward in their seats, they lifted their derrieres off their chairs the requisite inch or so, and sat back down immediately. I noticed that Ost was wearing a plaid flannel shirt and a bullet-proof vest; the shirt was unbuttoned and the Velcro fasteners of the vest were undone. He was always complaining that it was too hot in the emergency room. "Whaddya runnin' here, Doc?" he liked to say. "A steambath?"

" 'Mornin', Doc," Ost greeted me. "You know Kelly here, right?"

"Yeah, sure." I saw Kelly all the time, although I usually saw Kelly with his partner, Greg Malinowski, and Ost with his, an energetic young woman named Jude Rainey. "But where's Malinowski and Jude

Rainey?" (Jude Rainey was, for some inexplicable reason, always called exactly that: Jude Rainey. Never just Jude, never just Rainey.)

"Sick leave and special assignment."

"You sound like you think that's funny," I said.

"Jude Rainey's in a lesbian bar these last two weeks," Kelly said without smiling. Kelly only smiled when nothing was going on.

"That true?"

Ost was looking slightly cross-eyed. "Yeah, she's on that case where the guy is cutting up gays. We got a few people in the bars."

I looked pointedly at the plaid flannel shirt and the bullet-proof vest. Then I angled myself sideways to see under the table; the rest of Ost's outfit consisted of very tight jeans and cowboy boots. With spurs.

"O.K., O.K.," he protested. Kelly examined the ceiling. "You gonna sit down, or what?"

I sat. My heart started going again. *Let go. Just let go. Grieve.*

Not yet.

"First, what happened?"

I gave a quick rundown, beginning with Shelley's arrival and ending with her death. I knew they had asked McCabe the same thing before me. I also knew that they wanted to hear it again, in my words, and that they would listen to the story several times more in the words of the hospital personnel they would interview after me. I ran through the five "W's and H"—what, when, where, who, why, and how—and Kelly let me talk mostly without interrupting, occasionally making notations in his notebook.

"Time arrived?"

"Uh, quarter after nine?"

"Time of death?"

"Approximately ten-twenty-five."

"You physician of record?"

"I pronounced, yes."

"Cause of death?"

I hesitated. Kelly looked up, resting his watery blue eyes on me expectantly. I guessed him to be in his middle to late forties, and his face was very Irish. There were two things that face could have been: a cop or a priest. For a second I saw his face over a clerical collar, and I wondered with a start if this were a hallucination Kelly could project into other persons' brains at will. "You already discussed this with Dr. McCabe, right?" I asked.

"Yes," Kelly said, watching me. Ost leaned forward in his chair.

I drained the rest of my coffee from the cup I had brought in with me and resisted the desire for a cigarette, gave up, and fished one out of my lab coat. Ost's arm came up immediately with his lighter.

"Thank you, Ozzie," I said. I took a long drag.

They were still waiting.

"Acute salicylate poisoning. Aspirin overdose," I sighed finally.

"You wish to state that the woman in question, Dr. Shelley Reinish, died of an overdose of aspirin?"

"Yes."

"You in full agreement with this diagnosis, Doc?"

I smoked my cigarette and stared at the wall. Over the coffeemaker, the nurses had pinned up a magazine ad showing a woman doctor, her lab coat open to reveal a shimmering pink underwear ensemble, questioning a patient at bedside. Behind her, two male doctors, fully clothed, conferred with each other somberly. The nurses had cut out male torsos from a men's underwear ad and taped them over the male bodies in the women's-underwear ad.

"Dr. Sutcliffe?"

I started. "I'm sorry," I apologized. "I agree with the diagnosis. I just have . . . a hard time convincing myself that Shelley killed herself, that's all."

The detectives nodded sympathetically in unison.

"How well did you know the deceased?" Kelly asked me gently.

I winced. "We worked together. We didn't see each other socially, except at staff parties—you know, the nurses' Christmas bash, that kind of thing. Of course, you know what kind of hours we work here, and we get to know each other pretty well in that sense . . ." I trailed off. "Oh, hell. She was hard to know. She was religious. That's hard for a lot of people to relate to." I seemed suddenly to be very angry about that, but I quickly quashed the anger, deciding I must be angry about something else. But I didn't know what.

Kelly got up and poured himself another cup of coffee. He spent a few seconds examining the doctors in their underwear in the ad over the coffeemaker, then sat down again. "Dr. Sutcliffe, did the deceased at any time give you any reason to believe that she might be thinking of killing herself?"

I shook my head.

"Would you say that you knew the deceased well enough, personally speaking, to make a judgment about her mental health? To tell whether she was, let's say, depressed, or upset about anything?"

I noticed that Kelly's voice was becoming positively hypnotic. I shook my head again.

Kelly sipped at his coffee and spent a few minutes looking at his notebook. Then he said, "You say you didn't know the deceased very well, but you also say you find it difficult to believe that she killed herself. Why? What's hard to believe?" He swiveled his eyes up and fixed me with his watery stare.

I had a sudden memory of Shelley Reinish in surgery, the day I had first worked with her, my first weekend on the house staff at University Hospital. Shelley had been a tiny bundle of efficiency, her doll-like hands never faltering, her mind as sharp and quick as a stiletto. "I don't think you have to know a person very well," I said slowly, "to tell whether he or she is under stress. I think . . . a person under a lot of stress would not be able to function as effectively as Shelley. I mean, I never noticed that her work suffered . . ." I trailed off again, lifting my hands helplessly. "I think I would have noticed something."

Kelly turned a page in his notebook. "Dr. McCabe says he noticed that Dr. Reinish had been looking tired recently. Would you agree with this? That she looked tired, or seemed under the weather?"

I stubbed out my cigarette and cleared my throat. "Kelly, listen. We're all tired here. Sure she seemed tired. She was on call every third night for a while when the other surgical resident went on maternity leave."

"So you would not say the deceased seemed unduly tired."

They were watching me again, but not directly. Kelly was affecting great interest in a speck of something he had discovered under his thumbnail, and Ost was pretending to have a wayward lash in his eye. Jesus, I thought. Do these guys go to school to learn this, or what?

"Look," I said. I laid both forearms flat on the table, hands splayed. "You guys and I have worked together I don't know how many times and I have always felt like we had a good working relationship, you know? Somebody dies, you come in here, I give you all the info you need. A case is a little complicated —some kind of weird gunshot wound, a bizarre combination of drugs in a suicide, whatever—no problem. I explain it to you till you understand what you need to know, and I don't talk down to you just because you're not nurses or doctors. Now do me a favor and knock off with this Kojak crap, huh? You wanna know do I think I knew 'the deceased,' as you call her, well enough to tell if she was suicidal or not? I didn't know her very well, but I see a lot of suicidal people in this place, and I think I can say that Shelley was not suicidal!''

The detectives of course did not react to this, except to fine-tune the blankness of their expressions.

"I mean," I said, calming down a little, "just a week ago I came into the doctors' lounge here—this room— and Shelley was sitting here at the table with some typed transcripts of her book. You knew she was writing a book, about surgery and men and women who become surgeons?"

"Dr. McCabe mentioned it," Ost conceded. "A journalistic account, sort of like that book that came out a few years ago about Bellevue. He said it had more conversations with doctors about their personal lives and how they decided to become doctors and that kind of stuff."

"Well," I went on, "she was all excited about this book. It was almost finished. Her typist was working on the first draft. I don't think I've ever seen her look as vibrant and alive as she looked that day, talking about the book and how it had already been accepted for publication and all. I just . . ." I stopped. I just what? Something wasn't right.

I went back in my mind to a week ago Monday, when I had come into the doctors' lounge to get a cup of coffee. Shelley had been sitting at the table drinking a can of soda, a manila folder open in front of her, pages of typed manuscript stacked in several neat little piles on the table.

"Look at this, Ev," she said when I sat down next to her. Her eyes were bright with excitement. "I got this guy I knew in med school who's a surgeon at Mass General to talk to me about dog lab. I heard about this one dog lab where they never anesthetized the dogs properly and they would howl the whole time you were operating them and it took me ages to track down someone who was in that class and get them to talk to me about it." She drained her can of soda, hopped out of her chair, and got herself another from the refrigerator.

I watched her gulp the soda and nodded. Horror stories from dog lab were apocryphal. All medical students had to practice surgery on dogs before they were allowed to operate on people, and everyone seemed to know someone who knew someone whose dog "got light" in the middle of surgery and whimpered or whined, unnerving the operating team. I didn't really see what Shelley was so excited about, but her excitement was infectious anyway, so I gave her a big fat grin and reached across the table and shook her hand in congratulation.

"Dr. Sutcliffe?"

I came back to the present, feeling slightly disoriented. "I don't know," I mumbled. "I'm just having trouble with this. I mean, you don't go out and sign a book contract and give your first draft to a typist and then a week and half later kill yourself."

"Let me get this straight," Kelly said. He ran the flat of his hand across his chin. "You were actually working with Dr. Reinish on this book as a kind of editor for her, weren't you?"

"Well, yeah," I said, surprised that they knew this. McCabe must have told them. "I have a master's in English and most of a Ph.D., and I used to teach English lit and creative writing at the women's college here at the University. Shelley knew this and asked me if I would mind proofreading her manuscript for her, and I agreed."

"So you not only worked with Dr. Reinish here at the hospital, you also spent time with her going over her manuscript."

I nodded.

"And you never got the idea that she might be thinking of killing herself, or that she might be depressed?"

"No. If anything I—" I cut myself off. I had an idea, but I wanted to hang on to it for a while. "I would have to say that I've found her very . . . positive . . . about things these last few weeks."

A little too positive maybe.

Kelly leaned forward. "Forgive me for pressing you on this point, Dr. Sutcliffe, but I don't quite understand how you say that you didn't know the deceased very well. It seems to me you must have known her pretty well, if you worked here with her at the hospital and on her book as well."

I thought about Shelley, her frizzy-haired head bent over her precious manuscript. "I didn't know her very well at all," I said sadly. "We never talked about anything except medicine. I knew her as a doctor. I knew her as a writer who wrote about doctors. We had a lot of respect for each other professionally. But I can't remember one single time she ever told me anything personal about herself."

"All right." Kelly nodded. "What do you make of the injection marks?"

"I think it's reasonable to assume she had blood drawn for tests, yesterday morning or maybe Sunday. That would explain the Band-Aids. When they draw your blood for tests, they always give you a Band-Aid." It did not explain, in my mind, why she had two puncture sites, one of which was on the back of her hand. You don't usually get blood drawn for tests from the back of your hand; that's where they put the IV when you have surgery.

But for some reason I didn't say this.

"Any other ideas on that?"

"No, when we got the SMAC machine running again last night—it was down for a while—we ordered a Chem 60 series and we didn't come up with any of the usual drugs in her blood. Of course, she could have shot herself up with something esoteric, I suppose. . . . You guys realize, of course, that you can't ask the computer *what* a person took, but only *if* a person took such-and-such. If you don't name the drug and run the specific test for that particular drug, the person could be full up to the gills with it and you would never know the difference."

"But your opinion is that she probably got blood tests and that's what those puncture marks are?"

"I would surmise that, yes."

"O.K., then let me ask you this: why would she have her blood tested?"

"There are a number of reasons she might have wanted her blood tested. Maybe she had a routine physical. She could have had tests because she thought she was pregnant—her husband thought she might be pregnant; he told us her period was three weeks overdue."

"Pregnant?" both detectives said simultaneously, sitting up in their chairs.

"Yeah, pregnant," I said, slightly bemused. "You know, with child. Knocked up."

And then I got a distinct blip on my radar screen. *They know something*, I realized. *They know something I don't.* I glanced at Ost sharply, his being the more readable face, but I came up with zip. I knew I would get zip if I asked, too; I had been around police too long. Very slowly I reached my hand across the table and picked up Ozzie's lighter. It had the slightly oily feel of very good, heavyweight gold and was engraved with the initials JTR. I turned it over in my hand a couple of times. "Special assignment, huh?" I said softly. I pushed the lighter back across the table. Not to Ost, but to a space equidistant between him and Kelly, so that Kelly could see the initials. Ost's gaze shot sideways and back again like a rubber band snapping.

"This is a personal-interest case," I said. "Not just another stiff on the table. You guys knew her too. You're overcompensating with this cops-and-robbers shit to get yourselves around the fact that you're dealing here with someone you knew."

Kelly stared at me. For a minute I thought I saw his priest's face again, with a twinkle in the eye. Then it was gone. Ost put Jude Rainey's lighter in the pocket of his plaid flannel shirt. "O.K.," he said. "O.K." He cleared his throat. "To your knowledge, was Dr. Reinish conscious when found?"

"No. To my knowledge she was not, but this is hearsay. I'm repeating to you what her husband said."

"His words as you recall them?"

I repeated what Rabbi Reinish had told us when he brought Shelley in.

"And she did not at any time regain consciousness?"

"No."

"Her husband was home at the time?"

"Ah, no, he came home and found her. Listen, I don't know this, I'm telling you what he *said.*"

The detectives nodded largely so that I would understand the point was taken. "And he told you this when?"

"As soon as he brought her in the door."

"And how did her husband seem to you?"

"How did he *seem?* Distraught."

"You believed what he was telling you?"

"Yes. Of course."

"Did they have any marital difficulties? To your knowledge."

I watched them registering the look of astonishment on my face.

"This is routine, O.K.?" Ost said. "We're not alleging anything, we're just asking the routine questions."

"I don't know," I said, trying to let this sink in. "She always talked about him affectionately, yeah, that's the word I'd use exactly: she talked about him affectionately. She called him 'the Bear.' 'I told the Bear this and he said such-and-such.' I think I used to hear her call him that while talking to him, too. 'What do you want for dinner, Bear?' They seemed to talk a lot on the phone."

"There was no one else. To your knowledge. Other than her husband." The detectives were developing a bizarre cadence, speaking very slowly and carefully. *We're sorry to ask you this, but,* their manner implied. *This is routine, O.K.?*

"I would tend to doubt it."

"O.K.," Ost said. I saw that they had exhausted this line of questioning and were selecting the next. "When was the last time you saw her before last evening when her husband brought her into the emergency room?"

I thought about this. "Last Monday. Not yesterday—a week ago."

"And she seemed how to you at that time?"

"I would say she seemed . . ." I paused, choosing my adjectives carefully. *"Energetic.* Positive."

"You spoke with her at this time."

"Yes."

"And you discussed what? In particular."

"We discussed her book." Dog lab. Unanesthetized dogs howling during surgery.

"She did not seem depressed to you, or tired, or in any other way not herself."

They say "tired" like it's a euphemism, I thought. A code word for what they're not telling me. Instinctively I began to cover my left flank. "No."

"Any adverse relationships."

"I'm sorry, any what?"

"Adverse relationships. Anybody she not get along with? She fight with anybody, anybody not like her, she not like anybody?"

I thought about Firenze throwing the scissors at her in surgery. But that was Firenze, he was always throwing things. "No."

"She in debt? To your knowledge."

"I have no idea."

"You discuss her finances with her ever?"

"No."

"Anybody you know she was close to? A good friend, somebody she would confide in?"

I shifted my weight in my chair. I saw Ost immediately cock his head slightly, a roe deer turning its ear to a faraway noise carried on the wind. This man is good, I thought. He's *very* good. I realized I had crossed my arms over my chest and I uncrossed them slowly. "She was not habitually an open person," I said. "Or, let me amend that: I did not find her very open, we did not confide in each other." I got out another cigarette, tried to busy myself with it without looking like I was seeking displacement activity. Which I was. Smoking too much.

Ost didn't produce his lighter. I produced mine. I flicked it and then set it down on the table.

They're going to think you're hiding something, I thought.

"She's in therapy, you know, psychoanalysis?"

For a minute Ost and I looked at one another. My heart was going again. *Bang-bang-bang.* I took a long drag and blew it out. "Dr. Carchiollo is her therapist," I said as levelly as possible.

"First name?"

"Philip. You know him."

"He on the staff here?"

"One of the psychiatric attendings."

"Short guy, blond hair, wire-rimmed glasses?"

"Yeah."

"I know him. He here tonight?"

"No." I cleared my throat. I didn't tell them I'd been calling Phil all evening. "He went off this morning—sorry, yesterday morning—at eight and he has two days off now. He works a two-on, two-off, five-on, five-off schedule."

Something was happening in Ost's face; there was a slight pulling back of the skin around the eyes, and he immediately put his hand over his mouth and leaned his elbow on the table. He was staring at me and I stared back, determined not to break eye contact. I crossed my arms again and left them crossed.

He looked pointedly at my fake malachite lighter on the table where I had put it. I began to count beats in my head. One. Two. Three. Then Ost moved his eyes to his notebook, and tied his bland expression back on where it had come loose around the edges.

And I wondered what he knew.

CHAPTER

8

The plaster room of University Hospital is sometimes an alcove, sometimes a corridor—it depends on whether the door to the abscess room at one end of it is open or shut. In either case, we're talking about a very small space here, maybe five feet by eight feet, situated off a corridor in a warren of alcoves and corridors known collectively as Holding. Holding is where you put patients who are not sick enough to be admitted but who are too sick to be sent home: people sleeping off drug OD's, little old ladies with no one at home to look after them, people who might be concussed that you want to watch for a while to see if they start exhibiting bizarre behavior or neurological signs. Cases like that. God knows why they put the plaster room in Holding and not in the main ER. There's no rhyme or reason to the floor plans of hospitals. They put the *morgue* elevator back there, too. Of course, the morgue elevator has to be near the ambulance bay, so maybe there's a reason for that. It is an indisputable fact, however, that the floor plan at University Hospital stands as an unparalleled master's thesis in warrens of alcoves and corridors: a veritable Escher drawing, where all things converge and yet nothing converges, and the staircases go this way and that in various feats of *trompe l'oeil*.

I realized I was yelling about it in my head.

I was, in fact, yelling *at someone* about it in my head, someone who was prepared to contradict my every thought.

I had absolutely no idea who this supposedly contrary someone was. The unseen adversary. The imaginary opponent. You, out there. Yeah. You. I remembered that scene from *Taxi Driver* where Robert De Niro talks to himself in the mirror: *You talkin' to me? Well, there's nobody else here.*

Yeah, but you're not even looking in the mirror, Sutcliffe, there really is nobody else here.

Besides which, this is something to get mad about? The floor plan in Holding?

I was at the moment striding purposefully toward the plaster room from the nurses' station, where I had gone to collect Jay Hollander's chart. One of the nurses grabbed me to sign something, and such was my momentum that she nearly wheeled me into an about-face doing it; my mind paused in its diatribe for a split second to rest itself, a pleasant blankness filled my head, I signed whatever it was, and then my mind and feet sallied forth again.

I kicked through the swinging doors to the ER and swept around a corner past the morgue elevator.

I have ascertained, through careful study over the years, that all builders of hospitals are graduates of the same demented school of architecture whose one inviolable maxim appears to be this: all hospital corridors *must* evoke as faithfully as possible the confusion felt by a tourist lost for the first time in Venice, Italy.

If you have ever been lost in Venice you know what I mean.

Just a minute. Time out. Pause for station identification.

Why are you going *on* about all this?

Good question.

I'm going on about all this because I was trying to talk to Jay Hollander in the plaster room a few minutes ago and in five minutes no fewer than three people—all lost—wandered in.

Or maybe I'm going on about all this because the interview with the detectives left a bad taste in my mouth, because I couldn't tell who'd won and who'd lost. Play by play I suspect we came out even, but I'm not really sure.

Or maybe I'm annoyed with myself because I'm obsessing at all over who won or who lost with the detectives. Shelley's dead and I'm wondering who *won*. What the hell kind of focus is that?

Or I'm upset because Shelley's dead, period.

Or because I can't get ahold of Phil. He could be lying under a snowdrift somewhere, knocked unconscious by a mugger and left to freeze to death. Or Beth could be in New York unbeknownst to me and he could be lying in her arms this very moment, damn his soul.

Or because I'm going to have to read Jay's X rays in the corridor since the person who set up the plaster room in Year One neglected to provide a light box, even though any sane and logical consideration of design for the plaster room should have included provision for the fact that orthopedists read a *hell* of a lot of X rays.

No, that's *not* it.

I thought we were talking about the plaster room.

No. The ostensible subject of conversation was the plaster room. But the hidden agenda was what? *You know what it is. Say it.*

Or because I'm so distracted by Hollander's jawline and high cheekbones—to say nothing of his shirtless hairy chest—that I simply can't see straight.

"Where are your postreduction X rays?" I yelled at Jay Hollander, barging into the plaster room. I tossed his chart on the stretcher and crossed my arms over my chest belligerently.

He was sitting on a stool next to the sink, leaning

his shoulders and the back of his head against the door to the abscess room. The stool was very low and he sat on it the way parents sit on kindergarten furniture on PTA night, their knees high and at awkward angles. His face blanked with surprise.

I stood there a moment glaring at him. Over his head and to the left of the door there was a picture of Mr. Rogers holding up a newly plastered forearm. Mr. Rogers looked pleased as punch to have his arm in a cast. I was not pleased as punch. I was losing all patience with everyone, myself, Hollander, and Mr. Rogers included; I turned on my heel and marched back into the corridor. My arm came up with a snap as I reached for the switch on the light box.

Jay slid up behind me and slung his good arm around my shoulder; the large manila envelope of X rays dangled loosely from his hand. He pressed his body up against my back, cast and all, and the cast came between us like a fence.

I was so unnerved by this I nearly turned on him with the same punch I once lanced on an Italian soldier who goosed me in the Vatican.

Get a grip on yourself, Sutcliffe.

"You drive me wild," Jay whispered in my ear. "Mad with desire. I throw myself at your feet."

I smiled and put my arm up the way you do when you turn over in the night to get gently away from your lover, who has tangled himself around you. "You did that already," I said. "Last week."

"I did? It didn't work?"

I took the envelope from his hand and pulled one of the X rays out of it. The X ray made a small *wopping* noise like a saw bending.

"What kind of perfume is this you have on?"

"Oh, Jay, you're so corny."

"Does that mean I'm cute? Say you think I'm cute."

I couldn't help myself. I laughed. I snapped the X rays up into the light box and made a great show of looking at them. He was hanging over my shoulder again and I pushed him away. "What do I have to do with you," I sighed, "wear one of those suits beekeepers wear when they go poking around the hives?"

"I know a wonderful seamstress in Paris who sews the latest thing in French beekeepers' suits. How about a weekend in Paris? You and me."

"No. Now get off me and let me look at these X rays."

Surprisingly, he moved away. I looked at the X rays for a few minutes. I could still feel the heat of Jay's breath against my ear despite the fact that he had removed himself to somewhere behind me. Never mind Jay; you can talk to Jay in a minute. Look at the X rays, sweetheart. Focus. Line of fracture; you're looking for the line of fracture. There you go. It's right in front of your face. *Now look at it.*

I said, "Manny did a good job. You can hardly see the line of fracture."

Jay's face did not reappear over my shoulder.

I waited a minute, willing him to come up behind me and put his arm around me again so I could push him away again.

Very good. You're in touch with your ambivalence. *You want him to make a pass at you so you can turn him down.*

O.K., so I find him attractive. That doesn't mean I want to go to bed with him.

Uh-huh.

All right, I find him *very* attractive. I find him so attractive I'm a wreck. I've always found him attractive.

That's not true, you've never paid any attention to him. He climbs all over you all the time. This is the first time you're getting whacked out about it.

So what's different? What's the new dynamic here?

There was a noise behind me like a body falling.

I turned around to find Hollander bent double over the plaster-room sink, taking huge breaths, his good hand fumbling for the faucet. He turned the water on hard and angled his head and neck under it.

"I can't breathe," he gasped.

I didn't move; for some reason I stood riveted to the spot. Or so I thought. Actually I must have moved, because the next time I looked, my hands were on Jay's shoulders and there was water spraying everywhere; we might as well have been in the shower together. He seemed hell-bent on drowning himself in the plaster-room sink or at least sabotaging his newly casted fracture. Concern for him welled up in me from as far south as my feet and throbbed in my bosom. *My poor, poor J.J.*

Meanwhile another part of me thought: What is this bullshit, why do men do stuff like this? (And why do women respond like earth mothers to it?) He knows he has a new cast and he's not supposed to get it wet, why can't he just sit down and put his head between his knees like a responsible, sensible person? So he feels faint. But you tell me, Dr. Hollander, when you have a patient who feels faint, what do you say to that patient? Do you say: Here, put your head in the sink and let me turn on the water? You do not. You say: Here, sit down on this stool and put your head between your knees.

Oh, Jay, Jay, let me help you, sweetheart.

He was heaving in huge amounts of air and water and coughing and gasping and spitting. *For God's sake, you're going to drown yourself, you asshole.* I turned off the faucet with a quick jerk of the wrist and hooked an arm around his shoulder and under one armpit, hauling him bodily out of the sink. "Get up," I said. "Sit down. Here's the stool; sit. Put your head between your knees." I went down on one knee in front of him, wrapping the cast in one towel and trying to dry his hair with another. He wasn't helping, of course—(*Do men ever help? . . . Not bloody likely. . . . My poor, poor J.J.*)—he was leaning so far forward the cast was jammed between his chest and his thighs, and his hair was dripping all over everything. Including me.

He sat up suddenly.

I hardly noticed when I kissed him. I had his head between my hands; I was drying his hair. He was breathing through his nose again, long deep breaths, but regular, and he opened his mouth and my mouth was there.

Very, very brief and very simple. A quick dart of the tongue.

That was it.

Nobody was surprised. Nobody was making a pass at anybody. If anything, I was being very motherly at the moment—perhaps in some bizarrely incestuous manner, but motherly all the same—I was fussing over him, drying his hair.

"You're killing me, Ev," Jay wheezed. "You wanna make me bald, or what?"

"You have nice hair," I murmured. I took the towel away and tried to arrange his damp hair with my fingers.

"There's a comb in my lab coat," he said.

Then he said, "I can't believe she killed herself."

I was sitting on my heels on the floor in front of him; then I was sitting with my back against the wall and my knees drawn up to my chest, looking at Hollander's face and seeing a look I had never seen before. I thought: *You don't know him.*

No, that's not true; you know him. You've just never seen anyone die in Jay's face before.

Hollander's Adam's apple went up and down in a long roll. "When do you get off?" he asked me.

"I'm off now. Bobbi Kaplowitz came in a little while ago and I signed out to her—except for you, I said I'd sign you out."

He nodded, took his eyes away from mine. Seemed

to think about this for a while. Sniffed, then swallowed again. Cleared his throat.

I sat very still. Hugged my knees to my chest.

So what's different? What's the new dynamic here?

"Look," he said. "I make a very good omelet, and . . . I thought maybe we could have breakfast and some coffee, and maybe later you could tell me what happened." He coughed. "With Shelley."

Yeah, and then what?

Don't be such a cynic.

"I'd like that," I said softly. "Let's just get you signed out, and then we'll go." I got to my feet and moved past him, squeezing his shoulder briefly with my hand.

The squeeze made everything simple; all the complexity and ambivalence between him and me suddenly evaporated.

The squeeze said: Yes.

CHAPTER

9

"This is nice, Jay," I said as he shut the door behind me. I walked from the foyer into the living room. "What did you do to the floor? It looks wonderful."

"I sanded it and then I put down a couple of coats of polyurethane. It was really awful; you should have seen it when I moved in. The guy before me must have glued his carpeting to the floor or something."

Hollander had one of the one-bedroom apartments in the doctors' residence. The one-bedrooms had living rooms twice as large as the living rooms in the two-bedroom apartments, which worked out to the total floor space of the one-bedrooms being roughly equal to that of the two-bedrooms. Alex McCabe and I had done a lot of speculating about this interesting fact one evening over a couple of beers. We had decided that the doctors' residence, having been built in the thirties, had been made for two types of (male) doctors: the bachelor and the married/family man. We figured they put the bachelor docs in the one-bedrooms and the married docs in the two-bedrooms, and thoughtfully provided a lot of living-room space for the bachelor docs because—hey, boys will be boys—bachelors throw a lot of parties, right? You need floor space for that, right?

"What's so funny?" Hollander asked.

"Nothing. I was just remembering the party you had here last summer."

"Oh, did you come to that? I had so many people in here I don't think I even got to say hello to everyone who came. God, and did they make a mess. It took me two days to clean up after it."

"You have any parties since then?"

"Hell, no. One was enough. Now I have intimate dinners *à deux*."

I was standing in the middle of the living room, where the furniture was. Hollander had left the entire room empty except for a six-by-nine-foot Oriental carpet in the center of it, flanked by two Japanese futon sofas. A large square mahogany coffee table with thick legs squatted on the carpet like a sumo wrestler. There was a two-foot-tall Chinese pottery horse in the middle of the table. The horse was a very nice ceramic of a type I had seen in the windows of galleries and antique shops on Madison Avenue; it was a kind of mottled brown color with what looked like faded patches of colored glazing. The carpet with its furniture was an island moored in the middle of a sea of polished oak flooring, and the setting seemed oddly familiar, as if I had seen it, say, in an Oriental-carpet ad on the back cover of *The New Yorker*. The feeling passed before I could get a grip on it. I looked around at the white walls, which were completely bare. There were shoji screens on the windows. It was very effective.

I was aware of Hollander behind me.

"I may tek madame's coat, pliz?" he breathed suggestively on my neck.

I obligingly shrugged out of my white lab coat.

"I may tek madame's stezzoscope?"

I took my stethoscope off my neck and handed it over my shoulder as imperiously as I could manage.

"I may tek ze rest of madame's outervear und undervear?"

"I don't think so."

"Pliz to excuse. I may show madame her table?"

I followed Jay into the kitchen, sat down on one of the Parisian café chairs, and leaned my arms on the marble tabletop. "You steal this table and chairs from Borgia's in the Village, or what?"

" 'Steal'? Madame. Your choice of words. Pierre will be deeply wounded."

"If madame doesn't throw up first."

"It's getting a little old, huh?" He opened the refrigerator and took out a carton of eggs and a cardboard basket of mushrooms with his good hand.

"No, seriously, I like the way you've decorated."

"Thank you."

"You need any help?"

"You wanna slice the mushrooms?"

"Sure."

A stick of butter sailed off the counter and landed on the floor. "Shit," Jay said. "The butter just did a backflip over the knife."

I got to my feet. "Here, let me help you."

He heaved a deep sigh.

Then he said, "I want to hear what happened with Shelley."

So I told him. We cooked the omelets and ate them, and I told him what I knew.

Late—it seemed like a good while later, but when I looked at my watch, it was only quarter after ten—I was sitting at the marble-topped table while Jay fussed with tea; he had insisted on making it by himself. ("Have to get used to this," he had said about his new cast.) Sun was streaming in the window, and outside, the air sparkled like crystal. I felt quiet inside, very much in the present moment and cut off from the past and the future.

"You talk to the detectives?" Jay asked, setting two mugs of tea on the table, one at a time.

My sense of time reluctantly elongated to include the past again. "Yeah," I said.

"Which ones?"

"Kelly and Ost."

"You want milk or sugar?"

"Milk, no sugar."

He got a carton of milk out of the fridge and sat down.

I wondered how he was in bed. He looked as if he could be either wildly passionate or exceptionally controlled. Hard to tell.

"Kelly got black hair, bushy eyebrows?"

"No, that's Malinowski. Kelly's got blond hair. Malinowski's partner."

Why do I read these two extremes from him, either wildly passionate or exceptionally controlled?

"Looks real Irish?"

"Yeah."

Wildly passionate. I hope.

Jay nodded. "I had him for that guy got knifed in the throat a coupla weeks ago. He kept wanting to know, 'Those his words exactly?' so whenever I repeated anything *I* had said, I said, 'Those are *my* words exactly.' Then he kept calling the guy 'the deceased,' like if he didn't I would forget the guy was dead or something. Made me wonder after a while if you gotta take a course at the academy, Police Jargon 101. We sound that bad? I mean doctors."

"Probably." I was looking at his hand, cradling the tea mug. Hollander had massive hands. They reminded me of the hands of a well-known baseball player who had come into the ER one night with his mother; by the end of the evening I had diagnosed the mother as suffering from a mild gastrointestinal disorder and I had diagnosed me as suffering from a whopping case of infatuation with the ball player.

"So, they say anything other than 'his words exactly?' "

"They asked me did I think Shelley was having an affair."

"An *affair?* Yeah, with the telephone maybe, talking to her husband all the time on it. Who do they think she was having an affair *with?*"

I looked very solemn. " 'We aren't alleging anything, this is just routine, O.K. ?' "

"Gotcha. Ten-four. What else?"

"Did I think she had any financial difficulties."

Jay gave me an odd look. "Did she?"

"Hell, *I* don't know. Do you?" I stood up. "You got an ashtray?"

"Table in the living room."

I took a step, then stopped, almost with one foot in the air. I was looking at Jay's face. "What?"

"Table in the living room."

"No. Tell me. What's the matter?"

He stood up, looking very worn-out, maybe in pain.

"Your arm hurt?"

"You didn't hear what happened last Friday, did you?" Jay asked suddenly.

Something changed in the room, as if a door at the end of a corridor had closed. Or opened.

"What happened last Friday?"

"McCabe didn't tell you, or Carchiollo?"

"No, what?"

"Shelley went to pieces in surgery," he said. "She opened the patient and left him on the table and walked out. The attending had to complete the operation."

I felt myself go very still.

"It doesn't surprise me she killed herself," he said quietly. He turned to walk into the living room. "It doesn't surprise me at all."

We were sitting on the futon couches opposite each other, our legs stretched out on the coffee table. I was looking at the horse.

"Imitation T'ang," Jay said. "I really like this particular piece; I think he looks very calm and alert."

I thought the horse looked agitated, nervous about something.

Or maybe the horse was meant to look like a warrior's horse, just getting pumped for battle.

Nope. Definitely a very agitated-looking horse.

Or maybe I'm the one who's agitated, nervous about something.

Hollander took a long, slow breath and let it out. "I came on at six-thirty Friday night and signed out from Paul Roussy," he said. "I had a kid from the women's college with flu who was dehydrated, so I started an IV for her. I had somebody in end-stage renal. I turfed him to the renal unit. I had a little old lady in no apparent distress from the nursing home. Real disoriented; probably just needed a little oxygen."

Nervous about what?

"We got a multiple-gunshot wound. I was in the utility room and it came over the squawkbox, and then the cops brought the guy in. Shot in the back, no chest, three abdominal, one in the ass, and one in the left thigh. BP one-fifteen over eighty, pulse eighty-five, and respirations twenty-five."

Maybe I'm nervous about going to bed with him.

But I didn't think that was it.

I tried to focus on what Jay was telling me.

I thought about Shelley and the Band-Aids on her arm.

I uncrossed my legs on Jay's coffee table and then crossed them the other way, being very careful not to bump the horse.

I thought about sitting in Shelley's living room, my feet on *her* coffee table. We used to sit there sometimes, side by side on the couch, our feet on the coffee table, going over her manuscript.

I pulled my legs in and folded them under me.

The nervousness I was feeling went away. Just like that, amazing me.

"Cops all over the place," Hollander was saying. "We got guys in uniforms, guys in soft clothes, we even got two cops with machine guns, and they're all bouncing off the walls from the adrenaline, higher than kites."

He stopped talking.

I looked at him. He was holding his head at a very unnatural angle, as if trying to see a long distance over a high wall.

"What?" I said.

"Is it the full moon?"

"Sorry?"

"It is, isn't it? And we're having this snowstorm. The barometric pressure must be up. Or down. Whichever is the way it goes when it storms. I forget, does it go up or down?"

"Up. I think. I don't remember."

What is he talking about?

"There are more suicides in the full moon," he said. "More crime. More rape. More people going nuts, coming unglued. Women get their periods then."

I said, suddenly realizing his tack, "You think Shelley killed herself because it's the full moon? I don't know, Jay. That's a little farfetched, don't you think?"

"Yeah, but listen, it's a storm, too. The barometric pressure *and* the full moon, you see what I'm saying?"

I looked sideways and back again.

"O.K., it's a thought," he said. "Never mind. You want a drink? You like Bloody Marys?"

"I don't think right now. You want one, go ahead." I got myself a cigarette and lit it. "On second thought, yeah. A Bloody Mary would be nice."

Hollander almost leapt off the couch.

Maybe he's the one who's nervous.

He ran into the kitchen, banged around for a minute, and ran back with two drinks, clutching one between his cast and his chest. He handed me the one he had in his good hand and flopped down on the couch, this time sitting on the same one I was sitting on.

Instinctively I put my knees up between him and me.

"O.K., O.K.," Jay said a little breathlessly. He drank half his drink in one gulp. "I'm telling you this. The cops are all over the place, we got cops in uniform, we got cops in clothes, we got cops with guns, I mean of the blow-'em-away variety. *Big* fuckers, like you see on *Miami Vice*. They say the guy's a hit man for Willie Jack. This patient. They seem to think that Willie Jack's the biggest dope-runner in the Valley. I think: Yeah, sure, they're high, there's been some shooting, they're exaggerating. Biggest dope-runner in the Valley, give me a break. So I got Barry Steinberg there, and we let the cops get the guy out of his clothes. The guy's unconscious. I don't know what they think he's going to do to us—but they're the cops and we're the public. We got to get protected and they got to save the world."

Jay drank the rest of his Bloody Mary and took a deep breath. His eyes went out of focus, darting around the room like birds scattering hysterically after you shoot into the trees. "When they get him out of his clothes, they let us in the room. Barry and I get the guy cathed and IV'd and blooded and we send for a cross-match and Kathy goes to do the spun 'crit. I get good breath sounds both sides and Barry gets blood in the urine. BP holding at one-fifteen over eighty. I remember I said to Barry, 'He's holding up pretty well for somebody with six bullets in him, don't you think?' and Barry said, 'Yeah, the guy's a gorilla, his feet go off the stretcher,' and Whizkid comes in and says, 'He probably got hired because you'd need a lot of bullets to stop him.' And then somebody said, 'Who's on for surgery?' and I said . . . I said, 'Shelley Reinish.' "

"You don't have to tell me this right now if it upsets you," I said quietly.

Jay looked at me as if I had just beamed down from the starship *Enterprise*. "Of course it upsets me," he said. "Doesn't it upset *you?* Shelley's dead and we didn't do anything. We didn't even see it coming. We're supposed to be doctors, for Chrissake. *We didn't even see it coming.* I mean, even *Attenborough,* he's standing around in the OR going, 'Dr. Reinish has had a slight attack of battle fatigue.' Battle fatigue? *Slight?* Gimme a break, she threw Lukinsky off his fucking *riser!*" "Wait a minute. Back up. Go back to where she comes in the ER. If that's important. Or start where you get to surgery."

"Mother Mary," he said. He put his hand up and pinched the bridge of his nose. "I needed a surgeon. The guy had six bullets in him, so I paged Shelley and Alex McCabe, but McCabe was in CAT Scan. I think. I don't know where he was. Shelley came." He picked up his empty glass, ate an ice cube, and appeared to think about things for a minute.

"Sometimes I wish I smoked," he said, looking at my cigarettes.

Then he went on: "So Shelley comes in, and she looks like you wouldn't believe. You know, she keeps her hair in a bun, wears all that eye makeup? She's so neat all the time? Always wears something nice? Tonight she's got on some shirt looks like she got it off the floor of the closet, it maybe even looks like Steve's been out jogging three days in a row in it. No makeup. Hair all loose on her shoulders, and it doesn't look like she's washed it for a while. You *ever* see her look like that? O.K., that's one thing. The second thing is, she's obviously not all there. She looks like she's been through a war; she's got the hundred-yard stare or whatever they used to call it in Vietnam. Out to lunch. So she's standing there looking at the patient like she's in some kind of a trance, and she's cracking her knuckles. You notice she was doing that a lot lately? Cracking her knuckles? She does one finger at a time: she pushes each one back all the way, then she pushes it forward all the way. I mean, she's beginning to make me think maybe she's got early-onset arthritis or something. I can't even tell you what it was like when she walked in the room. Man, she got more attention than the patient with the six bullets. She walked in and we looked at her and then we did double-takes and just *stared*.

"So Maggie Rourke says, 'Dr. Reinish, do you feel all right?'

"And Shelley says—like she just woke up and she woke up mad—*'Don't mother me, I am not in the mood.'*

"Then she wants to know what we're doing for the patient.

"So I tell her. I present the whole case like she's my preceptor in med school: we did this and that and that, blah-blah, the patient is blooded, tubed, drips going, type and cross-match ordered, OR notified standby, neuro paged, Kathy's doing the spun 'crit, the whole shit and shebang.

"Then Shelley says, 'Type and cross-match. Tube him for urine.'

"Everybody just sort of looks at her. I just finished telling her *we did that.*

"Then Barry says, 'Shelley—'

"She doesn't even let him finish. She says, *'What? Don't start telling me how to do my job! And knock it off with this are-you-all-right dreck! I'm fine!'*

"So what are we going to do here? She's obviously incompetent as far as anyone can see. Not like that's going to disqualify you from anything around this place—you know that cardiac surgeon who-shall-remain-nameless with the hands that shake and his residents do all his cases? I figure there isn't much we *can* do except cover for her, and maybe when she calms down later or gets in a better mood or something, maybe I can talk to her a little.

"Then all of a sudden she says, 'I'm sorry if I yelled at you. I've had a lot on my mind lately and it's not an easy time for me.'

"So of course we all relax a little when she says this. She sounds more like herself, you know? I think that was a mistake. We never shoulda let ourselves relax like that. I mean, *look at the way she looked.* She looked like shit. Anyone could tell by looking at her that she wasn't herself. But if she's not herself, that means we've got one more thing to worry about, right? And who has time to worry about one more thing when we've got this multiple-gunshot wound and the whole ER's full of cops going bonka-bonka-bonka off the walls? Oh, jeez, just the fucking *paperwork!* We're going to be filling out forms out the wazoo! But just the same, I figure somebody ought to go upstairs to surgery with Shelley, and Barry has the same idea. He's waving at me behind Shelley's back, making hand signals that I should go up with her.

"So I say, 'Let's get this guy upstairs.' Shelley grabs the stretcher rail on one side and I grab it on the other and we start movin' 'em out. This looks like a good moment, so I say—as neutrally as possible—'Listen, if you don't mind, Shel, I'd like to scrub in on this one,' and I make up some bullshit about how interesting it looks, I want to see where the bullets went, blah-blah, I don't get to scrub in on a lot of gunshot wounds. What I'm really thinking is, if she goes wacko bananas in the OR, I'm there to help cover. Bail her out if necessary. Yeah. Right. She *went* fuckin' wacko bananas in the OR. I was a fuckin' lot of help. I did *shit.* I need another drink."

"I'll get it," I said. I got up off the couch and went into the kitchen, only vaguely in my body; I left my presence in the living room with Shelley and Jay on their way to the OR. I rinsed Jay's glass out in the sink, got ice cubes out of the fridge, found vodka, found tomato juice. Went back. Handed over drink. Sat down. Did not sit with knees between me and Jay. Sat instead near him, legs folded under me Indian-style, my arm stretched straight along the back of the couch where his good arm was also stretched. Arm to arm. Curled my hand around the bulk of his forearm, fingers in the crook of his elbow. Lit a cigarette, and looked for a moment at the shoji screens over the windows. Light through shoji screens is timeless. Leaned forward for a split second to move ashtray into lap.

"O.K.," I said.

"Yeah," he said. Moved his fingers against my arm, a small, halfhearted sweep, then still.

"O.K., so we get upstairs. We hand the patient over to the OR team, go scrub. Shelley's not exactly communicative at the scrub sinks, and I figure I should leave her alone. She's not in the mood, as she says. I did ask her where Steve was, if he was home, because I was thinking of calling him later and sort of alerting him to the situation. But she tells me he's got a bar mitzvah in Philadelphia and he's staying through the weekend down there. He has to teach a class Monday night or something. I forget. Be home late Monday night, Tuesday. I think: Christ, *Tuesday*. What are we going to do with her until Tuesday? What if she flips out? So I say, 'You gonna talk to him on the phone sometime this weekend?' and she says, no, it's Shabbes. Well, maybe she'll talk to him Sunday, but she thinks he's going to see this rabbi friend of his in Cherry Hill on Sunday. I say, 'What friend?' I'm fishing for info, I want to know where Steve is if we need him. So I find out the guy's name and make a mental note of it.

"I finish scrubbing and Shelley's kind of dawdling along with her orange stick, going under her finger-nails, so I leave her at the sinks there and go into the OR. Dr. Attenborough is there. This is a big relief. This guy has got to be the best attending ever to set foot in a hospital, I kid you not. I see him and it's like a big weight is off my shoulders. He likes Shelley. He likes me. He hardly knows me from Adam, but he likes me. He likes everyone. Everything is hunky-dory. You know who he reminds me of? You're gonna laugh. Remember Ben Cartwright on *Bonanza*? Attenborough reminds me of Ben Cartwright. I keep waiting for him to walk into the OR in a cowboy hat. He's so tall he has to bend over for the nurse to tie his mask on. And he's so corny. You know he has those half-moon glasses he always has to have taped on his nose for surgery, and he always says the *exact same thing* to the nurse: 'Wouldn't want my glasses to fall off and land smack in the middle of the incision, would we, my dear?' I walk in the OR and this is exactly what he's saying to the nurse. She says back—I like this nurse, but I don't know who it was—she never took her mask off, so I didn't get to see her face—'Dr. Attenborough, you say that before every single operation. I think you ought to have a little talk with your scriptwriters and see if they can't come up with some new lines for you.' Attenborough laughs. If he wasn't scrubbed and gloved, he would probably slap his thigh, you can just see him doing that. Anyway. Attenborough sees me and says, 'Dr. Hollander! Haven't seen you in a while, my boy! Are you cutting this evening?' Yeah. Right. Am I cutting. I say, 'Oh, no, sir. Dr. Reinish will do the operating; I'm just here to hold retractors.' Which is true; I mean, what else am I going to do? So Attenborough says, 'Ah, yes, Dr. Reinish, a beautiful young lady and an excellent surgeon. Well, always glad to have another hand, Dr. Hollander.' Hoo boy. All I can think is: He'll say something real bright and bubbly to Shelley when she comes in and Shelley will tell him to fuck off. Well, not 'fuck off.' Shelley doesn't use language like that. Something . . . what's that Yiddish thing she says? I forget. Grow onions in your navel, or something.

"All of a sudden I realize that because it's Attenborough and not one of the other attendings, Shelley really is going to be operating herself. If one of the other attendings was there, he'd do the operating and the resident would assist, you know? But Attenborough always lets the resident cut; he figures he's just there like a consultant. So I start looking around for who's going to be on the right side of the table, who's going to be assisting Shelley. This is when I start getting real nervous.

"Then Howie Lukinsky comes in. Jesus, Joseph, and Mary, of all people. This is all we need, right? We got Attenborough. On one hand, if anything is going to go wrong, he's who you want to be there for it. He's calm, he doesn't yell at the residents. On the other hand, if you're in a bad mood, he's a little hard to take, because he's so gushy and bright-eyed and bushy-tailed. I'm already afraid Attenborough will be gushing around and Shelley will lose her temper and take a potshot at him. Now here's Lukinsky. Shelley can't stand Lukinsky. And of course when Lukinsky comes in and sees Attenborough, he goes right into his ass-kissing mode: 'Oh, Dr. Attenborough! How nice to see you again, sir! Howard Lukinsky, sir! It's an honor to be assisting you, sir!' I'm going to throw up. Attenborough's clearing his throat, he hates ass-kissing. Then Shelley comes in.

"You think she had the hundred-yard stare in the ER, she comes into the OR looking like I don't know what, one of the women in Charcot's madhouse. She's drying her hands with a sterile towel the way crazy people do, washing and drying their hands in the air with soap and water that isn't there. Attenborough sort of looks at her for a minute but I guess he decides to let it pass. I don't know what he thinks. He says, 'I believe you're cutting this evening, Dr. Reinish. Let's get started.'

"For a little while everything goes O.K. Shelley

makes the incision, we pack it with laps, Lukinsky and I have the retractors. Shelley gets a bullet out of the right kidney. Guy's left kidney is O.K. She's telling Attenborough what she's doing as she goes along and she's doing really O.K. here for someone who looks the way she does. Attenborough is nodding away the way he does when he thinks you know what you're doing, and I start to relax a little.

"That's another mistake. I relax and Lukinsky says, 'What do you propose for this patient, Dr. Attenborough, sir?'

"Of course, this is a big insult to Shelley, and Attenborough knows it. So he defers to her. He says, 'Dr. Reinish?'

"Shelley says, 'I'm going to take his kidney out.' Real snappish. I see trouble coming right away. You ever around when Steve used to tease Shelley about when she gets that edge in her voice? He's always saying, 'I hear that edge and I get out of the way.' I'm hearing that edge now, and I'm hoping Lukinsky has the sense to get out of the way.

"Fat chance. Lukinsky's an asshole. He not only doesn't get out of the way, he says, 'Dr. Attenborough, sir, what is *the procedure of choice* in a case such as this?'

"Oh, God, I think, here it comes.

"Attenborough sort of squares himself up and says, 'Dr. Lukinsky, I think you fail to see—' or something like that, but it's too late. Shelley throws her scalpel in the instruments tray. The scrub nurse just about jumps through the roof; you ever see Shelley throw anything down in surgery? *And then she leans over the patient and grabs Lukinsky by the front of his gown.*

"I'm yelling, *'Don't, Shelley. Don't!'*

"Shelley's yelling, *'You wanna do it? Huh? You wanna do the goddamn operation yourself? Go ahead! See how far you get!'*

"Attenborough's yelling, *'Dr. Reinish, I must ask*

you to control yourself! And don't touch anything, young lady! You've broken scrub!'

"The circulating nurse is running around to get Shelley another pair of gloves before she touches anything and makes the whole incision unsterile. I'm backing up with my hands in the air so nobody makes *me* unsterile. Lukinsky's gone all white around the eyes. Shelley's still got him by the front of his gown. He's standing on a riser—he isn't any taller than Shelley, I don't think—*she's* on a riser too—I'm thinking: Those risers aren't up to this, one of them will tip and someone will land on the floor. And then Shelley throws Lukinsky off his riser. *BAM!* He's flat on his back on the floor.

"Then Shelley starts screaming. That's not the word. Howling. She starts howling.

"I can't tell you what this does to me. It goes right through me, it gives me chills. I've never heard anything like it. This is too much for Attenborough, even. *He* breaks scrub. He grabs Shelley by both wrists and gets her down off her riser and away from the patient before she makes the whole incision unsterile, and he hands her over to the circulating nurse. I have to hand it to him. He just sort of quietly marches her the way parents march their kids, you know? Now go over here. Sit down. Be quiet. He's saying to her in a real fatherly kind of tone, 'Dr. Reinish, I want you to get some rest. I'll take over here.'

"So the circulating nurse takes Shelley out of the OR. Oh, man . . . I just . . . This isn't what I wanted. I felt so fucking *helpless.* I wanted to run out of the room after her and take care of her myself, you know? Make her lie down, and sit there and hold her hand or something until she calms down. But now I'm really stuck, I have to assist Attenborough, since Shelley's out; he says, 'Dr. Hollander, step in, please.' I say, 'Dr. Attenborough, I think I should tell you, this is my intern year.' He says, 'I know that, son, now let's get on here.'

"Then he says to Lukinsky, 'Dr. Lukinsky, the next time I see you in my OR, I want you to know something about protocol and simple etiquette. I will not stand for junior staff insulting my residents, do I make myself clear? Now, step out. Go have a cup of coffee, and one thing before you go: I might add that it is always best, professionally speaking, if incidents of this sort are not bandied about. Dr. Reinish has had a slight attack of battle fatigue. We all get to the end of our ropes sometimes. I trust you will keep this to yourself.'

"I wanted to say: That was not battle fatigue. I wanted to get the hell out of there. I felt like screaming myself. For a minute I actually considered screaming, I thought maybe if I started screaming, Attenborough would say, 'Step out,' and I could go see Shelley.

"But of course I didn't say it wasn't battle fatigue.

"Dr. Attenborough said, 'Step in.' And . . . I stepped in."

CHAPTER

10

Sometimes I get into a place in my head where I can't seem to think. I get there and an announcement comes over the internal P.A. system: *I'm not thinking anything right now. My mind is blank. I'm not feeling anything.*

I was in that place now.

I had a physical sense of Hollander sitting next to me, clenching and unclenching his jaw. But I wasn't looking at him. I was looking at the horse on the coffee table, ready to rear on its hind legs.

"Then what happened?" I said quietly.

"Attenborough took the guy's kidney out, fried his liver for a while with laser cautery—you ever smell that? I swear to God, it smells just like liver cooking, everybody's going, 'Where's the onions?' and then we unraveled all eighteen feet of bowel and started resecting."

Now he was swallowing.

After a while he said, "The nurse came back and said, 'Dr. Reinish is a little upset. I'd like to give her twenty milligrams of Valium.' Attenborough says O.K., that's a good idea. I'm thinking: A little upset. These people need their heads examined. But I didn't say anything.

"So we're resecting, and McCabe comes in. This is maybe an hour or two later. He tells Attenborough

114

Tony Firenze has a subdural hematoma coming in the next OR, and Attenborough says fine, we're going to close soon, Firenze should go ahead and open the skull and he'll be in in a little while.

"Then McCabe says—get this—he says, 'Hollander, can I talk to you for a minute?'

"What, is he crazy? I'm up to my elbows in bowel here. So I look at him: he wants to talk, he's going to have to talk here. Obviously.

"So he sort of tilts his head, like I should come out and talk to him in the hall. Attenborough sees this and says, 'Dr. McCabe, is something the matter?' and McCabe sort of shuffles around—he's standing there in street clothes holding a mask over his face—and then he says, 'Dr. Reinish is asleep on the floor under the scrub sinks.'

"Aw, Jesus. Give me a fucking break. She's a lot more than a *little* fucking upset if you ask me.

"Attenborough says, 'I told her to get some rest, but I didn't mean on the floor.' He tells McCabe in real vague terms—he's glossing the whole thing over—about Shelley's attack of 'battle fatigue.' He says, 'Dr. McCabe, maybe you could see that Dr. Reinish gets to her on-call room.'

"McCabe says, 'I'll take her home.' "

Hollander got up, wandered around the room aimlessly for a minute or two, and sat back down on the other futon sofa.

I said slowly, "*Alex* took Shelley home?"

Jay's face pulled wryly. "Himself."

"You don't like that."

"I don't like what?"

"That Alex took Shelley home."

"Skip it."

"No, tell me. What?"

Jay turned his head to the side and showed me his mountaineers's profile for a while.

I withdraw the question, I thought after a moment.

I said, "Do you know anything else about what happened after Alex took Shelley home? Did he come back to the hospital later, or what? Does anybody know what Shelley was so upset about?"

"I don't know," Jay said. He picked at a loose thread on his cast. "We got clobbered, you know. Alex took Shelley home, I came back downstairs to the ER, and all hell broke loose. First the paramedics brought in a woman who had hanged herself, and then two minutes later we got an MI." An MI is a myocardial infarction, or heart attack. "Steinberg and I were going nuts. Just when we got the woman stabilized and upstairs to the ICU and the MI down to the morgue—he died . . . actually, the woman died too, but later on in the ICU—there was some kind of shoot-out in that bar over on Broadway, and we got three gunshot wounds.

"McCabe came back from Shelley's right after the gunshot wounds came in. We had our hands full, to say the least. But he came over to me and said, 'I took Shelley home. I made her eat something before I left.' "

"Is that all he said?"

"That's it."

"Did you talk to Alex anytime over the weekend?"

"No, he was off. I tried calling him, but I think he told Kathy Haughey he was going to his grandmother's for the weekend." Hollander got up and went into the kitchen, taking his empty glass with him.

I lit another cigarette.

I tried to imagine Shelley with her hair unwashed and no makeup and looking strung-out. I tried to imagine her throwing Lukinsky off his riser and howling in the OR.

I wondered what she meant when she said, *I've had a lot on my mind lately and it's not an easy time for me.*

It did not make sense to me, that Shelley had been upset or concerned about something, or that sometime recently had not been "easy" for her. Obviously she had been upset about *something* enough to kill herself, but I was at a loss to say what. As far as I could tell, Shelley had been in love with her work, in love with the book she was writing, and in love with her husband. She did not seem to have any "adverse relationships," as the police so quaintly inquired after—if one discounted Tony Firenze, who seemed to relish the cultivation of adverse relationships.

But maybe I shouldn't discount Firenze so readily, I mused. I thought back on his drunken assault on me in the ER that morning. I had been humiliated by him, and it was only through sheer exhaustion and persistence of will that I had put the incident out of my mind. In my opinion Firenze was simply not worth fighting with. He was an inordinately competent surgeon and his decisions were invariably sound, even if his aggressiveness and belligerence were infuriating at times, and I generally let him have his way whenever there was a dispute about something.

Even when he threw me up against the wall, I thought ruefully. That really was going way too far.

I wondered if Shelley had been having a hard time with Firenze in surgery lately, and if he had been bullying her about whatever it was she had written or planned to write about him in her book. I wondered if there had been more episodes of temper on Firenze's part than the one I had heard about, when he'd thrown his scissors at her.

Firenze seemed to have the idea that I knew whatever Shelley was writing about him, but I didn't. Shelley had been feeding me the manuscript chapter by chapter as it came back from the typist, and I had only seen about half of the proposed number of chapters.

Maybe there was something about Firenze in a chapter I hadn't seen yet, something he knew about and was particularly infuriated by.

And maybe he had been bullying her about that.

But still, you don't go out and kill yourself because a colleague at work is bullying you.

"Ev, can you come in here and open this can, please?"

"Yeah." I ground my cigarette out in the ashtray and swished the last bit of my drink around in my mouth. The ice cubes clinked in the glass, sounding loud in Hollander's quiet living room. The outside light shone diffusely through the shoji screens. I wondered what time it was but didn't look at my watch; it didn't seem to be any time at all, and there didn't seem to be any point in looking. A very large sigh came out of me, and I stood up.

In the kitchen, Jay pushed a quart can of tomato juice and a can opener toward me on the counter. I let my two hands briefly cover his one as I took the can from him. The touch of his skin was dry and pleasant, but something struck me as odd, enough so that my mind jumped: *what?* His hand was leaving my hands. I watched it go, settle on the counter, rest comfortably with fingers splayed slightly next to the can of tomato juice.

I held the can so that my hand was next to him. There was brushing contact, and I realized suddenly what it was: the touch was even and unelectric.

Jay took his hand off the counter and moved away to open the refrigerator.

"Where's your glass?" I asked, punching two holes in the can with the can opener. Maybe he doesn't want to go to bed with me after all.

"Here. Where's yours? You want another?"

"Living room. Please."

Maybe he's upset about Shelley; maybe telling me that story upset him more, and he doesn't want to be with anyone right now.

"More ice?"

I nodded. Maybe I should go home.

He put a fresh tray of ice half-on, half-off the edge

of the counter, steadied it with his good hand, and snapped the other end of it with his casted forearm.

"You're getting pretty good with that," I said.

"Might as well. Gotta wear it for six weeks."

Maybe he really isn't interested in going to bed with me; maybe he only wants to flirt, play the game, tease. Maybe I've misread him.

I fixed two more drinks.

He took his glass and wandered back into the living room.

I leaned on the kitchen counter and took a long pull of vodka and tomato juice. I had poured too much vodka in proportion to the juice; I could taste its sharp edge. I wanted a cigarette, but the pack was in the living room, and I didn't want to go in there right this minute. Hollander was in there. A little while ago I had thought he wanted me, and if he didn't want me, I wanted to be by myself a few minutes to regroup. Actually, if he didn't want me, I wanted to leave, but I couldn't think of a way to do that. For some reason, I felt stuck. I realized my mouth was dry and I thought about brushing my teeth—I carried a toothbrush in my lab coat at all times in a little plastic case for contingency during forty-eight-hour stretches in the ER. But Hollander might think it was strange if all of a sudden I asked for my lab coat and disappeared into the bathroom and then came out smelling of toothpaste. I really didn't want to leave, I wanted him to want me. But if he didn't want me, I wanted to leave. Or brush my teeth. Or have a cigarette. Or call Phil. Or go pay my respects to Rabbi Reinish; I needed to do that sometime today. What time was it?

Hollander reappeared in the doorway. "Are we all right in here?"

I smiled. My lips felt funny, as if my mouth might start twitching.

He seemed to watch me for a moment. I imagined

that he was assessing something about me, but I didn't know what.

"I thought you might like to look at my porcelains," he said.

"I would."

"There're in here."

I followed him into the bedroom, thinking: I don't want to be in here without a good reason. I walked to the middle of the room and then I started backing up again toward the door, just in case I had to get out of there fast.

The room was, by most standards, different. Hollander had a large futon mattress on the polished oak floor and a huge, imposing Oriental dresser against one wall. The dresser was as tall as I was and as wide as my arm span. On top of it there was a green-orange-and-ivory lead-glazed dog—or maybe it was a bear—with enormous grinning jaws and teeth that looked like they might drip saliva any minute. Jesus, I thought, what is *that* supposed to guard him from? The sight of it arrested me in my backward creep toward the door. I stopped feeling so vulnerable and started wondering how vulnerable Hollander was.

"That's Fu," Jay said. He was kneeling on the floor in the corner.

"Fu? Is that a kind of Chinese . . . ? Uh . . . What is that, a dog? Fu is a Chinese breed of dog?"

Jay looked amused. "It's a dog. His name is Fu."

O.K., I thought slowly, dragging the syllables out in my mind.

"Come down here," Jay said.

I took another step backward. Then I saw that Jay was kneeling on the floor next to a collection of porcelain figures; he seemed to have them marching in a line the way a schoolboy arranges toy soldiers. The figures were horses and some people, all facing the door, except one horse, which was facing the others.

Fascinated, I knelt down immediately. "These are

beautiful," I said. "But aren't you afraid someone will walk into them?"

He shook his head. "Not a lot of people come in here." He picked up the figure of an old man with a wide cone-shaped hat and two baskets and held it out to me. It seemed very small in his large hand.

I took it and admired it. "Are they part of a set?"

"Oh, no, they're all separate pieces. But I like to imagine them as a family. I pretend in my mind that they're all related. Have you ever seen a Bunraku troupe?"

"No, what's that?"

"Bunraku is traditional Japanese puppet theater."

I remembered that Hollander's father, who was a professor of Oriental studies at New York University, spent summers in Japan, and that Hollander himself had gone to Osaka University for his junior year in college.

"The guys who work the puppets stand right out in front of the audience," Jay was saying. "You can see them; they conceal themselves, if you want to call it that, by wearing all black—black clothes, socks, gloves, and hoods—and they do the puppets. After a while you don't see them anymore; you forget they're there. You just see the puppets. It's not like European puppetry, though, where the puppeteers hide behind a curtain or under a stage."

He took the little man back from me and replaced it in the procession of figures.

"Now, this one's been to the kitchen," Jay said, picking up the horse who was facing the others. He placed it in his casted hand and tapped it gently on the nose with a finger of his good hand, as if to chide it, or perhaps express affection to it. "He found out there's nothing worth seeing in the kitchen, so he's coming back to tell the others who are on their way to the kitchen to forget it." He put the horse down again. "These two"—he pointed at two others—"were in the bookcase in the foyer and they think they might like to go back there, but I have my vase there now, so they'll have to wait." He stood up. "I got this dresser in Bloomingdale's when they were doing their Chinese thing; do you like it?"

From my kneeling position, when I looked up, the dresser loomed, Jay loomed even higher, and the near-salivating dog loomed highest of all. I thought about crawling out of the room so I wouldn't have to stand up and compete with all this looming.

I realized I was beginning to feel very scattered again.

Why don't you just make a pass at me? Are you going to make me ask for it?

I stood up.

I wanted to touch him, but I didn't know how.

I couldn't even look at him.

I put my hand on the dresser instead, running my fingertips in the grooves of the intricate carving. "Yes," I said. I swallowed. "Very much. It's lovely."

He was standing next to me, neither close nor far. But my depth perception was distorted; I had no idea how far "far" was or how close "close" was. He was too close or he was too far; he was, wherever he was, out of my reach. My arms were too short or too long. I waved my hand hesitantly against the sleeve of Jay's shirt, fluttering one finger somewhere near his elbow.

He drew back, and looked away.

I turned and walked out of the bedroom.

I didn't want to be in there anyway, I thought. I'm going to get my lab coat and brush my teeth, and I don't care if he thinks I'm strange. And then I'm going to have a cigarette. Then I'm going home, and I'm going to—

I didn't even hear him come up behind me. He grabbed me by the arm and swung me around so hard and fast my back slammed up against the wall, and then his mouth was in my mouth and mine was in his.

CHAPTER

11

When I woke up it was dark. For a few minutes I thought I was in my own bed; the heat was coming up in the pipes with the same reassuring clank it came up with in my own apartment. But when I realized I was lying on a mattress with one foot on the floor, and that the mattress itself was on the floor, I sat up with a jolt.

Brushing against Hollander, who was sleeping like a dead person next to me, gave me another jolt. I had given him an injection of Demerol before we went to sleep because his arm was bothering him, and when he didn't stir I hastily took his pulse. I thought: I probably shouldn't have given him the Demerol when he'd been drinking. But I saw he was O.K.; he'd sleep it off. A long sleep would be good for him. His skin was cold and sweaty, but his pulse was strong. Leaning over him, I put my ear next to his mouth and listened to his breathing, which was even and deep.

Having reassured myself that I had not committed gross medical malpractice on Jay with the Demerol, I rolled over and swept the bare floor with my hand until I discovered my watch. After that I crept out of bed and felt my way along the bedroom wall into the hall, and from there to the bathroom. Although there were nearly three hundred apartments in the doctors' residence, there were only four different apartment layouts. Jay's apartment had exactly the same floor plan as Alex McCabe's, and was the mirror image of mine.

There was something very reassuring about this, although I wasn't quite sure what.

There was something *not* very reassuring about my reflection in Hollander's bathroom mirror when I switched the light on and got a good look at myself.

"Oh, *Christ,*" I groaned out loud.

I had a large purple hickey high on the right front of my throat.

Terrific. Wait till Phil sees this.

I went into Hollander's kitchen stark naked and called Phil again. When I got no answer, I called his beeper. When he didn't answer that either, I felt considerably less guilty and got dressed. After that I went back into the kitchen, put water on to boil, and found a small tin of Chinese black tea. This discovery pleased me immensely; I am a tea drinker by habit, and drink coffee only when there's no tea. Jay drinks tea, I thought. Phil never drinks tea; he drinks coffee. Fuck you, Phil. *Where the hell are you?*

Waiting for the water to boil, I called Time and found out it was six P.M. My watch had told me it was six but my circadian rhythm had gone out of whack way back in medical school and I was so perpetually exhausted from nights on and nights off that I sometimes couldn't tell by myself whether it was six P.M. or six A.M. . For all I knew, Hollander and I had slept right around the clock.

A feeling of disorientation swept over me. It didn't seem to help to know that it was six P.M. Tuesday and not six A.M. Wednesday. I leaned my elbows on Hollander's spotless kitchen counter and stretched my legs in a runner's stretch, first one, then the other, counting twenty beats for each stretch. I seemed mad at someone, but I wasn't sure whom. Shelley, for killing herself. Phil, for being AWOL. Jay, for taking me to bed. Me, for going to bed with him. Me, for being preoccupied with myself and my sex life when here a colleague of mine had killed herself. For shutting my feelings about Shelley up someplace where I couldn't get at them. For thinking of her in abstract terms—"my colleague" instead of "my friend." For not being her friend when here she was unraveling right in front of my nose. For not having a fucking *clue* why she killed herself. *For not doing a goddamn thing to prevent it.*

I remembered the time I had been suturing in the ER—a hapless intern exactly four days and ten hours out of medical school—and Shelley, in a pique about something else entirely, had stormed into the room to see how I was doing. My patient had a gash with uneven edges on his brow, and I had carefully shaved the eyebrow and was now trying to close the ragged bits and pieces of skin. Unsuccessfully. I was thinking: This guy is going to have a very bad scar because I don't know how to do this. Why doesn't someone come in here and help me? Where's Dr. McCabe? Where's Dr. Reinish? To add to my misery, my patient was jumping about and bitching at me from under the sterile drapes that I had meticulously arranged over his face. It was four A.M., the patient had been in some kind of bar brawl on Broadway, and I suspected he was coked up to the eyeballs. And then Shelley came storming in. "What did you shave his eyebrow for? *You never, never shave the eyebrow!*"

It was the only time she had ever yelled at me.

I put one foot on Hollander's kitchen counter and bent my forehead to my ankle.

I'm not sure I ever forgave her for it.

I forgive you now, I thought, putting my one foot back on the floor and the other on the counter. Forehead to ankle again. Count to twenty. I forgive you. Please forgive me back. For not being there for you. Foot back on floor. Deep knee-bend. For not grieving for you now.

I don't know how to grieve for you, Shelley.

Leah Ruth Robinson

Do you know where you are? What day is it? Who's the President?

It's Tuesday, and it's six P.M.

Shelley's dead.

Phil's AWOL.

You have a hickey on your throat that Jay gave you and you're going to have to explain to Phil.

Phil drinks coffee, Jay and I drink tea.

Jay and I also drink booze and fuck each other's brains out in the afternoon and sleep until it's dark and I don't know what day it is.

The water was boiling. I turned it off.

I thought: Don't forget to call the medical examiner's office in the morning and get Shelley's case report.

God, I dreaded that phone call. I should have made McCabe pronounce. McCabe's senior to me; he's the chief resident; it was his job to pronounce.

I opened a drawer looking for a spoon and found Hollander's cache of medical junk: a blood-pressure cuff; various freebies from the drug companies—throwaway penlights, ball-point pens with the names of drugs in loud large letters on the sides of them, pads of paper with drug names printed on the tops of the sheets; a few needles and syringes in their wrappers; an empty box of burette IV tubing. Jesus, I thought, look at all this crap. I had a drawer just like this in my own kitchen, where I unloaded all the stuff that wound up in my lab-coat pockets in the course of forty-eight hours on call. The damned medical profession follows you home; you never get away from it. I should have stuck with teaching Shakespeare at the university's women's college. Never mind the fact that some of my students had been rich little chickies from Long Island who came to class in fur coats and clanked jewelry larger than Hell's Angels' chains in my face when I tried to explain why they were not doing well in my class. Never mind the surly little brains from the Bronx High School of Science who wanted to be doctors and

126

took offense at the notion that they were required to take freshman English with me. Never mind the faculty politics and infighting. I'll take it back in a minute, just don't make me physician of record for Shelley's death or the lover Phil left to go AWOL or the woman who just got out of Jay Hollander's bed with an enormous hickey on her neck.

Get a grip on yourself, Sutcliffe, I thought.

I wrinkled my nose at the mediciny smell that wafted out of the drawer, then shut it and found a spoon in another.

I made my tea and sat down with it at the kitchen table, warming my hands on the mug and holding my face over the steam wafting up from it.

I thought about how Jay was in bed.

Excellent. A+. Ten out of ten. Trust the nurses to know what they were talking about; nurses *always* know what they're talking about, I thought ruefully. I would take what they had to say over what any doctor had to say any day. I sipped my tea and saw Jay's shoulder against my nose again. He had let himself go with a passion that shocked me. I wondered idly why I hadn't expected that of him.

I also wondered idly whom else he had slept with at the hospital. I had no idea. The nurses all seemed possessed of the intelligence that he was a passionate and enthusiastic bed partner—which I could now verify—but who among them was the one who kissed and told? Or maybe there was more than just one.

And then I wondered why I had gone to bed with him.

The question hung in the air over Hollander's marble-topped bistro table.

It was not a question I particularly wanted to ask myself or have asked of me—especially not while I was sitting at Hollander's kitchen table. I felt myself backing up from it, wondering why I had posed the question at all; then with a kind of exasperated belligerence I felt myself downshift from reverse into drive and I accelerated right into the question head-on.

I imagined myself pouring coffee for Phil and saying, "Well, it's like this: Jay drinks tea and I drink tea and you drink coffee, Phil, and while we're on this topic, *where the fuck were you when Shelley died?"*

That's not answering the question, Sutcliffe. That's avoiding the question by asking some other dumb question. Furthermore, asking Phil *where the fuck were you when Shelley died?*—as if that's a way to excuse yourself for going to bed with Jay—is just not going to hold water. It's not going to hold water for Jay and it's not going to hold water for Phil and it's not going to hold water for you either.

Shit, I thought. I put my head down on the table.

Try again.

I suddenly began to imagine another person sitting in the kitchen with me, a person who knew me better than I knew myself and was now present to comment on all my darker impulses and unconscious motives, a person who said:

You slept with Hollander because Shelley died.

The imaginary person across the table from me became Phil.

I could see him sitting there, the way I had seen him the very first time we had had a drink together. It was the previous September, and I had invited him over for a drink because he had mentioned to me during the course of the day at the hospital that it was his birthday and he was lonely because his girlfriend was in London on business.

One of the things we had talked about had been how, the day Phil's mother blew an aneurysm and died, Phil's sister called a man she had been seeing at college and went over to his apartment and lost her virginity.

"A lot of people want to have sex when someone close dies," Phil said. "It's a common reaction. One of my patients lost her daughter—the child was hit and killed by a car—and she told me that all she could think of after the funeral was how she wished all the people would leave so she and her husband could go to bed. And my roommate in college, when his father died and he couldn't get a flight to Kansas until the next morning, he went out and got drunk and bought himself a prostitute. He had never been with a prostitute, and he was appalled at himself. And then here's my sister: a nice Irish-Italian girl, right? A whole pack of brothers to defend her honor and a lot of family pressure to stay a virgin until she married, and we're talking what, 1970? In 1970 nice girls still didn't do it, especially not nice Irish or Italian girls. But my parents were in Italy at the time on vacation—when my mother died—and it was just me and my sister alone in the house, and off she went. I was frantic at the time when she stayed out all night and didn't call me. I nearly sent the police after her."

Like I'm thinking about sending the police after you now, I thought to Phil's imaginary presence.

Oh, I miss you. Where are you?

I don't want Hollander, I want you.

I sat up and drank my tea and didn't know what to do with myself. I wanted to see Phil across the table from me, I wanted to look in his green eyes the color of grapes and reach a hand out and ruffle his blond hair that was always a little too long between trips to the barber. I wanted to take his hands and say: *I love you, marry me.*

Great. Hell of a way to let Phil know how much you love him, sleeping with someone else.

I thought about getting my things and leaving. I could sneak out before Hollander woke up.

But it didn't seem too fair to Hollander.

Oh, now we're going to worry about being fair to Hollander. Why didn't you worry about being fair to Hollander before you slept with him? Why didn't it occur to you this morning that you just wanted to get laid because Shelley died? And that Hollander was handy and Phil wasn't? Or that maybe you're just a little mad at Phil for sleeping with Beth and you went to bed with Hollander to get back at Phil?

My heart sank. I went into the living room, got my cigarettes, came back into the kitchen, sat down again, lit up, and brooded.

This is a fine mess, but . . . you're not going to sort it out right this minute.

I heard Paul Roussy's voice in my head: *You don't have to solve all the world's problems in the next five minutes.* Paul said this to me rather frequently, whenever he felt I was "fussing." The last time he had said to me, "Ev, you're fussing, relax," I had countered, "I can't relax! If I relax I feel like Scarlett O'Hara worrying about it 'tomorrow.' I have to worry about everything today!"

Shelley had been present for that little exchange, and she had said with a smile, "Worry about half of it today and the other half of it tomorrow, how's that?"

I realized how much I had gone to Shelley to calm down. Whenever I was "fussing." Whenever I was out of touch with my own inner serenity.

Whenever I had had it up to here pretending to be an honorary man in a man's world.

Whenever I needed the company of a mother, or a sister, or a daughter.

Whenever I wanted to be in that gentle place inside myself where women meet other women.

I sat there for a very long time, smoking cigarettes while my tea got cold.

And then I made my mind focus on Shelley's suicide.

Don't forget to call the medical examiner's office tomorrow.

Go see Steve Reinish this evening and offer your condolences.

Call Shelley's typist if Steve hasn't done that already.

Call the police if Phil hasn't turned up by midnight; by midnight it will be more than twenty-four hours since anyone's seen him. They won't look for anyone until it's at least twenty-four hours.

Maybe if I called Ost or Kelly now, though, they could start looking for Phil. But I didn't think I really wanted to do that. I didn't think I could stand the look on their faces if I called like some hysterical wife and said he was missing and then they found him with some perfectly plausible explanation about where he'd been all this time. Wait till midnight.

Call Ost tomorrow after you get the case report and explain it to him if it needs explaining.

What were the detectives talking about when they kept asking me if I thought Shelley looked "tired"?

Shelley had not seemed tired to me at any time I could remember recently. On the other hand, now that I thought about it quietly for the first time since she'd died, I *had* noticed something "funny" about her. . . . What was it? Why had I been so defensive about the fact that she'd killed herself? Why had I wanted to argue with the detective about it when I'd gone to the lab on my own two feet and stood there while Ramesh Christopher ran the serum salicylate? A serum level of eighty-five milligrams of salicylate is a fucking dose of salicylate. She must have swallowed a hell of a lot of aspirin to produce those results; you couldn't possibly take that much by accident.

I remembered how I kept saying to the detectives that she had seemed *positive* these last few weeks. My words exactly: *positive*. She'd signed the book contract; she was excited about her book. The last time I'd seen her, she'd been babbling about dog lab.

A red flag went up in my brain and I realized the same red flag had gone up while I was talking to Ost and Kelly.

Think about this a minute: who the hell gets excited about poorly anesthetized dogs howling during surgery?

Who babbles?

Who drinks two cans of TAB in five minutes?

Somebody on amphetamines, that's who.

I put my mug of tea down on the table with a clunk.

Back up a minute. Amphetamines? *Shelley?*

But I couldn't back up as much as I wanted to. I wanted to back up far enough that I could say to myself: It's out of the question; Shelley would not abuse drugs.

But the evidence was staring me in the face: People on amphetamines don't sleep much. People on amphetamines look tired and drink a lot of fluids. They have large enthusiasms over small details, an abnormal ability to focus on the task at hand, seemingly boundless energy, and the proverbial verbal diarrhea, better known perhaps as babbling.

Lordy, Lordy, as McCabe would say.

That's another thing: McCabe. McCabe had taken her home after she flipped out in surgery.

Call McCabe when you get home later.

I went into the living room, got my toothbrush and a small notebook out of the pocket of my lab coat, brushed my teeth in the bathroom, clambered into bed with Jay for a minute to take his pulse and listen to his breathing, clambered out again, covered him up to the chin with the covers, and went back to the kitchen. I made more tea and called Phil and Phil's beeper and got no answer again.

As I made a list of the things I wanted to do and wrote them in my notebook, I lit another cigarette.

Then I wrote: *Possible amphetamine abuse.*

I thought about all the crazies I had ever seen in my years of medical training.

I wrote: *Acute psychotic break.*

Then I wrote: *Differential diagnosis?*

It's not always easy to tell the difference between someone who's undergoing an acute psychotic break and someone who's been "doing Dex," as people in medicine usually refer to amphetamine abuse. Dexedrine is the amphetamine of choice for medical personnel, since they can get their hands on it fairly easily if they want it. There had been no amphetamines in Shelley's system when we'd run the Chem 60 series on her blood, or the computer would have kicked out a value for it. So I knew she hadn't had any right before she died. But I couldn't remember offhand what the clearance rate for Dex was; the body gets rid of drugs in a certain number of hours after they've been taken, but the rate at which it gets rid of them varies from drug to drug. I'd have to look up clearance rates for the major amphetamines.

I wrote: *Clearance rate Dex?*

O.K., now what?

I tried to think back over Shelley's behavior the last several weeks.

I imagined Detectives Ost and Kelly sitting across from me at Hollander's kitchen table, and one of them asking me, "Dr. Sutcliffe, when did you first notice this alleged amphetamine abuse?" I would have to admit that I had not noticed it before last Monday, when Shelley had been babbling about dog lab. I would have to admit in fact that I had not even noticed it then; I was noticing it now, as I thought about it with the clear hindsight of knowing that since then she'd killed herself. At the time I had noticed unwarranted excitement over dog lab, and the consumption of two cans of Tab in five minutes.

Not a whole hell of a lot on which to base a sane and carefully arrived-at diagnosis.

I went back to *Acute psychotic break.* Basically the same signs as amphetamine abuse, although Phil would have to tell you the psychiatric terms for these.

I wrote: *Ask Phil signs psychotic break.*

Yeah, if we ever find him.

I decided I was not going to call Phil again. Fuck him. Let him come home and find out from someone else that one of his patients killed herself while he was incommunicado.

Let him try to find out where *I* am. I don't have an answering machine.

Well, he could call my beeper, I suppose. . . .

I remembered that I'd turned my beeper off after breakfast.

Good.

There was a thud against the wall and then Hollander stumbled into the kitchen and fell into the other chair. He smiled at me stupidly with his eyes half-shut and put his head on the table. "Christ," he groaned. "That Demerol really punched my lights out. *You* were wonderful. Will you make me a cup of tea?" He raised his head from the table, squinted at me, gave up, and laid it back down again. "Oh, God. I'll never walk again. Want to send out for Chinese? I'm famished. You can feed it to me while I sleep."

I leaned over and ruffled his hair, giving him a kiss on the cheek. I felt very disloyal kissing him: disloyal to Phil, disloyal to Jay, disloyal to myself. I thought: Oh, hell, worry about half of it today and the other half tomorrow.

Hollander hummed happily when I kissed him.

I made him a cup of tea, put it on the table, and curled the fingers of his good hand around it.

"I don't think I can drink this," he said into the marble tabletop, without opening his eyes. "Can you give it to me IV?"

I said with a smile, "How about I wrap your arm up in a plastic garbage bag and you take a cold shower?"

"Oh, God, no." He sat up. After smiling at me and squinting at the tea for a while, he drank some and went through an exaggerated pantomime of opening his eyes. "I think I need toothpicks to keep my eyelids open—like Aristotle Onassis, when he had the myasthenia gravis. Here. Watch this. I'm going to wink at you." He slowly closed one eye and opened it again. "Is that coordination, or what?"

I laughed. "How's your arm?"

"Heavy. My neck muscles are all in knots from it. You can give me a massage later. You know how to give a massage, don't you? You seem to know how to do everything." His voice softened. "You're a very sexy lady. You wouldn't consider leaving Carchiollo for me, would you?"

There was a silence while he looked at me and I looked at my mug of tea.

"Sorry," he said after a while.

I smiled and shook my head.

He took my hand in his. "It's O.K.," he said. "I have bad luck with women, anyway. My last lover threw me out because it was Christmas."

"What?"

"She said, 'It's Christmas and I always break up with my lover right before Christmas. Good-bye.' "

I looked at him. He was smiling. I couldn't tell if he was serious or not, and I didn't know what to say.

He gave my hand a squeeze and let go of it. "So, you want Chinese? How about moo shu pork? Or don't you eat pork?"

"I eat pork."

"O.K. You like scallops?"

"Fine."

"Can I stand up? I think I can stand up. Feat of modern medicine, watch this." He stood up. "I was O.K. in bed, wasn't I?"

I looked up sharply. He was examining the marble tabletop, a bundle of male anxiety. "Oh, Jay!" I cried. "Of course you were. You were wonderful." I got out of my chair and put my arms around him and kissed his neck.

He held me tightly with his good arm and moved his mouth in my hair, angling his fractured arm sideways so the cast wasn't between us. He had pulled on a pair of jeans when he'd gotten up, but nothing else, and I laid my head against his bare shoulder.

We stood like that for a while.

Suddenly, holding me even more tightly, he said, "Shelley bought a car two weeks ago. A sixty-eight Volvo. I asked her why she didn't buy a new one instead of an old used one. You know what she said? She said she didn't want a car with square headlights, she wanted one with *round* headlights."

He let go of me abruptly and pulled a Chinese takeout menu out from under a magnet on the refrigerator door.

I sat back down and watched him order the food.

When he had sat back down as well, he said, "Listen. I want to ask you something." He drank the rest of his tea in one gulp. "Did you notice anything . . . funny about Shelley recently? I mean, before all this happened."

"Yeah, I was thinking about this before you got up," I said.

Then I stopped. I thought: Don't say anything about the amphetamines for a minute. See what he's noticed.

I said, "I don't know what to think. Nobody close to me has ever gone over the edge, you know? Of course I see patients at the hospital suffering acute psychotic breaks, but they're already in the throes of it by the time I see them and I never have any idea what happened to lead up to it. And then, if you ask the family members what happened, they're all poor historians—you get a real confused history out of them. When did you first notice such-and-such? They don't know. They've been busy denying and making excuses and hoping it will all go away. Sure, So-and-so has been behaving a little strangely lately, but they never expected *this*. In fact, the family members are all standing in the hall looking dazed as hell. I never used to believe them. I used to think to myself: Oh, come on, how could you not notice? Your brother or sister or whoever is in there tied down with restraints, with razor cuts all over his or her face, and you didn't notice anything but a little strange behavior? That's a little hard to believe. You don't get up one morning and out of the clear blue sky cut yourself up with razors." I took a deep breath. "But I'll tell you something, I believe all those family members now. When Shelley killed herself, it just shocked the hell out of me. If anything, that's a mild way of putting it."

"Yeah, me too," Jay said. He thought for a moment, stretching his neck to one side and then to the other. "I noticed she seemed tired lately," he said. "I mean, before all this happened, before she became unglued. Will you get me my sling? My neck's bothering me."

I went into the bedroom, spent a moment contemplating Fu, the Chinese watchdog, and got Jay's sling. Went back to the kitchen. While I was pinning the sling on, Jay said, "I don't know. She *looked* tired. But she seemed very energetic at the same time, you know? She used to bring her manuscript to work and sit in the doctors' lounge all night working on it while everyone else was grabbing a few z's. Thanks. That's much better. You take good care of me. I don't know how the hell anyone does a residency and writes a book at the same time. When did she ever eat or sleep? Christ, the last few times I was on with her she didn't eat *or* sleep—not that I saw her anyway—she just saw her patients and sat in the doctors' lounge working on her book."

Didn't sleep or eat, I noted. *Possible amphetamine abuse.*

"And I noticed her wringing her hands," Jay went on. "I started noticing that about a couple of weeks ago, I think."

I had forgotten the hand-wringing. Another red flag went up in my brain, but when I tried to focus on it, it was gone. I snapped my fingers impatiently. "What's that a sign of?"

"The only thing I can think is early-onset arthritis. But maybe it wasn't an underlying disease process; maybe it was just a nervous tic or something."

"Any drugs you might take for an arthritic condition that have the side effect of toxic psychosis?"

"Good question, Ev." He regarded me momentarily with respect. "A *very* good question."

The doorbell rang.

"Food's here; they're getting quick," Jay said. "You wanna get it? There's money in the bookcase next to the door."

I fetched the food, paying the deliveryman with a twenty-dollar bill I found under the foot of a porcelain horse in the bookcase. When I came back, Jay was rummaging in a drawer. "I got chopsticks here someplace," he said. "How about some double-aught suture? I got that too. When I was in med school in Mexico," he went on, sitting down and handing me a pair of ivory chopsticks decorated with red Chinese lettering, "we had amoeba infections all the time from the water. I remember one guy flipping out from the medication. He'd been winding up for a breakdown for a long time and his wife had just left him. She said there was nothing for her to do down there, it was boring and too hot and she couldn't learn Spanish no matter how hard she tried—and they put him on that stuff for amoeba and he went right out the window. The guys in his house had to chase him down the street one night; he ran out of the house screaming and wearing nothing but his stethoscope. Doped him to the eyeballs on Haldol and Artane and shipped him out on the next flight to Houston." He piled my plate with some of the seafood dish he'd ordered and handed me a couple of pancakes for the moo shu pork. "That was the diagnosis: toxic psychosis. You may be onto something there."

I ate a few scallops and made notes in my head:
*Possible underlying disease process; toxic psychosis due
to what drug? Concurrent amphetamine use contraindi-
cated? Chief complaint: pain in hands. Possible joint
pathology?*

I said, "Is this shrimp?"

"Yeah."

"I'm allergic to shrimp."

"Oh," he said.

We both burst out laughing. I started picking out
the shrimp with my chopsticks and throwing them
onto his plate. I got a little ditzy and threw a few
pieces in his lap.

"Wait a minute, wait a minute!" he cried, jumping
up. "The woman's throwing shrimp at me! Stop it!"
He leaned over the table and kissed me flat out.

"Jay, for God's sake, I have food in my mouth. Let
me swallow."

"I don't care. I love you."

"No, you don't. C'mon. Sit down."

He sat down. "How do you know?" he asked. "Can't
you tell?"

I put my chopsticks down on the side of my plate.

He was shaking his head at me. "Forget it," he
said.

I was appalled. I didn't know what to say. I thought
in my head: But you sleep with women all the time.
All the nurses say how good you are in bed.

"I want to get married," Jay said. "I'm ready. I
keep looking for someone to get married *to*. I guess
I'm not doing too well in the looking department. I
used to think that maybe I went with women who
didn't want to get married, but this woman I was with
last summer broke up with me and married someone
else right away. He's not even a doctor. He's a medic.
She's a nurse. So then I went out with a doctor.
I figured a woman doctor wants to marry another
doctor, she's not going to dump me for a medic.

But *she* breaks up with me because it's Christmas. What kind of reason is that for someone to break up with you?"

"Oh, Jay," I said, feeling enormously stupid.

"She was a shrink, the Christmas lady. Maybe she thought I was nuts, I don't know. I guess if you're a shrink, you can't marry someone who's nuts." He shrugged as if none of this mattered very much to him anyway, then shoveled a few pieces of food into his mouth and appeared to swallow it without chewing.

"I'm sure she didn't think you were nuts," I said desperately. "You're not nuts."

"Maybe wanting to get married is nuts," he said. "You're not married. How old are you now, thirty-four? Thirty-five? But you're going out with a shrink too. Maybe it's just shrinks who don't want to get married, huh? Maybe the shrinks are all in cahoots together. Maybe Carchiollo told her marrying me was a bad idea. Eat your food. It's getting cold. You can give me the shrimp; just don't throw them at me. You can still eat this dish, can't you? I mean, you're not allergic to the scallops too because they cooked them with the shrimp? If you can't eat it, you can eat the pork and I'll eat the shrimp and scallops." He picked up his plate, slanted it over mine, and began tipping the moo shu pork off his plate onto mine.

"Jay, stop this," I said, grabbing his wrist. "I like you very much. I enjoyed being with you very much. My relationship with Phil is a little fucked-up right now and I was upset about Shelley killing herself and I've always been attracted to you. I'm sorry if I wasn't very responsible, maybe I shouldn't have slept with you. I guess I didn't realize that it wasn't more . . . uh . . ." I trailed off helplessly.

"Casual for me?" he supplied. "It's O.K. I've heard it before. Will you let go of my arm, please? It's the only one I've got right now that works. I don't want to talk about this any more right now. I want to eat. You going to eat the seafood or you want the pork?"

"I'm fine. I'll eat what I've got here. I'll give you the shrimp, O.K.? I can eat the scallops."

"O.K.," he said. "I'm sorry for being such a mess. I'll be O.K. It's not your fault. Don't worry about me."

But I did think it was my fault; I thought: Why didn't I see this coming? How could I have been so cavalier about going to bed with him? I put shrimp on Jay's plate one by one with my chopsticks, feeling awkward. I ate my scallops and moo shu pork with difficulty. I was miserable.

"I'm going back to bed," he said when he had finished eating. "Wanna come?"

I said, "I think I should probably go back upstairs."

He nodded and got up from the table.

"Say hi to Carchiollo for me," he said, walking out of the kitchen. "No hard feelings. Life goes on. *As the World Turns. General Hospital.*"

I heard him shut the bedroom door behind him.

I waited a few minutes to see if Hollander was going to come out of the bedroom; in fact, I stood in the living room and smoked a cigarette. When I had smoked the cigarette and he still hadn't come out, I got my lab coat and quietly let myself out of the apartment.

CHAPTER

12

"Where the hell have *you* been since you got off this morning?" Alex McCabe demanded as I let him in the front door of my apartment. "It's almost ten o'clock." He gave me a kiss on the cheek and swept past me into the kitchen. "If you're going to turn your beeper off like that, the least you could do is buy an answering machine. What happened in here?"

"What do you mean, 'What happened in here?' " I asked with a smile, wrapping my head in a towel and following him into the kitchen. When I'd come back from Hollander's I'd gone in to take a shower, and I was still toweling my hair dry.

"You washed the dishes," Alex said. He bent over the sink and peered at it skeptically, his face inches from the Formica countertop.

"Actually," I said dryly, "I didn't wash them. I hid them down the drain."

"Ah. That explains it." He straightened up. "That's a nice robe. Is that the one Phil got from his great-uncle when the old man died? Uncle had nice taste." Alex opened a cabinet and took down two beer mugs. "For your pleasure, my lady doctorship," he went on expansively, "I have here six bottles of McEwan's imported Scots ale."

"Six? Are we getting drunk?"

"A Boy Scout is always prepared. I'll put four in the fridge for later."

There was a stunned silence while we both examined the interior of the refrigerator.

"Lordy, Lordy," Alex said. "No, don't tell me. You were cited by the Board of Health. They closed your stranger-than-science experiments down. They threatened you with a violation. You begged. You pleaded. My God, you even *defrosted.*"

After a minute I said, "Only Phil can clean the inside of a fridge like that. He defrosts with a hair dryer. He must have done it after I went to the hospital the other night."

Alex shut the refrigerator. "Or Jay Hollander," he said. "Where is your bottle opener? I have no idea where you keep things when they aren't dirty and in the sink. Hollander and Carchiollo were running neck and neck in the Cleanest-and/or-Most-Anal-Retentive-Doctor-of-the-Year Contest the last time I looked. I take back every nasty thing I've ever said about Carchiollo. This is truly amazing. The whole place is clean."

I opened a drawer and handed him the opener. He popped the bottle tops, poured the ale, and handed me a mug. "What's *that* for?" he asked, registering the expression on my face.

I took the beer and drank a huge draft of it. "That's not funny, Alex," I said.

"What's not funny?"

I didn't say anything.

"Am I missing something here? Are you upset about something?"

"Alex . . ."

"Oh," he said. "I see Carchiollo's back. You two have a fight before or after?"

"Before or after what?" I asked, totally confused now. "*Is* he back? Have you seen him? I've been calling him all day."

Alex looked at me oddly. "I *am* missing something here," he said. "You haven't seem Carchiollo all day?"

"No."

"Then who the hell did that to your neck?" he asked, putting out his hand and fingering the purple spot high on my throat.

"Oh, shit," I said.

"Ev, what is this?" he said, laughing now. "No, don't tell me before I sit down." He sat down at the kitchen table. "I'm all agog," he said. "Who done it?"

"You don't want to know."

"I assure you: I want to know. I am, in fact, nearly horizontal with curiosity."

I took a deep breath and let it out again. "Hollander."

"*Hollander?* You have something going with *Hollander?* Since when?"

"Since this morning."

"Oh," Alex said, considering this as if he were considering a farfetched medical opinion. "Ah . . . Was the operation a success? Or is that an indelicate question?"

"Probably."

"Probably a success or probably an indelicate question?"

I laughed. "Probably an indelicate question."

"I see. You understand, however, that one cannot resist asking."

"Of course."

"You understand, moreover, that one cannot resist further asking whether or not Phil is to be appraised of the . . . shall we say . . . *situation,* given the rather undeniable physical evidence betraying the nature of the situation, plainly visible upon gross examination . . ."

I looked at the ceiling.

" . . . which reveals a round, purple contusion approximately two centimeters in diameter—"

I cleared my throat.

"You shall not deter me from my inquiry, Ev. The

144

caring physician pursues a thorough history-taking with gentleness and persistence. However, the *important* question is not whether His Doctorship Carchiollo is to be appraised of the situation. Forgive me for obfuscating. The important question is"—McCabe paused for dramatic effect—"this: Who cleaned your fridge, Hollander or Carchiollo?"

"Carchiollo," I said, grinning. "I assume."

"You assume? Let us pursue this *rationally*. Does Hollander have keys to your apartment?"

"Not the last time I looked."

"Perhaps you should look again. Did Kathy Haughey ever tell you about her floors?"

I did a double-take over my beer mug. "What do Kathy Haughey's floors have to do with this?"

"I assume you know about the Kathy Haughey/Jay Hollander connection. Kathy gave Jay keys to her apartment—"

"Wait a minute," I said. "Kathy and Jay had an affair? Before she married Bob? Jay said he was with a nurse last summer who left him to marry a medic, but he didn't say who. This is the first time I'm putting this together."

"Oh," Alex said. "They weren't together very long. She doesn't say much about it; I heard this from Gary Seligman, our local washerwoman. The man is a veritable fount of information."

"I know. So tell me about the floors."

"Kathy and Jay had just started going together. She was going down to the Jersey shore for a week and needed someone to feed her cat, so she asked Jay. When she came back the cat was under the bed and Jay had sanded and polyurethaned the floors. Not only that, he had painted the kitchen. Kathy told Seligman she had serious doubts about Hollander after that. However, I believe Kathy is also the source of the persistent rumor rampant among the nurses that Hollander scores ten out of ten in a certain age-old

activity to which you yourself have recently been privy."
Alex coughed delicately. "I say, old chapette, might
there be any truth to this persistent and constantly
rampant rumor? I ask merely in the interest of scien-
tific inquiry. You understand." He smiled widely,
stretching the corners of his mustache nearly to his
ears.

"You look like Bill Cosby," I said. "That is some
shit-eating grin you have there."

"We try to please. You are evading the question.
Also, your robe is falling open."

"Sorry." I pulled the robe together. Then for a
moment I went out of my body, out of my kitchen
where I was sitting companionably with Alex McCabe;
mentally I flew up seven floors to Phil's apartment
directly over mine, and stood in the middle of Phil's
bedroom and looked at the pictures on Phil's dresser:
the great-uncle wearing the robe I was now pulling
closer about myself; Beth in her spaghetti-strap negligee; me in my old orange ski jacket with the Austrian
ski patches, standing on the front steps of the Museum
of Natural History. I came back into myself with a
chill and looked at the clean sink and counters in my
kitchen and I thought this: *Phil was cleaning my refrigerator while Shelley was dying.*

"What?" Alex said.

"It ambushes me," I said. "The fact that Shelley's
dead. I try not to think about it and I forget for a
while and do something else, and then I remember
and it hits me like a ton of bricks. And then I feel
guilty that I'm not thinking about it *all* the time. I
mean, how can I just put Shelley out of my mind like
this?"

Alex reached out and took my hand. I looked at his
brown hand covering my white one, and at the gold
family-crest ring that had belonged to his grandfather
the Scots whiskey merchant. "People die," Alex said
simply. "We think about them and then we don't

think about them for a while, and after that we think about them again, and life goes on. But I know what you mean." He squeezed my hand, and I watched his amber-colored eyes go out of focus.

"I was with Hollander all day," I said. "He told me about Shelley going to pieces in the OR. And that you took her home."

Alex let go of my hand. But his eyes did not come back; they remained in the middle distance, vaguely aimed at a spot on my kitchen wall just to the side of my left elbow.

"I took her home," he repeated after a while.

"Tell me."

"I don't know if I can anymore. I keep thinking I should have done this, or I should have done that, and now I'm not altogether sure what exactly I did do." He pulled at his mustache, grooming it over his top lip. "But I do know this: Shelley was definitely on the verge. I am not Phil Carchiollo, but this was no little bout of forty-eight-hours-on-duty surgical blues. Shelley was winding up for a full-blown, clinically diagnosable, acute psychotic break."

CHAPTER

13

"I was in CAT Scan when they brought in the multiple gunshot wound," Alex was saying.

We were still seated at the kitchen table, and we had opened the second bottles of ale. I had also excused myself briefly to get dressed, and was now wearing a pair of Phil's jeans and one of his old sweaters.

"That's the patient Hollander was telling you about, the one they were operating when Shelley had her 'slight attack of battle fatigue,' as Attenborough so kindly understated it. The ER paged me and I called in, but they told me Shelley was there, and also Barry Steinberg and Hollander. They weren't calling a code, so I didn't go down. Tony Firenze was with me in CAT Scan. Our patient was a junkie who had what looked to Tony like a probable subdural hematoma; he had been assaulted with a golf club of all things, according to the police. The patient was fairly alert when he was brought in; he got off the stretcher, walked around, told me his head hurt, but after that his mental status began to wax and wane, and he seized a couple of times in the ER. The CAT scan showed some mid-line shift. There were no ICU beds available, so Tony and I parked the patient in the recovery room—the only monitored setting we could find for him—went and had dinner, and then came back to look at him again. By that time he appeared to need surgery, so we took him up.

"When we came into the surgical suites we found Shelley on the floor under the scrub sinks."

Alex paused. He was not a man who characteristically discussed his feelings, and I saw immediately that he wanted to discuss them now, but was not sure how to go about it. I waited quietly, watching him.

"It was very disturbing for me to find her like that," he said eventually. "I got the same feeling I get when one of the kids from the university comes in after there's been a motor-vehicle accident or a mugging. I thought someone had hurt Shelley, and I was alarmed. Or that she had fallen at the sinks while scrubbing and had knocked herself unconscious.

"When Tony and I got down on the floor, we had trouble waking her. She appeared drunk, or possibly drugged, which turned out later to be the case. But we couldn't determine that at the time. At first Shelley insisted that she had not taken anything and that she was only *sleeping*. Under the scrub sinks? Not a likely place for a snooze. We wanted to take her to her on-call room, but she kept saying she couldn't go there because she might be needed in surgery. A fairly ludicrous assertion, since she was obviously not in any shape to be doing surgery. She looked, in fact, simply terrible. Her hair was all undone. She was disheveled. I had never seen her look like that.

"Finally she admitted that she had taken twenty milligrams of Valium. We had no idea, of course, that she had been given it, and had not taken it herself."

Alex began patting himself, searching for his cigarettes. He patted the left breast of his golf shirt, where there was no pocket, both front pockets of his chinos, and then both back pockets. His crumpled pack of low-tars was on the table. I pushed the pack toward him, and he looked sheepish.

"It's not easy for me to talk about this," he murmured, lighting up.

"I know," I said.

"Shelley was not what one would call coherent," Alex went on, inhaling deeply. "Firenze and I were not inclined to leave her there under the scrub sinks, but she refused to be moved. She began to talk about Attenborough. 'Ask Attenborough,' she kept saying. Firenze thought Attenborough was in surgery, so I decided to go ask him. I left Tony with Shelley and got myself a mask and went around the surgical suites until I was able to find Attenborough. Hollander was assisting, as Hollander told you. I told Attenborough that Firenze had a subdural hematoma and Attenborough said fine, he was just about ready to close, Firenze should go ahead and open the skull. Then I said that Dr. Reinish was asleep under the scrub sinks, which was when Attenborough made his speech about battle fatigue. I really did not know what to think when I heard this. Attenborough is an old Boston Brahmin, and I know his type: half the time he's so damned busy being gracious that he doesn't see what's right in front of his face because it might be impolite to do so. There was a possibility, of course, that Shelley had actually had 'a slight attack of battle fatigue' and had then declined precipitously after receiving the Valium and installing herself under the scrub sinks. But I didn't think so. However, one does not argue with Attenborough; he becomes sharp."

"Hollander compared Attenborough to Lorne Greene on *Bonanza*," I said dryly.

Alex looked bemused. "Surely you jest."

"I speak the truth. Verily."

"Lorne Greene is five-foot-six. Attenborough is nearly a foot taller than that."

I lifted my shoulders with a smile.

"Hollander has an interesting view of the world," Alex mused, scratching his jaw and producing a sandpapery sound. "I have to say this, though: while Attenborough was politely glossing over Shelley's behavior in the OR, whatever it might have been, I noticed that Hollander was looking distinctly wild-eyed. I really did want to hear what Hollander had to say about it, because I was immediately curious to see how his account would differ from Attenborough's. In fact, I tried to get it across to Hollander that I wanted to talk to him after he was through in the OR, but he seemed very confused when I suggested it, so I gave up and went away."

"I think Hollander thought you wanted him to come out right that minute and discuss it on the spot."

"Oh, yes. Certainly. People leave the OR all the time to have casual chats in the hall. Ev, the man has socks missing from his seabag. He is entirely too subjective about things. You talk to him and he panics. How did you ever get him into bed?"

"Actually," I said, *"he* got *me* into bed."

Alex blinked. "That's what Kathy Haughey says too, according to Gary Seligman," he said slowly. "I find that hard to believe. No, I take that back. Hollander can be very appealing. He has a very attractive intensity, and a playfulness that I can see women responding to. But I digress. I told Attenborough I would take Shelley home.

"Which was not an easy task. First, I had to get her on her feet. Then I had to find her lab coat, because she had her house keys in her coat. That was great fun; if I hadn't been so anxious about the entire scenario, I would have appreciated it as a brilliantly comical exercise in playing the buffo. I had to go into the women's locker room—luckily it was vacant at the time—and then determine which locker Shelley had deposited her belongings in; Shelley was not a great deal of help in this undertaking. I sat her down on the bench and she slid right off onto the floor like Shirley MacLaine playing a drunk scene. I tried Shelley's key in at least five lockers before I found her things. Then I had to get her moving again. I considered throwing her over my shoulder, but I thought that might inspire undue comment on the part of anyone we happened to encounter, especially individuals who might not be able to recognize me as a physician in mufti; all they would see would be a black man abducting a helpless white maiden with flowing red hair. I figured no amount of protestation on my part would disabuse them of the notion I was absconding with her for evil and despicable purposes. Who's that guy in *The Magic Flute*? Monasero? Monastraso? The black guy who abducts Pamina? Never mind. I finally gave up the idea of carrying her, and in an inspired moment threw her on a stretcher and pushed her all the way through the hospital and then down through the tunnel to the doctors' residence. At that point I had to abandon the stretcher for the stairs. The door to the lobby where you get the elevator was locked, of course. I was standing at the foot of the stairs trying to decide how to maneuver two flights when Shelley sat up as if someone had rung Chinese gongs in her ears, leapt off the stretcher, and bounded up the two flights of stairs all by herself. With me clomping up after her in hot pursuit.

"This was, to say the least, surprising. One minute she's in a drugged stupor and the next she's moving up those stairs with all the determination and vigor of a gazelle moving across the Serengeti with a cheetah on her heels. Perhaps that is not a good analogy. Allow me to retract it. I was certainly no cheetah moving after her. I was gasping for breath by the time I reached the second-floor landing; furthermore, I was in a daze of speculation over Shelley's hop-to-it recovery from the effects of the Valium.

"When I came through the door onto the second floor, Shelley was standing at the end of the hall. She had . . . her shoulders hunched . . . This is difficult to describe." Alex got up abruptly from his chair, stood in the middle of the kitchen, and hunched his shoulders at me in a way that suggested a jungle cat poised to attack. "And she was breathing like this." Alex hissed air around his teeth. Then he sat down again.

"She was at the end of the hall," he went on, grinding out his cigarette. "As you know, the lighting in the corridors of this place is generally less brilliant than is desirable. There she was. Hunching her shoulders, and breathing like that. Ev, the hair literally stood up on the back of my neck. It was terrible. I was afraid of her, and then I was afraid *for* her. And then it stopped. Just like that." Alex snapped his fingers. "Whatever it was in her that I saw there for a moment passed like rigor passes after a seizure. Her body relaxed. Her breathing became normal. But as I walked toward her, I had the distinct impression that—this may sound odd—that she was somehow *sinking*. I realized that when you look someone in the eyes, you have the impression that they are right there behind their eyeballs; their soul, or their spirit, or their life force, whatever—it's right there behind the eyes; the *person* is right behind the eyes. But when I looked at Shelley I thought: She's not right there behind her eyes. I could see her in there someplace, but it was as if she had sunk very far away in there; I looked in her eyes and her soul had sunk to the bottom of a well.

"I must have known in that moment that she was psychotic, but for some reason I denied it. I asked her if Steve was home. She said he wasn't. I asked her where he was. By this time I had taken her keys from her and had the door to her apartment open. She said something in Hebrew. I think. I said, 'Shelley, speak English.' She went into the apartment and I went in after her and closed the door. She said, 'There is nothing new under the sun. Steve has too many books. I wrote the librarian a letter about him. I threw Lukinsky off his riser. Do you want some aspirin?'

"Now, this gave me pause. Did I want some aspirin. Not did I want a drink, or a cup of tea or coffee, but did I want some *aspirin*. I declined politely. But something happened to me in that moment. I've given a considerable amount of thought to this since Shelley died. I think . . . I believe, at that moment, I simply determined to go on as if she were not incoherent. To ignore the fact that she was ill. To pretend that any minute now she would become well, sound of mind." Alex slapped the table in rhythm with his speech cadence. "I began to speak very slowly to her, as if she were a child. I spoke quietly and simply. But I was speaking to her as if she were a *sane* child. When, of course, she was neither sane nor a child. She was not well, and she needed my help. *Which I did not give her.* I gave her Mom-Dad behavior. So much for all my professional training, eh wot?"

Alex barked a terrible laugh which was not a laugh.

I reached out and took his hands in mine, but he pulled away immediately.

"Nisht," he said. "As Shelley would say."

I lit a cigarette.

"God," he groaned, "I *hate* this." He took a deep breath. "She offered me aspirin. I declined. Then she offered me wine. To tell the truth, I needed a drink. She went into the kitchen and I followed her; she moved some books and I sat down at the kitchen table. She had a point about Steve's books—that he had too many—I have to say that. There were books everywhere. She gave me a glass of some kind of kosher Israeli wine and poured one for herself. And then, before I realized what she was doing, she took a vial of pills from the kitchen counter, shook out four or five, tossed them back, and chugged at least half her wine down on top of them—about three or four ounces.

"I jumped out of my chair so fast trying to stop her swallowing those pills, I very nearly turned over the table. I shouted, *'Shelley, what is this?'* and lunged for the pills. She put her hand behind her back with the vial and backed away from me, looking very frightened. It stopped me in my tracks. I was loath to *wrestle* the damned pills away from her—the idea of wrestling the pills away from her seemed too much like an aggressive act to me, I guess, and she was looking very threatened. So I planted my feet on the floor and scolded her like a schoolteacher. I felt absurd. I said, 'Shelley, you give me those pills this minute.' She began to behave like a *very* frightened animal. She was *cowering.* I said, 'Shelley, *please* tell me what those pills are.' She said, in a very small voice, 'Aspirin.' I said, 'Shelley, those are not aspirin'—I had seen them, and they were round and red—'and you either give me those pills right this minute, or so help me God I will put my finger down your throat until you barf them up.' I was becoming slightly shrill. Not only that, I had her by the shoulders by this time and I was actually *shaking* her, so help me God.

"She was beyond it, so to speak, and I was out of control. I imagined Steve coming home at that moment and finding this wild-eyed, incoherent colleague of his wife's shaking her until her teeth rattled, and I began to feel even more absurd. I stopped shaking her. I decided to try a different tack. I said, 'Shelley, these look very good to me, and I might like to take one myself. Can you tell me what they are? I hate to take anything when I don't know what it is.' She had offered me some, after all. I spoke in a very confidential tone of voice. Right away she said, 'Ibuprofen,' and handed the vial right over. I shook a few pills out and looked at them; they were indeed Ibuprofen, four hundred milligrams. I said, 'Ah. Yes, of course.' As if I understood *perfectly* why she might be washing down handfuls of Ibuprofen with Israeli table wine. Ibuprofen is the drug of choice for rheumatoid arthritis and osteoarthritis, for God's sake. Keeping my voice as level and reasonable as possible, I said, 'Why are you taking this, Shelley?' Meanwhile, of course, I was trying desperately to deduce to what extent five tablets of Ibuprofen four-hundred milligrams washed down with four or five ounces of wine might affect a one-hundred-and-ten-pound person who had had twenty milligrams of Valium approximately five hours earlier. I eventually decided that it would not, in all probability, effect cardiorespiratory collapse. I resisted the urge to start shaking her again.

"Shelley was not immediately forthcoming with information, so I decided to sit down again. I told *her* to sit down. We sat. I was beginning to feel as if I were smack in the middle of a Woody Allen movie about slightly demented but lovable New York sophisticates. Everything I considered saying to Shelley and everything I imagined her saying to me in response seemed to have a slight air of comic timing about it.

"I realized, very slowly, that I had to make some kind of decision and do something. But I didn't know what. While I was thinking this, I got out a cigarette and asked for an ashtray."

Alex stood up abruptly, and continued: "Which turned out to be, in Shelley's mind, a symbolic request of sorts. My asking for an ashtray." He took an unsteady step toward the refrigerator, opened it, and got out the last two bottles of ale. When he sat down again, I saw that something in his face had changed.

I thought the same thing I had thought about Hollander that morning, so many hours ago, in the plaster room: *I don't know him.* And the second thought came closely on the heels of the first, just as it had with Hollander: *You know him. You've just never seen him when someone has died.*

I took the two bottles of ale from Alex and opened them.

Alex turned sideways in his chair and began to talk to the far wall of my kitchen.

"She began to rant. I hesitate to use the word. She was not shouting, or even raising her voice; she was, in fact, speaking to me in a rational, even tone of voice. It was perhaps the rationality that was the ranting. The *tone* was rational. The content of what she had to say was not. She told me that smoking was bad for the body. Then she took an orange from a bowl of fruit on the table and offered it to me as an example of what was good for the body, as opposed to bad. She said, 'Oranges are round. Eggs are round. You have to think of your body as the source of your being and what you eat as the source of your body. Cigarette smoking is bad for the body. It violates the earth quality of the body. Earth to earth, dust to dust, ashes to ashes. If you develop a sense of your body as the source of your being, then you don't have to pay attention to your body anymore. You can purge yourself of your body.'

"Then she began to talk about salt. 'Salt is very good for you,' she said. She peeled the orange and salted it and ate a few sections of it and offered some to me. I declined. She said, 'Would you like an egg? Eggs are round.' She got a few hard-boiled eggs out of the refrigerator and peeled *them* and salted them and offered me one. I ate it. Then she got out a tomato, which she told me was round as well, and cut it up into sections and salted *that*. I ate some tomato. She peeled another orange. This went on and on. Tomatoes, oranges, eggs. All round. She said, 'You need salt for electrolyte balance.' She told me that the Romans used to pay their armies with salt instead of money and that's where we get our word 'salary' from—from the Latin word for 'salt.' Then she said that eggs were in the Passover story, and that the egg was the sign of the full-life cycle. She said, 'Life and death, life and death.' She explained the Talmudic concept of *Yezer Ha-ra*, the Evil Influence, and *Yezer Ha-tov*, the Good Influence. We went round and round about the two

Yezers for quite a long time. Going round about the two *Yezers* put me into a trance after a while.

"After that she began to talk about Steve's library books and the *Yezer Ha-ra*, the Evil Influence. Steve had too many library books. This was bad for the body, but I forget how exactly. From that we got onto the topic of Hollander's horses. This mystified me entirely until I was able to make the connection between the fact that Steve had too many library books and Jay had too many horses. Then we heard about Tony Firenze's surgical scissors; too many of those as well, and also bad for the body. We went back to Steve's books. Shelley claimed to have written letters to all the librarians of all the libraries from which Steve had borrowed the books, telling the librarians that it was bad for the body, et cetera. She wanted to show me the letters. I insisted that was not necessary. She began to talk about writing letters to police and curators about Hollander's horses, and I began to wonder to whom she was going to write about Firenze's scissors: Attenborough, no doubt, or the American Medical Association. Or perhaps the FBI.

"Then she said her hands hurt, which was bad for the body, and that she was *pregnant,* and that was *also* bad for the body. *And that she was going to have an abortion because her hands hurt."*

Alex put a large hand over his eyes, and sat very still.

It took me a minute to find my voice. It seemed to have fallen down my trachea and landed in my lungs somewhere, and my lungs at the moment had ground to a halt. "An *abortion?"* I squeaked eventually.

Shelley have an abortion? A rabbi's wife?

Alex seemed to be trying to find his voice as well. He ran his hand down from his eyes over his mouth and to his throat, then dropped it to his lap. After what seemed like a very long time he said, "I got up from Shelley's kitchen table and I called the ER and asked for Phil Carchiollo.

"He came on the line and spoke to me, and then he came right over, and I left him there with her."

"What?"

"I left. I couldn't get out of there fast enough. I shut the apartment door behind me and ran down the hall."

"Phil came over?"

"Yes. I called Phil. He came over. I left."

"Phil saw her like that?"

"Yes!" Alex cried. "He's the goddamned psychiatric *attending,* for Chrissake! What's the matter with you?"

"Why didn't anyone tell me about all this?" I shrieked. *"Why didn't you call me? Why didn't Phil tell me any of this?"*

Alex blinked at me. "Ev."

"What?"

"Rest yourself."

I glared. "That's not funny."

"I am not trying to be funny. Calm down."

"You calm down. I don't notice that you're so fucking calm yourself."

"Fine. I'll calm down. We'll both calm down. O.K.?"

There was a beat while we looked at each other.

Alex said, "Are we calm now?"

I said again, "Why didn't you tell me, Alex?"

"Ev, when was I supposed to tell you? In the first place, I didn't see you over the weekend; I got in my car Saturday morning and drove to Boston to see my family. I didn't come back until Monday noon, when I had to show up at the hospital. In the second place, I assumed that Carchiollo would have told you. The next time I saw you was at the hospital when Shelley . . . when she coded. When she died."

"Afterward. Why didn't you tell me afterward? We were on all night together."

"I was upset."

"You were *upset*? *I* was upset. We were *all* upset. You should have told me."

"I told you: I thought you knew! I heard Carchiollo on the phone when I called you to come over Monday night when Hollander broke his arm! Carchiollo was with you!" Alex began to bang the flat of his hand on the table.

I sat back in my chair and rammed a cigarette between my teeth. "Did you tell the police?"

"Of course I told the police."

"What, that Shelley looked *tired?*"

"I told them what happened. I told them everything. Of course I told them."

My hands were shaking. Alex took the matches out of my hand and lit my cigarette for me.

"Did you talk to Phil later that night? After you left him with Shelley?"

"Yes, I saw him after he came back to the ER."

"And? What did he say?"

Alex exhaled loudly. "He did not think she was psychotic. He diagnosed her as being 'somewhat loose.' "

"Loose" was psychiatric shorthand for "loosening of associations," or rambling, disconnected talk. *"Loose?"* I repeated incredulously. "That's it? Phil thought Shelley was *loose?"*

" 'Somewhat loose and exhibiting signs of concrete thinking.' Which I think means she was losing her sense of humor."

"Don't be sarcastic, Alex. 'Concrete thinking' means losing your sense of humor and not being capable of abstract thinking, but that kind of humorlessness is a serious sign of being out of touch with yourself."

"Oh, yes. Definitely. She was definitely out of touch with herself. You don't kill yourself because you're a 'little loose' or 'exhibiting signs of concrete thinking.' You don't kill yourself because you're a little out of touch with yourself. Carchiollo missed the call. Face up to it. *He missed the goddamn call."*

I put my feet on the floor and reached for my beer. "Alex," I said quietly, "do you think Shelley was taking anything?"

"What, you mean the Ibuprofen?"

"No. Dex or something."

"Amphetamines," Alex said. He didn't lift the end of the word into a question, but rather sat on it with his voice, pausing, thinking. "Yes. I did think that. I thought it when she jumped off the stretcher and bounded up the stairs. She'd had twenty milligrams of Valium and she jumped up like I'd set the stretcher on fire. Not exactly typical. Twenty milligrams is a whopping dose of Valium. You'd think she would have been more sedated." He scratched his jaw. "But then I thought it was just battle fatigue; that she was wired, and it would take more than twenty mg's to knock her out."

The phone on the wall behind my head rang, jolting me out of my skin. I batted at it, knocking it off into my hand. "Sutcliffe!" I yelled into the mouthpiece.

There was a silence on the other end. Then a shuffling noise, then Hollander's distinctive voice. "Ev?"

I received a strange bolt of lightning square to the middle of my breastbone. I waited a beat to let the fire of it dissipate. "Hi, Jay," I said.

"What's going on?"

"Nothing. I'm talking to Alex McCabe."

Silence.

"I'm a little upset right now," I said awkwardly.

"Oh," he said. Pause. "I thought I would go see Steve. He's sitting *shiva,* you know."

I nodded, encouraging him to go on, unable to respond with my voice. Then I realized he couldn't see me nodding. "Good," I said stupidly. "Please give him my regards. Tell him I'll come see him tomorrow."

"I go jogging with him three times a week," Hollander said. "And we lift weights together in the gym once or twice a week. I thought it would be good if I was with him for a little while this evening."

I looked at Alex, who was staring at the far wall of the kitchen with somber concentration.

Hollander went on, "I thought I would tell you . . . you know, where I was. In case you called me and I wasn't home."

"Jay," I said slowly.

"You're mad at me."

"No, of course not." *Say something. You've been in this position before with men. He wants reassurance you still want him.*

"Never mind," he said. "You can't talk now." Pause. "Will you call me later?"

"Yes, of course. A little later."

He didn't say anything. I imagined him nodding into the phone, thinking perhaps that *I* could see *him.*

"I'll call you later," I said.

"O.K." He hung up.

I slowly replaced the phone in its cradle.

"Hollander?" Alex asked.

"He wanted to tell me where he was in case I called him while he was out. He's going down to see Steve Reinish to sit *shiva* with him and he was worried I'd call and he wouldn't be there."

Alex grinned. " 'Did my heart love till now?' " he quoted. " 'Forswear it, sight! For I n'er saw true love, till this night.' "

"That's 'true *beauty.*' 'For I n'er saw true *beauty* till this night.' "

Alex waved a hand dismissively. "You need to talk to that man," he said. "Before he polyurethanes your floors and paints your kitchen. The whole thing sounds very unhealthy, Ev. You're not his mother. He doesn't have to tell you where he is every minute."

"I shouldn't have slept with him," I said. "I didn't realize he was that vulnerable. I thought he was supposed to be such a ladies' man."

"A lesson learned is a penny earned," Alex said with mock sobriety.

"Don't make fun of him."

"You're right. I apologize. Just go straighten it out tomorrow. Tell him you're in love with Carchiollo. Which you are. *Why,* I don't know, but that's immaterial."

We both laughed.

"I think it's 'a penny saved is a penny earned,' " I said.

"I defer, once more, to your infinitely superior learning. And on that cheerful note, Ev, if you'll excuse me, I have to grab some old racko time-ola. Are you on tomorrow?"

"Eight to eight P.M."

"Lucky you." He yawned. "I have noon till eight the following morning." He reached out a hand and ruffled my hair.

"How'd you pull that?"

"We lost a surgeon recently, remember? Somebody's got to cover."

Then he was gone, and I was alone.

CHAPTER

14

I was standing in front of my open refrigerator door thinking: Great. He cleans the fucking refrigerator but where is he when I need him?

Not only that, but Phil threw out all my food. O.K., so maybe it was a little old in his opinion. Phil threw out cooked chicken legs after two days; I threw them out after a week. When I was a kid my mother used to hand me pieces of cheese out of the fridge that were occasionally moldy, and she always said, "A little penicillin—it's good for you." I subscribed to her theory in good faith. Phil did not.

I still had half a bottle of ale left in my beer mug and I sat down at the kitchen table again to drink it. There had been very little drinking in my house when I was growing up, except for the Jewish holidays, when there was always wine on the table. I had developed a taste for beer during my college days, and had grown accustomed to ale with meals when I was studying at Oxford during my summer of research there, way back in that other life when I had been pursuing a doctorate in English literature.

Draining the last of the ale from my mug, I got up again and wandered restlessly into the living room, took down an old battered copy of *Twelfth Night* from the top shelf of my bookcase, thumbed through it, then put it back again.

I picked up the latest issue of *The New England Journal of Medicine* and put it down again immediately.

I called Phil; no answer.

I called Hollander, having no idea what I would say to him, and hung up with relief when he didn't answer either.

I sat down with the newspaper. A three-column headline on the front page informed me that New York City was completely snowbound; accumulations had reached twenty-eight inches in some parts of the city and Long Island, and in places drifts had blown ten feet high. There were pictures of people digging out their cars, children playing in the snow in Central Park, and would-be travelers sleeping on the floor at Kennedy Airport after their flights had been grounded by the storm.

I thought about Rabbi Reinish with snow in his beard and his wife thrown over his shoulder, banging on the door to the ambulance bay.

Laying the newspaper across my knees, I wondered what had gone through Shelley's mind Monday morning. Had she noticed the snow starting up, falling softly outside her window at first, then more steadily as the storm swept into the city? I saw her as I was used to seeing her: in her blue OR scrubs, her flaming red hair gathered up in a turn-of-the-century bun. Her implausibly blue eyes bright with intelligence. Her tiny hands working the needle-holder in surgery; I heard the *click-clack* as the needle-holder opened and shut.

Had she been hysterical in her decision to kill herself, or calm?

And how did she manage to swallow all that aspirin? She'd have had to down it by the handful to consume the amount she had.

Did it make her gag?

I had a patient once in the ER who told me that he had tried to kill himself by swallowing an entire bottle of aspirin. I wasn't seeing this patient for the aspirin overdose; I was seeing him two years later to sew up his face after he got hit over the head with a gun butt on Amsterdam Avenue at three A.M., but he told me about the overdose while I was suturing him. He said, "Those dudes try to take me down, but you know, I got nine lives; I try to kill myself two years ago but it just make me throw up the whole fuckin' night." So I asked, "What did you take?" and he said, "Aspirin. Man, don't ever try to take you'self out with that shit, it make you sicker than a *dog*. God damn, it make you sick."

Getting up from the couch, I rummaged in the closet until I found my Austrian mountain boots, grabbed my old orange ski jacket with the ski patches from Brand and Vorarlberg and St. Moritz, sat down for a minute to pull on my boots and lace them up, got up again, and left the apartment.

Outside on the street the air was so frigid the bones in my face throbbed when I drew breath. I sucked the dagger-cold air into my lungs. I was outside myself; my mind was in the *off* mode. Automatic pilot. Without considering where I wanted to go, I set off toward Broadway. My legs worked by themselves; they plunked one foot down in front of the other, left-right, left-right, *hut*. I was a passive passenger.

I felt very alone and very alive suddenly, as if being alive were something I had won in some long-forgotten war. I got out a cigarette and lit it in cupped hands, my back to the wind. The street was quiet; the side streets had not been plowed yet, so there was no traffic. I stopped walking for a minute and puffed on my cigarette.

I wondered why I identified with soldiers all the time.

Rabbi Reinish had been a soldier for two years in the Israeli Army, "way back when," as Shelley used to say, waving her hand behind herself with a smile. No, wait—it wasn't Steve who'd been the soldier; it was Shelley's brother, and it was the American Army. Steve had been in the Israeli Army, but as a medic. That was it: Shelley's brother was in the U.S. Army before he decided to become a rabbi, and Steve was in the Israeli Army before he decided to become a rabbi, and that's how Shelley had met Steve: her brother had brought him home one Friday night for Shabbes.

I wondered why, when I thought: *I'm alive,* I immediately thought: *I've been through a war, and I've won being alive like a medal.*

Maybe it was all the blood, the bones sticking out of people, the gunshot wounds, the stab wounds.

Maybe it was all those war movies I'd seen, where the men saw things and then seemed alive to themselves in a different way than they had seemed to themselves before the war.

The man I had been living with when I entered medical school, a gentle sort of man who taught English and German in a fancy boys' prep school on the East Side, had said to me during my first summer clerkship—the summer clerkship during which I met Shelley—"You're different; you've changed."

I said, "I haven't changed, I've changed *professions.*"

He said, "No, *you've* changed. You're cold now, and nothing bothers you anymore."

I said, "Richard, I can't talk about this anymore, I have to get some sleep."

He said, "Fine, you sleep."

He began packing his things into old blue shopping bags with "Brooks Brothers" written on the sides in white script. I watched him pack the first bag and shake the creases out of the second bag, laying his shirts out on the living-room couch. Then I went to sleep. I had been on call the night before, and I slept like a dead person. When I got up the next day I looked at the couch where Richard's shirts had been in neat little piles the night before and I waited to feel something. I waited to feel something about the gaps in the bookshelves where Richard had kept his books; about the empty dresser drawers, the blank wall in the living room where Richard's cousin's painting had hung for the last two years, the empty space on the kitchen counter where he had kept his coffeemaker and coffee grinder.

And when I didn't feel anything I went to the hospital.

I did feel one thing: as if I were in my body more than usual. I went around the entire day waiting to feel something emotionally, but instead kept being distracted by a funny looseness in my knees and centering of strength in my thighs. I had had that feeling before; it had started my first day on the wards. It was a bizarre feeling, especially since it alternated with panic from one minute to the next; I was either in a panic or thinking I was able to leap tall buildings in a single bound. It was all the more bizarre when I noticed, after I had had a few patients die on me, that I seemed to get this feeling in my legs—this *physical* feeling—in lieu of an *emotional* feeling from the patients' dying. Someone would die and I would think: When am I going to feel something? What's wrong with me? And then sometime later I would think: I'm alive. I'm in my body. My legs are strong.

Standing in the snow smoking my cigarette, I decided: You kick enough feelings down the basement stairs and it makes your legs strong.

Like you kicked your feelings for Shelley down the basement stairs.

Throwing my cigarette in the snow, I started walking again, and there it was: the old familiar looseness in the knees, the power in the thighs.

I stopped abruptly and held my body as still as I could hold it. I let the air out of my lungs. Over on Broadway a bus went by, the chains on its wheels grinding. But on the side street it was calm, and quiet, and I willed my body as still as I could make it.

Oh, Shelley, I thought, I don't know how to mourn you.

And then the tears came. I took a great wracking gulp of ice-cold air and stood on the sidewalk and cried.

CHAPTER

15

I marched past the triage window, past a dozen miserable-looking people waiting for medical attention, and around a corner into the main hospital corridor.

I had no idea what I was doing in the hospital.

As I passed the sign that said "NOT AN EXIT FOR STAFF," I wondered for the thousandth time where in God's name they *wanted* us to go in and out of the hospital when it was after hours. I followed the green line on the floor that took you to X Ray; or was that the blue line? Maybe the red one. No, the red one went to the ICU. . . .

I was still crying.

This is great, Sutcliffe. Here you are waltzing through the hospital, a total mess, completely out of control. What are you going to say if you bump into someone?

I'm going to say I'm crying because Shelley's dead, what the hell is the matter with that?

Crying made me think of my old grandmother, Bubba Hazel. When I was little and my parents punished me and I cried, Bubba Hazel always had a cookie for me. She would push the cookie up my sleeve so my parents wouldn't see, and then she would shake her finger at me with a great show of ferocity and say, "So much crying even a baby doesn't do. Stop! Enough!"

Stopping in front of the main elevator banks, I got out a Kleenex and blew my nose.

I'll go check my mail, I decided.

Then it came to me:

There's something from Shelley in your mailbox.

With a sinking feeling I realized I had seen Shelley later than I mentioned. I had told the detectives I hadn't seen her since the previous Monday, but I had seen her Thursday morning.

She was running somewhere, barreling along in the curious way she did when she had to get somewhere fast but wasn't wearing the right shoes and had too much junk in the pockets of her lab coat to run without losing it all up and down the corridor. She would sort of hunker down, jam her hands into the pockets of her lab coat to hold down whatever she had in there—pens, notebooks, stethoscope, neuro hammer, plastic slide charts for figuring out fluid input/output— and off she would go, churning her legs under herself like dual propellers on a boat, her skirt flapping in the wind.

She shouted at me as she ran by me: "Latest transcript back from the typist. In your box!"

Oh, Christ, I thought.

The elevator doors opened and I staggered on like a drunk person. It occurred to me that maybe I *was* drunk. How much did you drink with Alex? Three bottles of beer? No wonder you're a little out of it. Alex can drink three bottles of beer without batting an eyelid; you can't. I sagged against the far wall of the elevator as the doors clanked shut again. A premed student with a handful of bloods for the lab looked at me and then looked away again. I wondered what he was doing there; premeds were supposed to be out of the hospital by ten P.M. It was almost one A.M. The premed got off on four, the lab floor. I stumbled out of the elevator on the twelfth floor.

You *are* drunk, you dumb shit.

I leaned against the wall and thought: I'll just stand here a minute and see if I get a little less drunk. How come I wasn't drunk while I was talking to Alex? How come I wasn't drunk when I got my coat to go outside? How come I only got drunk when I got into the elevator? There must be some medical explanation for this, some physiological mechanism of the metabolism of alcohol that I'm missing here. . . . Let's see . . . I couldn't think of any physiological mechanism. All I could think of was a story Bubba Hazel told me once, about her cousin's friend who drank a lot at a party and it was very cold outside, and she walked out the door from the house where the party was and the cold air hit her in the face and she passed out immediately and fell right down the front steps of the house.

No, wait a minute, is that how it went?

I couldn't remember.

I'll put this together if it kills me.

Let's see, you drink alcohol and the capillaries dilate . . .

I let my knees go limp and slid my back down the wall until I was sitting on the floor. I'll just sit here a minute.

While I was sitting on the floor recuperating, I began to worry about the transcript of Shelley's manuscript waiting for me in my mailbox. I began particularly to worry about finding out whatever it was that Shelley had written about Tony Firenze. I didn't want to have any more altercations with Firenze, and I wondered what my responsibility in the whole matter was now that Shelley was dead. Who was going to see this book through publication? Me? Shelley's husband? Her parents? Shelley's husband was a rabbi and Shelley's parents were Oriental-art dealers. They presumably would like to see her book published and would look to me to continue the work I was doing with the book, since I was a physician and they were not physicians. And out of loyalty to Shelley I would certainly like to continue.

But I really did not feel like fighting with Tony Firenze about it, and knowing Firenze, he would probably hold me personally responsible for whatever Shelley had written about him.

Firenze was not the only person who was unhappy about Shelley's book. Phil, for instance. In his interview with Shelley, he had discussed his ambivalence about University Hospital's treatment of "bag people," the homeless mentally ill. University, like all New York City hospitals, had a hit-or-miss policy of treatment for these people, doing what it could to treat only the most acutely ill and turning the less nutsy cases right back out on the streets again. Phil was concerned that the hospital might not take his criticisms kindly, and that he would suffer endless political ramifications for his opinions. When Shelley had interviewed McCabe, he had commented at great length about the triage of surgical patients; it was his opinion that certain surgical procedures were offered to the poor exclusively by whim of the attending surgical staff, who agreed to take only the cases they thought would be interesting or instructional to the residents. McCabe was not too happy about seeing his opinions in print either. I was, in fact, one of the few people who had talked to Shelley for her book and had not expressed reservations afterward about having done so. I had talked about the ethics of "slow code" resuscitations of the terminally ill and DNR (Do Not Resuscitate) orders in patients' charts, and I had liked what Shelley wrote about me.

So what does this boil down to, exactly? I asked myself. Are you just giving in to Firenze's temper tantrums again? Why not stand up to him for a change?

I was puzzled that Firenze did not seem to know what Shelley had written about him. Didn't he remember what he had discussed with her?

Or was there something else, something he had not intentionally discussed with her, something she had overheard him say in surgery?

I got unsteadily to my feet. It might be a good idea, I thought, if I read the rest of the book before I started worrying about it.

The twelfth floor was very quiet. There was nothing up there except the on-call rooms and the doctors' mailboxes, and it was a standing joke among the doctors that no matter how many times you went in and out of your on-call room in a given day, you would never bump into anyone in the halls on the twelfth floor. I stood for a minute listening. The quiet began to give me the creeps. There was still a little snow on my boots, what hadn't already melted, and I banged each boot on the wall to knock it off. Banging my boots on the wall made me feel a little easier. It also made me feel slightly less drunk, somehow.

I moved toward the doctors' mailboxes, a bank of cubbyholes built into the wall; the cubbyholes were open so the doctors could leave notes for one another. I made my boots go *clump* on the floor as I moved.

I stopped and listened again.

Then I turned around and peered down the corridor.

I didn't remember it being so creepy up there.

My heart began to knock inside my chest, not a bad knock, but just a light knock to let me know it was there. Knock, knock, I'm here if you need me.

I turned around again and snuck up to my mailbox, darted in my hand, and yanked out the mail. There were no snakes in there as far as I could see; no hand coming out of the wall to grab me. I backed away from the boxes anyway. Flipping through the mail quickly, I looked behind myself for predators. Several white envelopes, regular mail, and a few blue inter-hospital envelopes, but none large enough to hold a transcript from Shelley's book, were in the stack. A flier about some speaker for Grand Psychiatric Rounds;

I threw it in the wastebasket immediately. Sometimes my relationship with Phil seemed like Grand Psychiatric Rounds; I didn't need to overindulge. Two fliers about meetings I was supposed to attend; I'd think about them. A postcard from my brother Alan with foreign stamps on it; where the hell was he *now?* Guy goes out of the country more than a fucking diplomat; that's what happens when you have a rich lover, I guess. Greetings from Mykonos, Greece. I turned the card over and looked at three very tanned and very naked men lying facedown on colorful towels on a beach. Very funny, Alan. An envelope addressed to me in handwriting I didn't recognize. A flier from a medical journal; file thirteen for that one as well.

I looked at the envelope with the handwriting I didn't recognize; it said: "SUTCLIFFE YOUR EYES ONLY." Not exactly written by someone with all his oars in the water, as McCabe would say.

Or her oars. I realized with a jab to the breastbone that it was from Shelley.

YOUR EYES ONLY. Oh, Shelley. . . . What happened to you?

I turned the envelope upside down to slide the letter out—it wasn't sealed—and something fell out and went *ping* on the floor.

A key.

As I bent to retrieve it, I felt sick. It was a hospital key, easily recognizable by the oversize, square top.

I unfolded the letter in the envelope. It was a handwritten note on a slip of paper torn from one of the freebie pads the drug companies like to pepper the hospital with; the name of an overprescribed tranquilizer proclaimed itself in large red letters on the top. Underneath the screaming red lettering was written, in block letters: "TRANSCRIPT ON DESK ON-CALL ROOM READ IT."

I wondered briefly and sadly if, when you became psychotic, you lost your ability to punctuate your sen-

tences. Or if everything became so urgent it could only
be conveyed in upper-case letters.

I wondered why Shelley had chosen to leave the
memo in my mailbox. Why she hadn't just handed me
the manuscript, or called me on the phone at home to
tell me she was bringing it over, as she normally did?

Had she already made plans to kill herself? Did she
want me to go to her on-call room after she was dead
to get the transcript?

But that would show a lot of forethought on Shelley's part, a careful premeditation that didn't exactly
jibe with the hysterical handwriting here.

The chief of Psychiatric Services told me once over
coffee in the doctors' cafeteria that people who were
going to kill themselves usually worked things through
very carefully before they actually did it. They picked
the way they would do it, too, choosing a method that
had the most symbolic control, say, for example, drowning. "If someone wants to drown himself," the chief
had said, "and you row out in a boat and point a gun
at him, he'll swim to shore before he'll let you shoot
him in the water. A patient who wants to kill himself
usually feels he has no control over anything going on
in his life; the only thing he does have control over is
the method and time he has chosen to end his own
life."

I looked at the handwriting on the envelope and the
note in my hands.

I pictured Shelley treading water, and me, in a
rowboat, pointing a gun at her.

Shelley, still treading water, says to me, "Oh, wait a
minute, I forgot to give you this," and tosses a soggy
envelope inscribed in waterproof ink "SUTCLIFFE YOUR
EYES ONLY" into the bottom of the boat. The key falls
out onto the wet floorboards and Shelley says, " 'Bye
now," and disappears under the water and doesn't
come up again.

The key fell out of my hands and *pinged* on the floor again.

I looked at it for a while before my eyes focused and I bent to pick it up again.

O.K., Shelley, I thought. I'm here for you now. I'll go read your transcript, and God rest your soul.

"Ev," a voice behind me said.

I screamed.

A hand came down on my shoulder and reflexively I snapped my elbow back, feeling it connect with the soft flesh of someone's belly.

Without looking back, I ran down the hall, my heart clawing in my chest to get out.

CHAPTER

16

I held Paul Roussy by the shoulders. He was doubled over, gasping, and I said over and over again, "Are you O.K.? I'm sorry. Jesus. You scared the fucking *shit* out of me, sneaking up on me like that. You sure you don't want to sit down?"

Roussy made a noise like a vacuum cleaner.

"Take deep breaths. You'll get your breath back in a minute."

He nodded.

"Sit down."

He shook his head.

"Some . . . bedside . . . manner," he said after a while.

"You O.K. now?" I let go of his shoulder. "What are you doing up here, anyway?"

"What d'ya mean, what am I doing up here?" He took a deep breath, his arms still crossed protectively over his solar plexus. "I'm going to my on-call room. What're *you* doing up here? You're not on tonight, are you?"

"Checking my mail."

"Huh. You got a black belt in that, checking your mail? Who'd you think I was, anyway? Godzilla?"

"I'm sorry. I'm a little jumpy."

"A little." He straightened up. "Whoosh. I thought I'd forgotten how to breathe there for a minute. Listen, did McCabe find you? He was looking for you earlier."

"Yeah, we had a couple of beers."

He nodded. "Somethin' about Shelley, huh?"

I looked down at the key and note and envelope, scrunched up in my hand. I opened my hand and started smoothing the note out.

"That why you're jumpy?"

I nodded.

He made a sucking noise against his teeth. "Wanna talk?"

I looked up. Paul Roussy was probably my closest confidant among my hospital colleagues, excepting Phil, of course. Paul and I had had many a heart-to-heart in the wee hours of nights on call together.

"I'm off," he said. "I got off at six, but I'm staying in my on-call room to sleep 'cause I got my sister and her husband and two kids in my house this week and I need some space from all that."

"Thanks," I said. "I'm a little strung-out."

When we got to Roussy's on-call room he plugged in an electric kettle. "You want tea or coffee?"

"Tea." I sat down on one of the two beds. Roussy sat on the other—Indian-style, his forearms resting on his knees. He was a large man, broad across the chest and shoulders and pudgy around the waist, with straw-colored hair cut in a style I associated with TV sportscasters or Italian kids from Staten Island. He was twenty-five years old, divorced, and had a four-year-old daughter who lived with her mother in Texas. He and his ex-wife screamed at one another regularly on the telephone, Roussy sometimes holding up his end of the argument in the middle of the nurses' station in the ER, but I had never heard him so much as raise his voice at anyone else. I knew him to be one of the most patient individuals on earth—interactions with his ex-wife excepted—and one of the kindest.

He smiled at me to encourage me to talk.

"I feel I was a bad friend to her," I said, my voice catching in my throat. I thought I was going to start crying again, and I was embarrassed. Jesus, *get a grip on yourself.*

Roussy nodded. "We all feel like that," he said simply, getting up to fix two mugs of tea. "You want Coffeemate or sugar in this?"

I shook my head.

He put the mug into my hands and I held it gratefully, warming myself.

"You can't feel responsible for Shelley's death," he said, sitting down again. "They bang that into our heads at Al-Anon and ACOA. You're not responsible for anything anyone else does."

I nodded. Roussy's mother was an alcoholic and his wife had started drinking heavily after their child was born, and after his divorce he had started attending meetings at Al-Anon and Adult Children of Alcoholics. I said, "I don't feel *responsible,* but I feel I could have been a better friend to her."

"Yeah, but that's feeling responsible. You feel you could have helped her by being a better friend and then maybe she wouldn't have killed herself, right?"

"But I didn't even know she was *depressed.* I didn't know anything was the matter. Last week when she was talking to me about her book, she acted a little strange, and I didn't notice."

"What's 'strange'?"

I blew on my tea and took a sip. It was still too hot to drink. "She was . . . I don't know, I've been thinking maybe she was taking amphetamines or something, she was kind of agitated and talking fast . . ."

"When, this one time? Or you noticed this over a while?"

I thought about it. "I guess I mean that one time. I don't think I noticed it before. But that's the point, I really didn't pay that much attention to her. I feel if I had been a better friend and had been paying

180

more attention to her on a regular basis, I might have noticed more what was going on with her."

"I don't think that's true, necessarily. Did her husband notice it?"

"I don't know, I didn't ask him. I haven't talked to him."

"Well, if it makes you feel better, I didn't notice it either. I feel bad about that too. But I don't know her that well—didn't know her that well. And you have to take that into consideration too. Shelley was a kind of private person. She didn't talk to everyone about herself; in fact, I get the impression she didn't talk to very many people at all on a personal level. You're saying that you weren't a very good friend to her, but maybe that's because she didn't . . ." Roussy trailed off, searching for the right word. "She didn't let you in, you know?" He took a thoughtful sip from his mug. "And I never had the idea she was taking amphetamines. . . . You sure she wasn't just wound up? She have a code right before you saw her? Or just come out of the OR? You get a difficult case and pump adrenaline, you're going to be a little up for a while afterward."

"No, I don't think it was that; I've seen her after she's been in the OR." I thought about the two cans of Tab. "I think she was either amphetaminy or winding up to be psychotic."

"You think that at the time, or you think that now that she's killed herself?"

"Well, I think that now. Thinking back."

"Yeah, but what's that? Monday-morning quarterbacking."

I frowned.

"What's Carchiollo say?"

"I don't know. I don't know where he is. I've been trying to call him since she died, but I can't get ahold of him. That's another thing that's making me upset." I got out my cigarettes. "You have an ashtray?"

"No, just use the floor." He took a breath and blew

it out slowly. "Listen, we're doctors. We see crazy people all the time, we ought to know it when we see it. On one hand you feel bad because you didn't see it coming, but on the other hand we didn't see her when she was off duty—I don't think she socialized much with the other doctors, I think she saw her husband's circle of friends, you know? And we didn't sit in her head either. And she could have . . . um . . . gone downhill rapidly in a few days. She could have held it all inside for a long time, and then gone downhill so fast the few days before she killed herself we might not have had time to put it together even if we had seen it. *I* didn't see it coming. One of the nurses said she was strung out over the weekend. McCabe tell you about Friday night? O.K., so you know about that. But Carchiollo saw her Friday night too. So, whatever he thought, he probably did for her what she needed, whatever it was. If he thought she was psychotic, I'm sure he would have hauled her ass into the hospital. So if she's his patient and he didn't call it, you can't take it on yourself because *you* didn't call it."

"Yeah, but, Paul, there's more to it than this. I'm not a very good friend to most of my women friends." I laughed self-consciously. "What am I talking about, women friends? I don't have any women friends, all my friends are men."

"O.K., but why is there something wrong with that? You don't have any sisters, you have two brothers. Shelley didn't have any sisters either, so maybe neither of you made friends with other girls very well."

I smiled. "Girls?"

Paul looked at the ceiling. "Aw, Jesus. *Women.* O.K. ? I don't know what's wrong with that word."

"There's nothing wrong with that word, it's for persons eighteen years old or younger."

Roussy waved his hand dismissively. "Ah'm jes' a Texas *boy*, O.K.? Don't get on my case about that right now. Pay attention to what I'm saying here.

Shelley didn't have any sisters, and you don't have any sisters. And from what I could make out the only time I met Shelley's mother, she didn't have a very close relationship with her either. Her mother came to have lunch with Shelley one day and Shelley brought her over to the hospital to show her around, and her mother just kept going on and on about this important Korean artist she had to go meet, something to do with the art gallery. She didn't seem the least bit interested in the hospital or what Shelley did here. Every time Shelley tried to say something about the hospital, her mother would interrupt and talk about the gallery. She even complained to Shelley in front of me that Shelley never worked in the gallery anymore the way she used to do when she was in college. Can you imagine? Shelley's a surgeon, and her mother is pissed off because she doesn't have time for the art gallery anymore, or time to help her parents entertain Korean artists or Japanese art dealers."

I shook my head. "It's not just Shelley's problem, Paul. I had a woman friend in med school. I loved her very much, in fact, I loved her with a kind of passion that I usually only have when I love men. I wasn't interested in her *sexually,* I'm not saying that. But whenever we had a fight it really hurt me, and I got just as upset about fighting with her as I get when I fight with my *lover.*"

"I think you've told me about her, this is Rebecca Bayard, right? Works at the medical examiner's office?"

"Right, Beck Bayard."

"Ev, from what you've told me about her, she sounds like a really difficult person."

"She is. But that's not the point."

"This is the woman your old lover Richard went to to commiserate with when he left you and she took him to bed?"

"That's not the point, either."

"I think it's a valid point, your lover leaves you and

goes to see your best friend because he needs a shoul der to cry on and she takes him to bed. What kind o' friend is she to you if she does that?"

"Paul, will you shut up a second and listen to me? It was months after Beck and I fell out with one another that Richard went over there. So, as far as I'm con cerned, he wasn't my lover anymore and she wasn' my friend anymore, and if they want to go to bed fine. Didn't you go to bed with your sister-in-law once after you and your wife split up?"

Roussy looked sideways and grinned wolfishly. "I was drunk."

"Yeah, I've heard that before." We both laughed, a little wryly, but sharing the wryness comfortably. "Now listen," I said, getting serious again. "I need to talk about this. I really feel that one of the things wrong with my friendship with Beck was that I didn't know how to be friends with a woman. I didn't know how to pay attention to her when she talked to me the way I pay attention to a man when *he* talks to me. She used to complain to me about it too. It made her really mad. She'd tell me things and I'd forget them. She said I never forgot anything a man told me—which is true, I have a really good memory for conversations I have with men—but that I forgot things *she* told me all the time. And it's *true*. I really *didn't* listen to her half the time. Because I didn't take her as seriously as I took my men friends. I need that male attention, I need that male affirmation."

Paul looked at me curiously. "Do either of Beck's parents drink?"

"Paul, Al-Anon and ACOA help you a lot, but don't get one-dimensional."

"Do they drink?"

"They drink socially. I've been to their house."

"What about your own parents?"

I shook my head. "On the Jewish holidays we had wine, and schnapps for the guests if they wanted it.

And when their bridge group came there were drinks. My parents played bridge twice a month with four or five other couples and they rotated to one another's houses."

"Did the people get drunk?"

"Yeah, well, they got pretty boisterous. One of the men made a pass at me in the kitchen when I was fifteen. Well, not a *pass;* he tried to kiss me. I didn't let him. It wasn't a good experience, though. It gave me the creeps, and I wouldn't go near that man for a while. But there was something else."

"What else?"

"It's not important." I dropped my cigarette on the floor and put my foot on it.

Paul said, "Ev."

I looked up and saw that he was watching me *very* closely.

"What else about that man?" he asked quietly.

I finished my tea and put the mug down on the bedside table. I fingered the handle of the mug. "My mother had an affair with him."

"Hm. What happened?"

"His wife came to the house and made a scene. I don't want to talk about it right now."

Roussy leaned over and touched my knee. I jumped.

He said, "Do you ever talk about it?"

I picked up my tea mug, looked at it, and put it down again. After a while I shook my head.

Roussy was very still.

"It wasn't the only affair she had," I said.

"What about your father?"

I shrugged. "He knew. I think he knew about all of them. He used to make excuses to us—to me and my brothers—when my mother didn't come home in the evening. He'd say she was at the hospital. But then the hospital would call, and we knew she wasn't at the hospital. Or I knew. I don't know what my brothers thought. They're younger than me; Alan is four years younger and Craig is five years younger. So when I was fifteen, Craig was only ten."

"But everybody knew after the wife of this man came over," Roussy said gently.

"Objection," I said, smiling. My smile felt crooked. "Prosecution is leading the witness."

"What else about your mother?"

"Paul . . ." I said helplessly.

"Ev, you're talking to me about your relationship with Rebecca Bayard and your relationship with Shelley and you're telling me you think you don't know how to be good friends with women. But maybe it's not your problem, maybe it's your mother's problem. How did you feel about these affairs?"

"Paul, I don't think you can blame everything on your parents. I like my parents. I *love* my parents. My dad was very present, very *there* for me, for me and my brothers. He didn't think it was my mother's job to take care of us by herself; he thought fathers should do their fair share around the house and with the children. He cooked, he cleaned, he was always available to talk or listen to all the little problems kids have. He's very good with kids; he's a pediatrician." I stopped. Then I said, "I'm talking about *him,* huh? I'm not talking about *her.*"

Paul said, "What happened when the wife came over? The wife of the guy your mother had the affair with."

"She screamed and carried on and said if my father would keep his wife in line this kind of shit wouldn't happen. She said—oh, God, Paul, I haven't thought about this *in years,* I think I forgot all this stuff—she said, 'So what's *your* problem, Sandy? You don't fuck her enough? You can't get it up, she had to get it from *my* husband?' Oh, it was *awful.* I was in the kitchen with Craig and Alan listening to all this—Mrs. Shapiro was *screaming* and we could hear every word. We couldn't hear what Dad was saying back, he must have been talking very quietly.

"After Mrs. Shapiro left, my father came in the kitchen and gave everyone a dish of ice cream and sat down with us at the table. He said . . ."

I had to stop and think for a minute.

"He said . . . Well, he told us. He said, 'Your mother is having an affair with Mr. Shapiro.' I remember now he had to stop and explain this to Craig. He said, 'That means that sometimes when she doesn't come home at night she sleeps in bed with Mr. Shapiro. Now, Adele—Mrs. Shapiro—is a little upset about this right now, so you mustn't think bad things about her because she was screaming like that. When you get married and you stand under the *chuppah* together it means you promise not to sleep with anyone except the person you're getting married to, but this is a hard promise to keep sometimes, and your mother's having a little trouble keeping that promise right now.' Then he said, 'Now, I don't want you to say anything about this to your mother. This is a problem mothers and fathers have to talk about with each other; it's a very complicated problem and if you kids get in on the act it will only get more complicated. So don't say anything about this to Mom. You can talk to me about it if you have some thoughts or questions later, but not while Mom is in the house, O.K.?' "

Paul asked, "Was your father always so reasonable? Wasn't he upset your mother was stepping out on him like this?"

"Oh, no, he wasn't always that reasonable. Half the time he was just plain pissed off; he would stand at the bottom of the hall stairs and yell upstairs at her." I started to laugh. "He would get very exasperated."

"Yell what?"

"Oh, things like, *'The goddamn war is over, Joan! This is not London! This is not the blitz!'* " I deepened my voice to imitate my father's, waving my arms a little the way he used to wave his when he got mad. *" 'This is not 1942 and you're not driving an ambulance anymore, you think you could park the goddamn thing once and for all, Joan?'* My mother was in London during the war," I explained. "She drove an ambulance and pulled dead bodies out of the rubble and that kind of thing. My father used to say she missed the war, that life wasn't exciting enough for her anymore."

"Did you talk to your dad about it later? About the affairs? He said you could talk to him about it if you wanted."

"No."

"Did you discuss it with your mother?"

I looked at the floor.

"You did discuss it with her?"

"One day I got mad at her because she wasn't there for something, I don't remember what it was, and I said, 'Why don't you stay home with Dad instead of fucking around with all these other men?' I used those words, too. I even said it in front of my father. He jumped up right away and yelled at me, 'You are out of line, young lady! Don't you *ever* let me hear you talk to your mother like that again, do you hear me?' "

"What did your mother do?"

"She didn't do anything. She didn't react at all. But that's like her, she never tells you what she's feeling. She keeps it all in, she's always in control."

"No she's not, not if she has all these affairs. That's being out of control, that's acting out."

"No, she's always *in control.* She's in control of herself and she's in control of you too. I learned that fast enough, growing up. But I don't want to say she was a bad mother, because she wasn't. She wasn't always there, but if you did anything that made her proud, she told you how proud she was of you, and she told all the other mothers too. She was always on the phone telling the other mothers if I did well in school or if Alan did well in art school—he was very talented as a kid, he painted, and won prizes in art shows—and I'd hear her telling people on the phone about it. I think . . ."

"Do you trust her?"

I blinked. An odd question. "Yeah, I trust her a lot, now. Since I've grown up she's been . . . well, a lot more *there*. I think maybe she didn't do too well with kids, you know? She's been a lot more interested in me since I've become an adult, and when I went to college she stopped having affairs. Now when I call up we have really good conversations, and we're good friends, and I can tell her anything I want. She's especially understanding when I have problems with men. . . . Well, I guess she has a lot of experience with men." I smiled.

Roussy nodded. "Yeah, I like my mom a lot more as an adult. And she's sober now, too. She's been sober now for a couple of years. She still acts out, sometimes, but she knows I go to ACOA, and we talk about it. We can talk now in a way we couldn't talk when I was a teenager. But that's true of most families; teenagers are difficult people for their parents to deal with, especially if the parent has problems of his own to deal with. But you should think about all this further. Between your mother and Mrs. Shapiro—boy, *she* sounds like a real winner—you didn't have very good role models for women in your immediate environment. You may have decided that only men could be trusted. And if your mother was controlling, you may have decided too that women are controlling, and when you form relationships with women now as an adult, you may suspect they will try to control you, and you may not be able to trust them."

My mind was off on a tangent; I had started thinking about Shelley again. "Alex says Shelley told him she was pregnant and she was going to have an abortion," I said, changing the subject. "I don't know what to make of that."

Roussy looked surprised. "An abortion? Can you do that if you're so Jewish-religious? I thought religious Jews were like the Catholics on that score."

"Yeah, me too. I don't know."

"I know she was ambivalent about having kids," Paul said after a moment. "We talked about it one night when we were on call together. Recently, in fact. It was one of the few times I ever talked to her, you know, *personally*. I was talking about my own fears of abandoning my daughter, not being a good father to her, especially since she lives so far away, and Shelley started talking about her own fears about being a mother. She had the usual conflicts: career versus children and all that. She wanted children eventually, but her husband was foaming at the mouth to have them. Shelley said that she thought he'd make a wonderful father, but that he was pressuring her a lot to stay home with a baby for a year or two. She didn't know how she could; you just can't take two years out from your surgical residency and get back in when you want to."

I made a derisive noise in the back of my throat. "Typical husband's view of the world," I said.

"Not really. Steve isn't your usual chauvinist. He's very pro-women. He used to lobby in some group for the ordination of women as rabbis. The Conservative Jews didn't ordain women until just recently, you know, although the Reform have for about fifteen years now. Steve just happens to be one of those men who are in awe of motherhood. The miraculous birth event and the sacrosanct bonding between mother and child, that kind of thing. He's older, too. He's thirty-eight. He wants to get on with the show."

"She never talked to *me* about anything like that," I said enviously. "She never told me anything personal about herself at all."

Roussy gave me an assessing look. Then he examined his tea mug for a while, turning it in small circles on the tabletop between the two beds. Eventually he said, "She didn't feel she could. Discuss personal things with you like that, I mean."

I felt as if I had been struck a blow. "What?"

"You were always so businesslike with her," Paul said. He stopped playing with his tea mug. "She always figured you only wanted to talk about medicine. She used to say that you were one of those women for whom it was a point of honor to act like a man and be treated like a man, and that you didn't like women who wanted to act like women."

I was stunned. "Shelley said that?"

"I probably shouldn't tell you this," Paul apologized.

"No, please. What else did she say?"

Paul cleared his throat. "Uh . . . she said you reminded her of one of those chimps at the institute in Atlanta where they're teaching sign language for the deaf to primates. They gave this one chimp a pile of pictures of chimps and humans and told the chimp to sort them into piles. The chimp did this but put her own picture in the humans' pile. Shelley said if you had to do this with pictures of men and women you would put your own picture in the men's pile."

"She said this to you during this conversation you were having about having babies?"

Paul was beginning to look decidedly uncomfortable. He sighed a large sigh. "We were talking about Melanie Charnock and how she used to have her babysitter bring her baby over so she could nurse it in the doctors' lounge, and your name came into the conversation because you told Shelley it embarrassed you that Melanie was doing this. And Shelley said to me it embarrassed you when women did women's things in public, that no man would nurse a baby in public. Well, of course not. Men don't nurse babies." He coughed.

I said, "What else did Shelley say?"

Paul looked at the floor.

I said, "Paul, I'm telling you I have trouble relating to my women friends and you're talking to me about my mother when you know all along this stuff Shelley has to say about me? Jesus. Just tell me what the fuck she said." I got up off the bed and went over to the window and looked out. I thought: *I'm mad.* Then: I'm hurt. I'm hurt because she had this to say about me.

I fished my cigarettes out of my shirt pocket and lit one with my lighter. *You're smoking too much.*

I remembered pushing Jude Rainey's lighter across the table to the detectives and them saying to me, *Any adverse relationships? Anybody she didn't like?*

I wondered how much Shelley really liked me.

That's dumb, Ev. Of course she liked you. You just can't take criticism from women.

I went back to the bed and sat down on it again.

"I want to know what else Shelley said about me," I told Paul.

"She said you don't like women who are women, Ev. I have to say I thought about it at the time she said it and I agreed with her. I'm not making a value judgment here, and neither was Shelley. This is simply the way you are. Shelley said that she'd seen you talk to women, and you talk differently to a woman if she's wearing a dress. You like women who wear pants, or who dress like lady lawyers in three-piece suits. Shelley is—*was*—a really feminine person, and . . . She felt . . . She felt you never took her seriously because of that. You took her seriously as a *physician*. But not as a *person*."

"I don't know what you're talking about," I said testily. "I took Shelley very seriously. I worked with her on her book. She was the one who wouldn't talk to me about personal things."

"Did you talk to *her* about personal things?"

"No, of course not. But I sleep with her goddamn *shrink,* Paul! I couldn't go blabbing to her about my personal life when she was seeing my lover professionally. Phil would have had a cow."

"Well, then you didn't give her an opening. But you could have asked her about herself. Did you ever do that?"

"Well, no, but I don't like to do that."

"You like to do it with *men.* You're very solicitous of Hollander. Every time he so much as looks down in the mouth you're right there asking him all about it, trying to help him sort it out, whatever is bothering him. I've even heard you do it with Attenborough."

The entire exchange was surprising me enormously and I was fascinated; on one hand it made me jumpy and I was fighting that, but on the other hand I was beginning to feel *very* clearheaded and on top of things. Probably an illusion, I thought. Defense. Paul's making you jumpy telling you all this, so you're telling yourself how clearheaded you are. But I realized there was something else going on in this conversation, something I couldn't quite put my finger on.

I said, "Attenborough knows my father. And his son was in a motor-vehicle accident."

"Yes, but you *ask.* 'How's your son Christopher doing, Dr. Attenborough? It must be very difficult for you.' Christ, Ev, you practically pat him on the head, you're so solicitous."

"What are we really talking about here, Paul?" I asked quietly. "Are you being defensive because you're telling me that I'm not feminine enough for you? Just because I'm not like the women *you* like to go out with? Or are you feeling guilty you had this conversation about me with Shelley and I'm pressing you to repeat it to me?"

Paul thought about this. "Yeah," he said after a moment. "I'll be honest with you. Both those things, and I find you intimidating at times."

I did a double-take five miles wide. "You find me *intimidating?*"

"Yeah. I do. And so did Shelley. You have this way of saying what you think, and it shuts people up, and when you do that with me sometimes I just crawl away with my tail between my legs."

I realized I was staring at Paul, who was fidgeting under my stare. I got up again and went back to the window, turning my back to him. It was a trick I had learned with my patients; sometimes people need you not to be looking at them while they're talking to you. I smoked my cigarette for a few minutes and then dropped it on the floor and ground it out with my foot.

"I'm sorry," I said to Paul over my shoulder. "Next time I do that to you, you'll let me know, O.K.?" I looked down at 114th Street, twelve floors below. The Sanitation snowplows were getting around to the side streets. "What else with Shelley? Tell me, it's important to me."

"You told Shelley that in your opinion pregnancy was the invasion of the body snatchers," he went on in a flat voice. "And that if you ever got pregnant you'd go out and get a bell and hang it around your neck because it would make you feel like a cow. Shelley's feelings were hurt. How was she supposed to confide in you about her concerns about juggling a career and childbearing after your deprecatory remarks?" He stopped. I imagined he was catching himself, seeing his own defensiveness. He went on in a kinder tone: "I don't mean to be harsh about this, Ev. I don't even know why I'm telling you. Oh, forget it, *I* want you to know it. The point is, Shelley liked you. She wanted to be friends. That's one of the reasons she asked you to help her with her book. You were one of the few doctors she knew, she said, who was interested in and knowledgeable about things other than medicine. She liked talking to you about all the books you'd read and the time you spent doing research in Shakespeare at Oxford, and she liked hearing all your funny little stories about your students when you were teaching English lit at the university. She really liked you, Ev. And you never drew her out because she was this little feminine person who worried about pregnancy and motherhood."

I didn't know what to say. I fiddled with my cigarette lighter. I felt myself backing up from this conversation, backing up from Shelley's death, backing up from a lot of things. Hollander. Women in skirts. My old friend Beck Bayard, who slept with my lover Richard after he left me. I felt very inside myself, and that's where I wanted to be.

"I'm sorry," Paul said. "You look as though you're attempting a rather difficult instrument landing in the fog over there. I shouldn't have dumped all this on you just now. It wasn't a good time. It was thoughtless of me; I'm sorry."

"It's O.K." It wasn't, but it was a reliable exit line, something to say when there really wasn't anything to say. Absently, I fingered the small Star of David on its thin gold chain around my neck; a present from Phil the previous Hanukkah.

Where the hell was Phil?

"Excuse me," I said to Paul. I picked up the hospital phone and asked the night operator for an outside line and dialed Phil's number. No answer; no answering machine. I dialed his beeper. The operator told me in her thick Russian accent that he wasn't answering. I threw the receiver back into its cradle.

Did he know that Shelley had died?

"Who are you calling?" Paul asked.

"Carchiollo. I haven't been able to get ahold of him since Shelley died."

"Oh," said Roussy. He knew Phil and I were lovers. He also knew about Beth; I had told him the whole thing one night over a couple of beers. "You don't know where he is?"

"No. He was with me when Alex called me to come over and sign out from Hollander. I left him in my apartment and he said he was going to go upstairs to his. He apparently stayed there long enough to defrost the fridge and clean the kitchen before he went upstairs. Those were his last known whereabouts, as Kelly and Ost would undoubtedly say. They were asking me about Phil; they know he was Shelley's shrink."

Paul cleared his throat. "Beth in London?"

"Far as I know."

"He usually tells you when she's here in New York?"

"As far as I know, he *always* tells me when Beth is in New York."

"O.K., O.K., don't get defensive."

I turned around and looked at Roussy. We both laughed.

"Yeah," I said. "We're both a little defensive, huh?"

Paul grinned widely. "Uh . . . would you like me to call the precinct and register an hysterical plea to send forth the hounds? I will, if you like. I don't mind."

I shook my head with a smile.

"Sure?"

"It's O.K. He'll turn up."

"You let me know if you want me to. I don't mind lending my male voice of authority to the cause; I know the cops take men more seriously than women. Notice I didn't say 'girls.' "

I laughed. "For a male chauvinist, you can be pretty egalitarian," I said. I sat down again on the other bed. "Paul, you ever think about going into psychiatry?"

"All the time. It's a toss-up between that and pediatrics. How about you?"

"Me? I think I'll stay in the ER, become a shock-trauma doc. I like working under the gun. It keeps me on my toes."

"You never think about going into psychiatry?"

"Oh, hell no! I get enough from Phil. If he says to me one more time, 'How do you feel about that?' or 'You might want to take a look at that, explore that a little,' I think I'm going to throw up."

Paul laughed. "So what are you going to do now? You gonna go home and get some sleep?"

"I don't know. I slept most of the day, and now I'm wide-awake. I had a couple of beers with McCabe too, and I'm getting the boomerang from that now."

"Yeah, me too. You have a couple of beers and get a little drunk, then you're wide-awake a few hours later. When I got off at six I slept for a few hours. Then I went to a bar with my brother-in-law and had a few."

"Think we'll ever sleep the same hours other people sleep?"

"Who knows. I was talking to my brother-in-law about that. He's a firefighter in Houston, and he's usually on nights. He said he thinks sometimes that he's not on the same planet as other guys."

"You like your brother-in-law?"

"Yeah, he's good to my sister. But I have trouble talking to him sometimes; he kind of defers to me because I'm a *doctor*. He thinks that's a big deal. So I spend a lot of time bending over backward, trying to show I'm a regular guy. But listen, I want to ask you something. You ever think of going into therapy?"

I smiled. "You sound like Phil. Phil thinks everyone should be in therapy. Yeah, I've thought about it. But I talk to Phil, and McCabe, and I talk to you. And I think about things a lot."

"Well," he said, "I'm not saying you have problems. But you may want to talk to a therapist, you know, in a more formal setting, about some of the things you've been talking to me about tonight. You might find it helps you to get clear, you know?"

I nodded and stood up. "I'll think about it," I said. "I gotta go. Thanks for talking to me about Shelley."

"Yeah," he said. "It was good for me too."

I patted him on the shoulder and put my ski jacket back on and went out and shut the door behind myself.

When I put my hands in my pockets to get my gloves, I found Shelley's on-call room key.

Miles to go before you sleep, I thought. Miles to go.

CHAPTER

17

As I turned the key in the lock of Shelley's on-call room and pushed the heavy door in on its hinges, I thought about her family.

Shelley had never said much to me about her parents except that they were art dealers and that she and Steve sometimes went out with them when they were entertaining "visiting dignitaries."

I never got the idea that Shelley thought her parents were negligent of her because of their preoccupation with their business, as Roussy had seemed to imply. And the one time I had met them, the night at Lincoln Center, both Shelley and Steve seemed to be having a good time with her parents and their guest.

Even the following morning, when I saw her at the hospital, she had talked about the evening with pleasure. Or at least with good humor. Their guest had apparently suggested they eat in a Japanese restaurant, and Steve and Shelley had been hard put to explain to him why they couldn't eat sushi because it wasn't kosher.

I remembered her laughing about it.

I wondered how Steve was doing.

Maybe I should take Steve a casserole. But if I made him a casserole he wouldn't be able to eat it; it wouldn't be kosher.

When my grandfather died, my grandmother, Bubba

Hazel, wouldn't eat. My mother threatened to give her an IV. Bubba Hazel agreed to eat rice pudding and she ate that for days on end. Finally she agreed to eat chicken soup with matzoh balls.

Maybe I could go down to the kosher deli on Seventy-second Street and get Steve two quarts of chicken soup with matzoh balls.

I didn't know if he liked chicken soup with matzoh balls.

I realized I had been standing on the threshold of Shelley's on-call room for God knows how long because I was afraid to go in. I put the key in my pocket and let the door click shut behind me, and I looked around the room.

Two hospital beds with hospital chenille bedspreads. A bookcase full of medical journals no one ever read and medical texts that were so heavy they would give you respiratory arrest if you tried to put them on your chest to read while lying down.

A night table between the two beds with an ashtray and a pack of menthol Dunhills.

A desk, not hospital issue; probably the gift of a misty-eyed old geezer retiring from years and years of service on the hospital board of directors. Or maybe the gift of the wife of an old geezer donating the desk to the hospital after her husband's death, hoping to spice up the lives of the current generation of interns and residents a little.

A manila envelope on the desk. Not a blue hospital envelope but a manila envelope. Addressed to me, in large letters: "SUTCLIFFE."

My heart sank.

I moved to the closet and opened the door and counted the empty coat hangers: five.

I picked up the pack of Dunhills on the night table. Empty. I took the tinfoil lining out and peered inside.

I opened the drawer of the night table. Empty except for two pens and three pads of paper, all freebie promotionals from the drug companies.

I got down on the floor and checked under the beds.

I went into the bathroom and opened the medicine cabinet. Four toothbrushes. Three tubes of toothpaste, different brands. One blue mascara wand. Mouthwash. A silver St. Christopher's medal on a silver chain. Several vials of pills. I held the St. Christopher's medal in my hand a long time, looking at it, hefting it, dangling the medal on its chain, running the chain through my fingers. The chain was broken.

I took the vials down and opened each, shook out a few of the pills in my hand.

I looked at the pills. The red pills were Ibuprofen; the name was stamped on each pill by the drug company that manufactured it, along with the dosage. Four hundred milligrams, as McCabe had said. The light blue pills were Valium, ten milligrams. I wondered if Shelley had been taking Valium; judging from her antsy behavior, I wouldn't have thought so, but if she were used to ten milligrams of it on any kind of regular basis, it would explain how she could hop so quickly after taking the twenty milligrams Attenborough had ordered for her in the OR; the dosage would not have affected her as much as it would affect someone who never took Valium.

There was a third kind of pill in my hand, a triangular orange one stamped only with the code SKF E19. I looked at these for a while, and at the St. Christopher's medal. Then I put the pills back in the vials and put the vials in my pocket with the medal.

I went back into the room and opened all the desk drawers and found the usual stuff: more freebie promotionals from the drug companies—pads of paper, penlights, pens, slide rules for figuring out fluid input/output and electrolyte balance.

Sutcliffe, you going to look at what's in this manila

envelope, or what? You waiting for the blue moon, maybe?

I sat down on the bed and looked at the envelope. At Shelley's handwriting: "SUTCLIFFE."

I opened the envelope, turning it upside down so its contents slid out into my lap. The transcript from Shelley's typist was neatly typed, with large margins for my editorial comments. I scanned the first page. It was a chapter in which Shelley had interviewed a young Italian-American doctor, the only son of immigrants who, although they were proud their son had become a surgeon, worried who would take over the family electrical-supply business now that their son was occupied elsewhere.

Across the top of the first page Shelley had scrawled, "Pick a tense, Ev. Any tense."

I turned to the second page, looking for the name of the person Shelley was interviewing. She had a habit of introducing her interviewees by detailing their background before they decided to become doctors, then telling the reader the name of the interviewee only when that person decided to become a doctor, or went to medical school, or appeared on some ward as an intern or resident—or at whatever point Shelley came into the picture as interviewer. The implication was that we had all crawled out of the same primordial soup, but those of us destined to enter the healing arts evolved into a higher species upon receiving the call to medicine. The tone, I felt, was certainly elitist. "Put the name of the person you're interviewing in the first sentence," I had suggested. "Or at least the first paragraph."

I came to the name of the physician at the bottom of the third page of text, when he had got it into his head to go to medical school.

Dr. Anthony Firenze.

I had been slouching on the bed; I sat up now, very quickly. This must be what Tony doesn't want Shelley to print about him, I thought. This must be what the fuss is all about.

But when I had finished the fifteen typewritten pages, I was puzzled; I could find nothing in Shelley's interview with Firenze that would upset anyone, not even an emotionally volatile, old-fashioned surgeon. I reread the pages, carefully. I read about Firenze growing up the only son of Italian immigrants; how he had not gotten into medical school the first time he applied; how he had spent three years as a research assistant performing cardiac surgery on dogs; and how he had hired what he called a "presentation consultant" to help him prepare for his personal interviews when he applied the second time. He had been accepted to a medical school in Brooklyn, and he repeatedly stressed the importance of careful preparation for the personal interview during the medical-school-application process.

For this he threw me up against the wall?

For this he dug his fingers into my jaw and demanded what Shelley had written about him?

Was the consultation of a "presentation consultant" in his preparation for med-school applications somehow dishonorable in Tony's mind? If so, we could all reassure him that his sessions with this consultant had had no effect on his personality whatsoever, beyond helping him to make himself presentable in his med-school interviews. He was still his surly self, as far as I could tell.

I noticed that Shelley had made a note to herself to include this chapter with the material in the first section of the book, where she interviewed people about how they had gotten into medical school. Shelley had finished writing that section some time ago; the material she had been giving me lately was for the third section, where she talked to people about what they thought about having gotten *through* med school, now that they were interns and residents.

I wondered if Shelley had written a different chapter for Firenze than she had planned to write. Maybe she had interviewed him about being a resident, but when she saw how much it upset him, she wrote about his applying to med school instead.

But both Phil and Alex had expressed reservations to Shelley about their interviews with her, and she had not written different chapters for them; their chapters both fell into the third section of Shelley's book, where she got the physicians to talk about problems they had encountered with the medical establishment now that they were interns and residents.

Maybe Firenze had talked to Shelley about problems he had with the establishment in a way that would be particularly damaging to his career if he were to be quoted. And maybe he had made more of a fuss than Phil or Alex, who had both complained to Shelley rather politely. Firenze had complained vociferously, throwing his scissors at her in the OR.

In any case, if this were all Shelley had written about Tony, he had nothing to be upset about.

I turned to the other sheets of notepaper that had been in the envelope; Shelley often included handwritten notes of her impressions that she took down while the tape recorder was running at her interviews. I scanned the pages; she had apparently interviewed Firenze in his kitchen: there were descriptions of that, and also of his girlfriend, a violin teacher. Nothing incriminating there either. I looked at the handwriting, which was Shelley's normal hand, and then I looked at the way she had scrawled "SUTCLIFFE" on the envelope. The only word I could think of: *belligerent*. There was something belligerent about her loud, screaming scrawl.

Then I noticed a page of notes that had nothing to do with Firenze or anyone else Shelley had interviewed. Suddenly I realized the note was not in Shelley's handwriting; it was in Phil's.

I read that page over and over until my blood was cold and there was a buzz in my chest. Then I put that page in my pocket with the pills and St. Christopher's medal, and I got up and left the room.

I had to go back for the transcript of Shelley's book with its notes about Firenze.

I went back a second time for the empty packet of Dunhills.

After that I figured I had taken everything, and the next time my eyes focused I was looking at the front door of Phil's apartment, my key to his door in my hand.

I had trouble unlocking Phil's door. He'd been burgled a few months earlier and had had a complicated pair of deadlocks installed. I could never figure out whether the top lock went clockwise and the bottom lock went counter-clockwise or vice versa, or whether you opened the top first and then the bottom or the other way around. There was a cartoon taped to Phil's door and I looked at this while I fumbled with the locks and cursed. The cartoon had been drawn by one of Phil's patients and it showed a headless man walking into a doctor's office, holding his head out in both hands toward the doctor like a Halloween pumpkin.

I remembered Roussy telling me some time ago that Hollander had been burgled right after he moved into the building. Roussy said Jay had not only installed new locks, he had gone out and bought a twenty-two revolver and had joined a gun club in Westchester County so he could practice shooting it.

That seemed highly unlikely to me. Hollander did not seem to be a person who would do such a thing, but Roussy insisted it was true, and, moreover, that Steve Reinish knew how to shoot from his Army days and had gone once or twice with Jay to the gun club to give him some pointers on shooting.

That seemed even more unlikely. I couldn't imagine

either Jay or Steve taking potshots at targets at a gun club in Westchester County. Then again, I couldn't imagine a gun club in Westchester County. I associated Westchester with shopping malls and country clubs and wealthy women driving their kids in fancy cars to violin lessons after school. Many of the attendings at the hospital lived in Westchester and most of them seemed to drive to work in Mercedeses and Volvos and BMW's. Most of these attendings were male and I imagined them all with wives who played tennis and drove the kids places after school and went shopping at the malls and hung out at the country clubs on weekends.

That was unfair to doctors who didn't live like that, I knew. My own parents didn't drive cars like that or live like that or fit that stereotype.

When I got Phil's door open finally and stepped into the foyer, I stopped dead in my tracks.

"Phil?" I called tentatively.

No answer. The apartment was dark except for a soft light coming from Phil's study; Phil hated to come home to a dark apartment, and he had the light in his study on a timer to go on at dusk. The grandfather clock in the living room ticked; the refrigerator hummed in the kitchen. Other than that the place was eerily quiet.

Of course it's quiet, I thought. It's two o'clock in the fucking morning. Oh-dark-thirty-hours, as McCabe would say.

I was getting a very creepy feeling. I held the door open with one hand and straightened up like a deer in the woods, ready to bolt at a disturbing scent on the wind. Then I closed the door behind me and went on a reconnaissance tour of the apartment, slinking around on legs half-bent at the knees and turning on all the lights and opening all the closet doors, which made me feel like an idiot. I wondered what I thought I might find: a dead body sprawled across the floor in the bathroom? Bloody fingerprints on the wall near one of the light switches? Unidentifiable and suspicious-looking stains on the duvet folded neatly across the bottom of Phil's immaculately made bed? A note articulating God knows what dire deeds propped against the lamp on Phil's dresser? A typewritten treatise from Shelley, explaining why she had killed herself, scrupulously laid out on Phil's desk?

Going around the apartment a second time, I turned off all the lights again except the light in the study. I threw the envelope with Shelley's manuscript on Phil's desk. I took off my ski jacket, emptied the pockets onto the desk—the vials of pills, the St. Christopher's medal with the broken chain, the empty pack of menthol Dunhills, the page of notebook paper that Shelley had included with the manuscript that had nothing to do with her book—and dropped the jacket on the floor. Then I sat down at Phil's desk.

Sitting at Phil's desk made me feel slightly less melodramatic. I liked Phil's desk. It was an antique cherrywood secretary, the kind with a glass-paned cabinet of bookshelves on top and little cubbyholes underneath to sort bills and correspondence and other papers into. Phil was a lot more organized about money than I was, so he could afford things like antique furniture. He could save up and then buy the cherrywood secretary and the Oriental rug on the floor and the leather armchair with matching ottoman in the corner and the large comfortable couch with the soft Mexican blankets thrown all over it. He could take all sorts of wonderful photographs of himself and his family and friends to a good framer and then hang all these photographs in their lovely frames all over the walls, giving his study a warm, intimate atmosphere. He could afford nice touches such as Oriental tabletop lamps and a good painting here and there and pretty crystal vases and ashtrays. He could not only afford these things; he could choose things that went together in a stylish and understated, comfortable way without consulting me or Beth or his sister or an interior decorator. Which wasn't something most male doctors I knew could do. Most male doctors I knew had apartments like mine: things thrown together, medical journals piled everywhere helter-skelter, stacks of newspapers, clothes on the floor in the bedroom, dirty dishes in the sink.

Except Hollander, I thought. Hollander had an eye like Phil: he knew how to make his place look nice. And he was neat and orderly.

I opened one of the doors of the bookcase over the desk and pulled down Phil's *Physician's Desk Reference*, shook a few of the orange pills out of the vial, and matched them to a photograph in the front section of the *PDR*. Dexedrine, as I had thought. Five milligrams.

Amphetamines. Not a whopping dosage, but amphetamines all the same.

I spent a few minutes thinking about amphetamines, Ibuprofen, Valium, and aspirin. Steve Reinish had said that Shelley had taken a lot of aspirin, although why she would take aspirin if she were also taking Ibuprofen was beyond me; Ibuprofen was what they gave you for arthritic conditions when aspirin was not strong enough.

Maybe Shelley told Steve she was taking aspirin so he wouldn't ask why she was taking Ibuprofen.

Which was a good question; why *was* she taking the Ibuprofen?

Or the Dex and Valium, for that matter.

I thought about the aspirin for a while and got an idea that made me sit up straight in my chair. I went through Phil's stack of back issues of *The New England Journal of Medicine*, neatly arranged in chronological order. I found the issue I was looking for, then got down Phil's *Principles of Internal Medicine*, read the index for a while, and turned to the section titled "Systemic Lupus Erythematosus." I lit a cigarette and pulled my feet up under me, sitting Indian-style on Phil's leather swivel desk chair. I read all about systemic lupus erythematosus, smoking the cigarette in short determined draws. My mind was focused; I was doing what I did best: putting it all together, coming up with a diagnosis. Yup, I thought with a twinge of excitement, this is it. Sutcliffe, you're a brilliant diagnostician.

I read the article in the *Journal* entitled "Aspirin-induced Hepatotoxicity in Patients with Systemic Lupus Erythematosus." When I finished the article I lit another cigarette and thought about this information, my heart clunking in my chest.

Systemic lupus erythematosus, also called SLE or just lupus, is a disease of the body's immune system. It is similar to arthritis—its chief symptom is pain and swelling of the hands and feet—but it is a much more serious disease. Unlike arthritis, lupus can affect the kidneys and heart, and twenty percent of lupus patients die from kidney or heart failure within five years of initial diagnosis of the disease. Some patients with lupus have spontaneous remissions; others respond favorably to treatment with corticosteroids and aspirin, or corticosteroids and other painkillers like Ibuprofen. Some patients, on the other hand, do not respond at all to currently available medications.

Aspirin. Ibuprofen.

Shelley wringing her hands.

Steve Reinish: *She takes a lot of aspirin.*

McCabe: *What for?*

Reinish: *I don't know, headache, pain in the back—what d'you take aspirin for?*

"Aspirin-induced Hepatotoxicity in Patients with SLE." According to the article in the *Journal,* patients with lupus who take a lot of aspirin—and most patients with lupus take a lot of aspirin—could show wildly high SGOT levels, indicating liver-function breakdown. It was the liver's job to "clear" aspirin—process the aspirin so that it could be excreted by the body—and the physicians who had written this article had noticed that patients with SLE could not always clear all the aspirin they were swallowing, hence the high SGOT levels, signaling liver malfunction. SGOT was a liver-function test. Normal SGOT levels were something like five to forty units. I had noted on my report to the medical examiner that Shelley had shown a SGOT level of 924 units.

The Band-Aids on Shelley's arm and the punctures underneath. I'd explained to the detectives: *She could have had her blood tested, they usually give you Band-Aids when you have your blood tested.*

The detectives: *Why would she have her blood tested?*

For Lupus!

When you have lupus you need to have ten hours of sleep a day and make sure you rest frequently.

Or you can relapse.

Or exhibit signs of acute psychosis. With lupus, if you don't get your rest, you might just crack up.

Attenborough: *A slight attack of battle fatigue.*

I put my feet on the floor.

With lupus one shouldn't get pregnant. Pregnancy exacerbates the symptoms of the disease: the pain in the joints, the emotional mood sweeps and emotional outbursts, kidney problems, heart problems, a red rash that sometimes breaks out on the face and across the chest, giving the patient a formidable, florid visage (early observers of the disease had noted the formidability of the "look" of a person with lupus, comparing it with a wolfish appearance—"lupus" means "wolf" in Latin). Shelley had not had the rash on her face but she could have had it across her chest, or she might not have had it at all; about twenty percent of all patients with lupus never have the rash.

Shelley: *My hands hurt so I have to have the abortion.*

She had puncture marks in the crook of her elbow

and on the back of her hand. The crook of the elbow is where they usually draw blood for tests.

Like for a SGOT test.

The back of the hand is where they usually put the IV when you have a surgical procedure.

Like an abortion.

That about sums it up, I thought.

I tried to imagine what it must have been like for Shelley when she first noticed the symptoms creeping up on her. I tried to imagine what she thought the first time she gripped the scalpel in surgery and could not find a comfortable way to hold it. The first time she couldn't manage a tiny, minute suture because her hands were swelling and the manual dexterity needed for the job just wasn't there. Or the first time she became frightened by the extremity of an emotional response that just didn't have a basis in reality. The first time she saw the test results coming back, indicating a serious problem: kidney problems, or heart problems, or high SGOT levels signaling liver malfunction. Coming to grips with the knowledge that lupus was going to cut short her career as a surgeon. Coming to grips with the knowledge that lupus was going to severely shorten her lifespan. Wondering how long she could continue to funtion in surgery. Wondering how long she could hide her growing surgical incompetence from the other surgeons and physicians. Wondering how to tell Steve she couldn't bear the children he wanted so badly, finding out she was pregnant, agonizing over the decision to have an abortion.

Wondering what to kill herself with, and when.

CHAPTER

18

I heard the key turn in the lock of the front door and every joint in my body jerked. Catapulting to my feet, I ran into the foyer before I knew where my legs were going. With two quick turns of the wrist, I undid the deadbolts and yanked the door open.

"Hey," Phil said, giving me his five-hundred-watt smile.

I threw my arms around him.

"Mm," he said. Kissed me a big kiss, his mouth wide open. "You're nice to come home to." Kissed me again.

"Jesus, Phil, where have you *been?*"

"At the office. You know there's a power failure down there? The whole West Side between Fifty-ninth and Eighty-sixth Street or something. Phones and lights are out, *everything.* I was sitting in the office with candles on. Lucky Gina has this big candelabrum there, it takes six candles." Gina was the other shrink Phil shared his office with. "Hey. *Hey.* Let me take my *coat* off."

He was laughing at me, his warm intimate laugh, his laugh that said: Wanna go to bed?

I held him at arm's length and stared at him.

"Miss me?" He leaned forward to kiss me again.

I couldn't stop staring. Finally I said, "You shaved your beard."

"Yeah, how do I look? See this? You can see the scar on my chin where my brother Joey hit me with a hockey stick when I was seven years old."

I was dumbfounded. I looked at Phil's new beardless face, which I had never seen before, and I looked at the deep aqua ski jacket he was wearing. I had never seen the jacket before either. "Is this a new jacket?"

"Abercrombie's had a sale. I went down to the Seaport. You like the color?"

I let go of him and he took the jacket off, threw it over the back of the couch in the living room. "Let me go to the bathroom," he said over his shoulder as he went into the bedroom. "You want a glass of wine? There's a bottle of retsina in the fridge. Or if you'd rather have red, there's a zinfandel."

I heard the bathroom door close behind him. My knees were starting to shake. I sank down into the corner of one end of the couch and put my head back against the cushions.

I looked at the new aqua jacket on the other end of the couch.

When Phil came out of the bathroom I said, "Shelley Reinish took an OD of aspirin Monday night and killed herself."

"*What?*"

"Her husband brought her over right after I got to the ER, after McCabe called me. Completely unresponsive. Pupils dilated, no reflexes, very shocky. Arrested about fifteen minutes later. We ran a code on her for about an hour, but she was gone."

Phil had frozen mid-stride. Arms stiff and one foot in front of the other, he looked like a statue. "Mother of *God!*" he cried. He put a hand over his mouth.

I stared at him, thinking incongruously: He has all new clothes on. I've never seen that shirt before: a lumberjack plaid wool in nice pastels. The pants are new: charcoal-gray corduroy, baggy and fashionable.

The Timberland boots, laced halfway up his leg with the pants tucked inside: also new.

I wondered if he had new underwear on as well, and began to feel myself panicking at the thought of it. What if, instead of his usual brightly colored French briefs, he was wearing—Jesus—*boxer* shorts under his new corduroys?

Phil moved his legs in jerks like a young horse until he got himself over to the couch. He almost fell over me trying to sit down. "Mother of God," he said again, making the sign of the cross. "She never gave me a clue."

A feeling of desperation welled up in my chest, a feeling so huge I was at a loss to explain to myself where it had come from or where it was going—I was sure it was going to jump out of me and become a separate being of its own, with arms and legs and maybe a tail and surely a mouth which could scream long and hard—*What was it?*

I got to my feet and went into the kitchen and opened the refrigerator, took out the bottle of red wine that was in there, found Phil's corkscrew right where he always kept it, uncorked the bottle, poured two glasses, and thought: Bloody Marys with Hollander, beer with McCabe, tea with Roussy, wine with Phil; what next? Chicken soup with Rabbi Steve Reinish? Schnapps after the funeral?

I looked at my watch. Three-ten A.M. I had to be in the ER at eight A.M.; I had to think about getting to bed, getting to sleep.

Phil came into the kitchen and put his arms around me from behind and laid his head on my back. "Oh, God," he said. "I didn't call it."

I put my hands over his and asked, "Will you tell me about it? When McCabe called you Friday night and you went over there?"

He said, "Were you there? When she coded? What *happened?*"

"Phil, the police have been looking for you. They want to talk to you about it."

He let go of me and took a step backward. "The *police?* The police want to talk to me? *Did she leave a note?*"

"Ost and Kelly were there. They need to close the case as a suicide. They talked to all of us in the ER this morning."

Phil didn't say anything. He reached past me and took one of the glasses of wine and went back into the living room. After a minute I followed him, sitting down next to him on the couch again.

"I can't talk to the police," he said. "Do you know if she left a note?"

I lit two cigarettes and handed him one. He took a drag, said, "Uck," put it out, and got his own pack of Dunhill menthols out of his coat pocket.

I said, "Did Shelley have tests Monday morning for the lupus?"

He nodded dumbly. "Bloods. Chem 60. A few other things. Oh, Jesus."

"Not at the hospital."

"At the university clinic. Her friend Gail moonlights there. Gail sent the tests out to the lab they use. Shelley didn't want to have them in the hospital."

"They diagnose the lupus already? Or they just suspect it?"

"Suspect it, but you know how long it takes to rule out everything else. That's the thing with lupus." He turned his head very slowly, in a different time zone, to look at me. "I didn't realize she'd told you."

I drank some of my wine and put the glass on the floor next to my foot, stuck my cigarette in my mouth, and started unlacing my boots. In my mind I saw the Band-Aids on Shelley's arm, one at the crook of her elbow, the other on the back of her hand. I saw the nurse's freckled hand pulling the Band-Aids back and the puncture marks underneath. I heard her say, *Dr. McCabe, you'd better look at this.*

I took off one boot, then the other. I asked, very carefully, "Did you take her to have the abortion Sunday morning?"

"Jesus, she tell you that too? The whole idea was to keep everything a secret, not tell Steve about the lupus *or* the baby."

I sat up and looked him right in the eye. "Phil," I said quietly, taking my cigarette out of my mouth, "was the baby yours or Steve's, or didn't Shelley know?"

I watched the question dart around in Phil's eyes.

"What? You think . . . Steve's! Of course it was Steve's! What the hell's the matter with you? You think I had something going with Shelley? Jesus Christ! She was one of my *patients!* When did you talk to her? *What did she tell you?"*

I said, "You wanna tell me what your St. Christopher's medal was doing in Shelley's bed in her on-call room?"

"In her *bed?* What do you mean, in her *bed?* I didn't leave it in her bed, I left it in the bathroom, on the sink. I was washing my face and the chain got stuck on the water spout and broke and later on I realized that I left it there."

I didn't say anything. I watched him.

"She was emotionally labile—wide mood swings— you should know that, from the lupus. What did she tell you? If she told you we talked about it, you know, how we felt about each other—sexually—you should know I talked to her about transference and counter-transference and the whole thing of broad emotional sweeps with lupus. We weren't talking about actually getting *involved.* Shelley wouldn't do that and I certainly wouldn't do that, not have sex with one of my patients! We were talking about sexual feelings the patient has for the therapist, and how the patient transfers to the therapist feelings that the patient had for an early object—the mother, father, whatever—and that's transference, and the patient acts it out sexually. When the therapist does it with the patient, that's countertransference. Ev, you *know* all this—you rotated through psychiatry—the patient is *supposed* to transfer. It's part of the therapy. The therapist isn't supposed to do it—or at least not act it out—the therapist is supposed to examine why he has the countertransference and try to figure out why and how the patient is initiating it. What did Shelley *tell* you?"

I said, "Where did she get the Dex? You prescribe that for her?"

Phil almost fell off his end of the couch. *"Dex? Shelley was on Dex? Jesus motherfucking Christ!"*

"How could you go away and leave your beeper off like that when she was so shaky? When did you see her last? Sunday? Monday?"

"Don't!" Phil cried, leaping to his feet. *"That's not fair!"*

But I was not about to be derailed. Something cold was fanning out in my chest, a river under ice. "When did you see her last?"

Phil stared at me incredulously for a beat, then turned his back to me and walked across the room. He opened the bottom door of his grandfather clock and did something with the chains and pendulum. After a moment he came back to the couch and got another cigarette out of his coat pocket.

"You've got one in the ashtray," I pointed out.

He glared at me, lit the cigarette, and stubbed out the one in the ashtray. "I'm trying to remember that line from *Romeo and Juliet* you and McCabe quote back and forth to each other," he said bitterly. "Juliet to nurse after nurse tells her to marry what's-his-name, the other guy."

"Paris."

"The line; or are you conveniently forgetting it just now?" He spit this out.

" 'You have comforted me marvelous much,' " I quoted flatly. *"You* are evading the question."

"I'm evading the question," Phil repeated. "I see. *You* are *attacking* me. Don't try to turn it back on me."

"When did you see her last?" I repeated.

"When did *you?* You seem to have had a lengthy and detailed chat with her. Did you talk to her Monday morning? What is this, some kind of competition? Which one of us saw her last? Shelley kills herself and that's what's important to you? Which of us saw her last?"

"It's going to be pretty damned important to the police."

"What is this with the police?" Phil yelled. "Why am I on trial here all of a sudden? Do I demand this kind of accountability from you? There are certain things about my relationship with Shelley that I am not going to discuss with you, and that you have no right to ask about!" He began to pace back and forth in front of the couch, waving his arms until ash from his cigarette flew in all directions over his immaculate living room. "I am not going to tell you what Shelley and I talked about on Friday or any of the times I saw her the rest of the weekend! It isn't your business. If McCabe and Hollander want to shoot their mouths off, it's gossip. If I shoot mine off, it's a flagrant breach of patient confidentiality." He took a last drag of his cigarette and ground it out, half-smoked, in the ashtray.

"You can't claim patient confidentiality," I said. "She's dead."

"I open my mouth," Phil went on, not hearing me, "and the next thing I know, the cops will be taking a statement and then I'll find myself in the courtroom on the witness stand and my credibility as a psychiatrist will go right out the fucking window."

About to light another cigarette, I forgot it and the match I had struck burned down to my fingers. I dropped it on the carpet, then scrambled to put it out. "Phil," I said very quietly, striking another match, "who is talking about a courtroom? This is suicide, not murder."

Phil opened his mouth, shut it, then opened it again. "I am not suggesting it was murder," he said emphatically. "Where in God's name is your mind, Ev? All I'm saying is, if I make a habit of talking too freely to the police, I'll wind up in the courtroom when there's a questionable case. I'm not talking specifically about Shelley."

"I think you're being pretty damned defensive about the police," I said.

"*I'm* being defensive?" He made a rasping noise in his throat. "Oh yeah? You wanna tell me who the hell chewed your neck up like that? I didn't know adults went in for sucker-bites—or did you make it with a fifteen-year-old? We used to do that to each other in high school, have a hot date and neck at the drive-in. I'm being defensive? Jesus Christ, why don't we talk about who chewed your neck up and see how defensive *you* get!"

For a moment I didn't say anything. Inside my mouth, I carefully lined up the bottom row of teeth with the top row of teeth and inspected the arrangement with the tip of my tongue.

"Not so quick to discuss that, are you?" He sat down in his favorite wing chair, across from me, pushing the ottoman out of the way with his feet. He crossed his arms over his chest and stared at me belligerently.

"Should I be?" I asked coldly. "Quick to discuss it? In my opinion you're too damned quick to discuss your relationship with Beth. I frankly don't want to know about it."

"Let's not drag Beth into it."

"Why not?"

Phil laid his head back against the chair and regarded the ceiling for a while. "I have a right to know who it is."

"Oh, really? What's that, *droit du seigneur?*"

"Ev, what are you being so hostile for? I come in here, you tell me Shelley killed herself, then you *attack* me! Besides which, you've obviously been in the sack with someone else. What's that about?"

"I didn't know where you were!" I yelled.

Phil thought about this. "Oh," he said. "You felt abandoned, so you became hostile and slept with someone else because I abandoned you, is that it?"

I stared. It had taken me a great deal of thought throughout the course of the day to piece that insight together, and there was Phil coming up with that same conclusion in about seven seconds flat. "Oh, Jesus, Phil," I sighed elaborately. "Do you have to be so fucking analytical all the time?"

"Who was it?"

I took my glasses off and wiped them on my shirttail.

"Let me guess," he said with a great deal of resignation. "Hollander."

I didn't say anything.

Phil took his glasses off too, and laid them across his lap. He put a hand over his eyes dramatically. "At least tell me it was Roussy or someone else," he said. "Roussy is at least a nice guy. Hollander's totally incapable of having a real relationship. Or don't you know that? Or was this just some kind of sex to negate death, that kind of thing?" He put his glasses back on. "Let me guess. The police interview you, they interview Hollander, then you guys go back to your place for a little consolation in the sack, that it?"

"They didn't interview Hollander, as far as I know. He wasn't there when she died. McCabe and Roussy were there." I heard my voice becoming flat. "Afterward I took Hollander home—to his place. Manny Hernandez had casted Jay's arm and I helped Jay make breakfast, then Jay and I had a few Bloody

Marys and he told me what happened with Shelley in surgery Friday night."

"So you went to bed with him."

"Yes."

"So where do things stand? You going to sleep with him again, or this is a one-night stand?"

"A one-night stand." I swallowed. "I wish you'd tell me Beth was a one-night stand."

"Beth doesn't work in the same hospital you work in. I don't want to discuss Beth right now, we'll talk about Beth in a couple of days, O.K.?" Phil hooked a foot around one leg of the ottoman and pulled it flush against the chair. He began unlacing his new Timberland boots. "This business with Hollander bothers me," he said. "I don't like him; he's a manipulative son of a bitch, and I don't want to think about the two of you together. I can't picture it and I don't want to picture it." He dropped his boots to the floor and slung his legs over the ottoman. Clutching both arms of the wing chair, his legs straight out in front of him, he looked as if he were anticipating a particularly wild rollercoaster ride on a flying carpet.

"Hollander is completely paralyzed emotionally. His home situation was lousy. His father, the great antiquities expert at New York University, threw Jay's mother over for a seventeen-year-old Japanese girl—not even a grown woman—when Jay was four years old. Jay used to spend summers in Japan with them and he hated every minute of it. Didn't even get to see much of his father—the great man was galloping all around the country cataloging art objects, and there's Jay with the stepmother and the *amma*. Great stuff for a healthy adult psyche, don't you think?" Phil snorted derisively. "Jay doesn't like people, Ev. Jay likes *things*. Just look around his apartment for a minute. The man sinks a fucking fortune into Oriental porcelain and ceramics. You see that T'ang horse on the coffee table? That was in somebody's private collection; it was auctioned at Sotheby Parke Bernet and it went for several thousand dollars. Several *thousand,* Ev. Jay's twenty-six years old and he's coughing up thousands of dollars for *figurines.* He probably wanted to get you into bed because you were the only woman in the hospital he hadn't been to bed with.''

"Yes, I can see that one thing follows logically on the other," I said dryly. I was getting mad. "Anyone who would buy something at a Sotheby Parke Bernet auction couldn't possibly experience an emotional bonding with another human being during the sex act, is that what you're saying?"

"I am talking about the man's level of narcissistic injury! He is not—"

"He's not one of your patients," I shot in. "Or is he? Or can't you tell the difference? What's an *amma?*"

Phil reached for his wine. "That's great focus, Ev. The Japanese baby-sitter. The governess. The person you get to take care of your kid when you just can't make the time to take care of him yourself."

"I don't know, Phil," I mused. "Seems to me you're acting out a little unfocused hostility here. I'm the one that did you wrong, but you're mad at Hollander and it looks as if you're about to get mad at Hollander's *parents.* And since the Japanese word for 'baby-sitter' rolls so fluently off your tongue, I take it Hollander told you this story himself. Which means you're telling me all this in flagrant disregard of patient confidentiality. Which, if I remember correctly, you were all fired up about just a few minutes ago.''

"Jay Hollander is not one of my patients," Phil shot in hotly.

"So how do you know all this shit about his childhood and how he's 'paralyzed' emotionally because his father left his mother and the *amma* didn't speak English?"

"What?"

"The truth of the matter is this," I went on, feeling

anger slosh up my esophagus like hydrochloric acid, "people tell you things. You're like a father confessor. They just open up. They sit down with you for lunch in the hospital cafeteria and find themselves telling you their problems because you're such a good listener, and you've got that 'you-can-tell-me' air about you, that sympathetic look on your face. They should only hear you now, how you use what they tell you to make your own goddamn points!"

"What do you want me to tell you? I love you, and I don't like him! I don't want to see you get hurt!"

"Yeah, right," I said, and got to my feet. "Try again. More like, you want to fuck Beth, but you don't want me to fuck anyone but you. I'm supposed to make this big commitment to you, but you won't make it back." I faked a swoon and fell to my knees. ' "And all my fortunes at thy feet I'll lay, and follow thee my lord throughout the world!' " I lurched to my feet and went into the study and collected my jacket, the manila envelope with Shelley's manuscript in it, and the vials of pills. I left Phil's St. Christopher's medal on the desk along with the empty Dunhill pack. When I came out again I said, "There's one thing missing here, Phil: 'The exchange of thy faithful vow for mine.' Let me know when you want to make the swap."

I stomped out of the apartment, slamming the door behind me. I had gone down three flights of stairs before I realized I was in my stocking feet; I had left my mountain boots in Phil's apartment.

Feeling defeated, I sat down on the stairs in the hollow, chilly stairwell and stuck my umpteenth cigarette of the day into my mouth. My eyes stung and began to well over. Fumbling for my lighter in my pocket, I pulled out the piece of paper I had found in Shelley's manila envelope that had nothing to do with the manuscript.

On the piece of paper was the name of a well-known, expensive abortion clinic for the well-to-do, complete with address, telephone number, and the scrawled notation, "Sunday Feb 3rd 10am, npo 12hrs ā". *Npo* was the Latin instruction 'nothing by mouth'; when you have an abortion or any other surgical procedure, you can't eat or drink anything for twelve hours beforehand.

I smoked my cigarette and brushed tears away with the heel of my hand as I read the message underneath: "Don't worry, Shel, I'm in this with you as long as you want or need me. *Hah-sock* (or however you spell it). X X X."

Chazak was the Hebrew word for "courage."

The note was in Phil's distinctive, nearly illegible handwriting.

CHAPTER

19

"You missed all the excitement last night," Dr. Bobbi Kaplowitz told me cheerfully Wednesday morning. "We had this patient, we restrain her and she gets a Bic lighter out of her pocket and sets her stretcher on fire. The other patients are yelling, 'Fire! Fire!' We had her arrested for arson. You signing out from me?"

"Yeah," I said. I was still a little bleary-eyed.

"O.K., first: new med students rotate in today, but we keep the ones we've had the last six weeks too. So that's the four old ones and four new ones. Let's see . . ." Bobbi flipped through some typewritten memo sheets, her gold charm bracelet clanking. I always wondered why she wore such impractical jewelry on duty, including a diamond engagement ring the size of the Rock of Gibraltar. "You team with Hollander," she went on, "and you keep Whizkid Larson and Karen Eissfeldt. Your new guys are David Aubrey and Francis LeBaron. Hollander's going to be out a couple of days, so you have them by yourself until he comes back. The new people are with their preceptor for orientation right now; they'll be here at eight-thirty. You get Hollander home O.K. yesterday?"

The question made me blink. I nodded.

"He say how long he's going to stay out?"

I shook my head.

"It's lucky we got the extra med students to help,

with Hollander out and Shelley . . . Shelley . . ." Bobbi trailed off and sat very still for a moment. Then she heaved a shaky sigh and went on. "Roussy and I team, and we'll take the other four." She pulled a pile of charts down from the doctors' in-box. "There's an old guy with abdominal pains and diarrhea. My instinct tells me he's got a hot appendix, but I haven't had time to look at him. He only speaks Spanish, you'll have to get Carlos." Carlos was the ward clerk. "This woman over here"—Bobbi waved in the direction of a stretcher parked in the corridor—"has been seizing. If I get the story straight from her son—frankly, I think the son could use a psychiatric evaluation myself—she takes Dilantin but he doesn't know when she took it last. She also drinks. My opinion is she's going to need big-guns stuff."

I glanced over at the woman on the stretcher. Her son was sitting on a chair next to her, gesticulating into space.

"He won't take his sunglasses off," Bobbi said. "He says General Qaddafi is trying to shine a light into his eyes to see if he's lying or telling the truth."

"Ah. You page Psych?"

"Bet your sweet ass. I don't want to turn around and find out he just happens to have a gun on him to shoot Qaddafi with. The Psych nurse came over and talked to him a few minutes; I think she's paging Carchiollo out of Grand Rounds." She flipped to the next chart. "Um . . . Oh, this guy you know. The museum guard who got ethered during the robbery at the Museum of Natural History, remember? He asked for you when he came in this morning."

"Oh, I remember him," I said. I was beginning to focus. "We could hardly keep him down long enough to do the exam, he was so mad. He kept telling us he was going to 'sit up like a man' and not lie down 'like a weak woman.' Said he was in the Polish cavalry during the war. Did you see him? He talks like some casting director's notion of an actor to *play* someone in the Polish cavalry—you see that *mustache?* He talks like he learned syntax from Uncle Vanya! He looks at me and says, 'Ven you are goink to haf babies?' ''

Bobbi laughed heartily. "He thought you were the nurse, right?"

"Of course! Abdicating my God-given task of motherhood. He didn't want me to examine him."

"So what did you say to that?"

"I said this wasn't the old country, for one thing, and he had a hell of a gash over his eye, for another, and if I were home having babies, who would be here taking care of him, and then I asked him whether it did or did not follow logically that I would do a better job of sewing him up, being a woman, than a male physician. Women are better at sewing, right?"

"Barf," Bobbi said to this, with a grin.

"I know. *However,* he gave me a rather sly look and let me suture his eye. What is he here for now?"

"Chest pain. His wife dragged him in here about five this morning. He was doing the whole macho routine, denying up and down that anything was wrong. His wife may stay home and have babies, but he sure as hell listens to *her,* let me tell you."

"You run an EKG?"

"Yup; normal. We're waiting on the bloods. I don't think he infarcted. I think he has chest pain because he's upset over the robbery—that was a very humiliating experience for him. It's his job, and he's very much the macho man, and he's getting on—he's sixty-four."

I nodded. "I'll see what his bloods are." I took the museum guard's chart; across the top it read "ER233756 PAVELKA STANISLAW." "I'm surprised he asked for me."

"By name. Well, almost. 'Soot-klaf' he called you."

We laughed again, and Bobbi got up to go. She did a long, slow stretch and her more-than-ample breasts strained against her blouse. "Oh, one other thing," she said, stuffing her stethoscope in her purse, "we got a kid whose brother came after him with a meat cleaver. Caught him in the forearm." She made a chopping motion with the flat of her hand against her left elbow. "He's only about sixteen. Firenze is sewing him, so you don't really have to look at him, but you may want to see the wound. What a mess."

I winced. "They get the brother?"

"Upstairs in X Ray with a police escort—cops broke his nose. Anyway, I'm out of here."

I watched her move off down the hall, her heels clicking on the linoleum floor. It really is amazing, I thought, how Bobbi Kaplowitz always manages to look so glamorous in the ER.

"All right," I said to my two new med students, who were eyeing me nervously. "Mrs. Neville. Whadd'ya got?"

David Aubrey looked to me to be about twenty years old, which I assumed was impossible, and about to jump out of his skin, which was plausible. Francis LeBaron was more my own age and seemed more composed; I figured he could tell by looking at me that I was not the kind of resident who ate med students for breakfast.

Aubrey took a scattered breath and launched into the case presentation as if he were taking a wild leap off the high dive. "Neville is a sixty-seven-year-old white female," he intoned with as much authority as he could muster, "complaining of vertigo, angina, hemiparesis, and diminished motor power of the left leg. Patient states that she fell in her living room, this A.M., knocking her head on the television set. Patient denies previous cardiac history. She shows marked contusions on the left side periorbitally with some edema, is oriented times three and alert, pulse eighty-two respirations eighteen—"

"She lose consciousness?"

Aubrey planted both feet squarely under himself. "Negative."

I blinked. *"Negative?* Aubrey, this is hardly *Miami Vice."* I glanced at LeBaron and thought I detected a smile about his lips. "You ask her?"

Pause. "No," Aubrey admitted.

LeBaron grinned and I tried not to. "O.K.," I said gently. "Rule number one: don't try to bluff me. I'm not here to prove I know more than you do, and you're not here to prove you know as much as I do. If I ask you something and you don't know, you say you don't know. Any history of seizures, fainting spells, that kind of thing?"

"No," Aubrey said defensively. "I asked."

"Meds?"

"Ah . . . Tagamet, Tylenol, Dalmane, Benemid—"

"Benemid? What's that for?"

Aubrey looked like he might cry. "I don't know."

I smiled and squeezed his arm. "You're learning. You like 'Dave' or 'David' better?"

"I prefer 'David.' "

"How about you?" I asked LeBaron. "You like 'Frank', or 'Francis'?"

"Actually I'm called 'Kip,' " LeBaron said, smiling.

"O.K., you know what Benemid is for, Kip? Probenecid."

He shook his head. "That's the one she couldn't remember," he said. "She said, 'Benemid or something.' "

"Benemid is a renal tubular block," I explained. "Sometimes you see it given with penicillin; it prevents too much of the penicillin being excreted. It's not used so much now. Nowadays they only give you a shot of it right before they give you your shot of penicillin for gonorrhea. I don't think she's on that."

LeBaron laughed loudly, and after a moment Aubrey laughed as well.

"So, what do you think?" I asked.

"She's weak in the left leg—can't raise it, and also the left arm," LeBaron said. "Maybe some kind of CVA incident with the right hemisphere?"

"Stroke. O.K., that's a possibility. What do you want to order for that?"

"CAT scan?" Aubrey asked hopefully.

"Yes, if that's what you suspect. But let's go see her first."

"Mrs. Neville," I said when we entered the examining room, "I'm Dr. Sutcliffe. You don't look so good. What happened?"

Mrs. Neville turned her head so she could see me out of her right eye; her left eye was swollen nearly shut. "I fell on the TV," she said apologetically, as if she were troubling me needlessly. "I hit my eye, I think."

"I see that. You've got a hell of a shiner there. Were you alone?"

"Yes, my husband is in Boston for a conference."

"Is he a physician?"

"No, an attorney."

I nodded. "Dr. Aubrey tells me you take Tagamet, Tylenol, Dalmane, and what's the other one, Benadryl?"

"Yes, that's it. I couldn't remember before."

"You also take Artane with the Benadryl?"

"Yes, I'm sorry—I forgot to mention the Artane."

I looked pointedly at LeBaron and Aubrey. "You're having chest pain? Can you tell me about that?"

"I have a pain here," she said, passing a hand over her left rib cage. "It hurts when I breathe."

I nodded. "The pain steady, or it comes and goes?"

"It's fairly steady, when I inhale, I think."

"Any history of heart problems?"

She shook her head.

"Did you land on yourself funny when you fell? Hurt your ribs or your left side?"

"Yes, here on the left side, and I hurt my left arm too."

"Your arm hurt?"

"Yes, a bit."

I examined her left arm, then took her hand. "Squeeze my hand, please."

She squeezed.

"You're a little weak in your left arm?"

She nodded.

Gently I ran my hands over her left rib cage. "This hurt?"

She shook her head.

"This?"

She winced. "Yes."

"All right, we'll get you some X Rays. I don't think your arm is broken, but you may have cracked a rib or two. O.K.," I said to Aubrey and LeBaron, "you want to order films of the left arm and chest. Also, get her orbit X-rayed." The orbit is the bone over the eye. "While you're at it, go look up in the surgery text in the doctors' lounge how many pounds of pressure you need to break what bone—there's a chart in there somewhere that shows this—you'll see that it takes the most pounds of pressure to fracture the orbital bone. Mrs. Neville, did you lose consciousness?"

"I don't know. I don't think so."

I took Mrs. Neville's hands and held them up in the air until her arms were straight up. "Now, without holding your hands together, can you close your eyes and hold your arms up like this for a minute?" I let go of her hands. Mrs. Neville closed her eyes and managed to hold her arms up, but the left arm began to tremble noticeably. "O.K., you see this tremor?" I said to Aubrey and LeBaron. I took Mrs. Neville's hands and laid her arms down again. "Can you pick up your right leg? Good, you can put it down again. Your left leg?"

"I can't," she said.

"You have Parkinson's," I said.

"Yes."

"That's what you take the Benadryl and Artane for."

"Yes."

Next to me LeBaron's mouth fell open into a grin.

"Do you walk with a cane?" I asked.

"Yes, it has things on the bottom." Mrs. Neville imitated four feet with her hands.

"And you drag your left leg when you walk?"

"Yes."

"Were you dizzy when you fell, or you just fell?"

"I wasn't dizzy. I lost my balance when I tried to turn the TV off."

"You don't get dizzy or light-headed ever?"

"No."

"All right." I took Mrs. Neville's hand and squeezed it. "We'll get you some X Rays, and we'll take your blood, just for some routine tests. We need to do that." I turned her head and looked at her eye. "Some lacs here," I said to Aubrey and LeBaron. "But I don't think sutures are indicated. Very little bleeding."

"What do you do for lacerations like this?" Aubrey wanted to know.

"Nothing. You can swab around the eye a little with an alcohol wipe—make sure you don't get it in her eye—but other than that, just leave it. Maybe one or two butterflies. Come outside with me now."

We took our leave of Mrs. Neville, and outside in the corridor I said, "I am not going to postulate CVA. I think that's clear. David, when you present a case for your preceptor or at rounds, you want to be formal, the correct jargon and all, but that kind of stuff isn't necessary here. It's much better to say, 'Patient says she fell and hit her eye, and her chest and arm hurt,' than, 'Vertigo, angina, and hemiparesis.' Those are conclusions you were making about what she said, and I think you can see that's not what was going on with this patient at all. She wasn't dizzy and she didn't have angina. Your next patient, go a little slower and take the time to think things through and sort it out with the patient."

Aubrey nodded. He seemed to be relaxing somewhat, which pleased me. "O.K.," he said.

"Good." Then I said to LeBaron, "Don't stand by and watch, Kip. I can see you're a watcher, you learn by watching, and you're quick to learn, but I want you to get your hands dirty. What did you do before you decided to go to med school?"

LeBaron grinned. "I'm a Freudian analyst," he said.

I laughed. "That tack's not going to work here. I'm sure you know by experience that the one thing you need to know is the last thing the patient tells you, right? Mrs. Neville is a good example—you notice she didn't say, 'I'm weak in the left leg from Parkinson's so I lost my balance and fell on my television set.' You have to drag the information out of them sometimes. Either of you speak Spanish?"

"I do," Kip said.

"Enough to take a history?"

"I think so."

"O.K., you go see the patient who's complaining of abdominal pain and diarrhea, I think he's in cubicle B. If you don't understand him, get Carlos, the ward clerk. You know how to do a PE?" A PE is a physical exam.

"I'll try."

"O.K. David, you want to blood Mrs. Neville and then take her to X Ray?"

David looked panic-stricken. "O.K."

"You don't get it on the second stick, come get me. It's no big deal. We got an intern who still can't hit a vein. Don't worry about it, just try."

He nodded.

They went off, and I sat down in the nurses' station

to write in Mrs. Neville's chart. I lit a cigarette and thought this: I like this better than teaching English.

For the first time since Shelley had died I felt back in myself, and that Life Would Go On.

It made me feel guilty.

"Mr. Pavelka," I greeted the large man with the Polish cavalry officer's voluminous mustache, "I told you to come back on Friday to have your stitches out. This is only Wednesday. What's the matter?"

Pavelka smiled at me from his bed. He looked very tired. EKG leads were planted all over his hairy chest like mushrooms in a forest, their lines snaking every which way. A steady blip-blip emanated from the console over the bed.

"I dunno, Doctor," he said sadly. "I got some pain and my wife, she push me here like a small child. Maybe after all I am an old man, no good anymore for fighting off robbers in the night. Maybe now is time for Pavelka to go to God."

I blinked to keep my eyes from crossing. Good grief, I thought; who is this man's scriptwriter? I was used to male histrionics; I saw a large number of black and Hispanic patients, and I found many of the males to be either gruff or little-boy-like when faced with the prospect of being examined by a female physician. I realized they had to "do" something to retain their sense of masculinity in my presence, and I was generally affable about humoring their discomfort. Growing up the older sister of two brothers helped. "Mr. Pavelka," I said, "don't be ridiculous. You've got plenty of life left in you; let God wait."

"You know, when I was a young man, I rode with the Polish cavalry."

"Yes, I know." I smiled. "You told me the Nazis shot your horse out from under you. That wasn't worse than getting whopped over the head by a burglar, was it?"

He smiled as if I were missing the point. Don't patronize him, I thought. Let him talk. "What happened with the burglary? You want to tell me a little about that? What did the burglar take?"

"He took china statues." Pavelka spit this out as if he, Pavelka, had lost his masculinity over a very small trifle indeed. The corner of his mouth curled. "They were not so valuable. Not so valuable to rob a *museum*. A museum is a place for the people, for the people to come and learn."

I wondered if Pavelka had ever read Chekhov. "And he came up behind you, and he hit you? What did he hit you with?"

"He hit me with his fist. He was a very big man, with a very big fist. I would not have lost, I am strong myself, but he put the plastic thing over my face, with the smell. It made me faint."

"Yes, I remember. He ethered you. Ether would knock anyone out, you know; they used to use it in surgery to anesthetize the patients, before they came up with more advanced methods of anesthesia. You wave it under the nose of the biggest football player on TV and you'd drop him in two seconds flat. I wouldn't be embarrassed about it, if I were you. Ether is strong stuff."

Pavelka waved one of his hands impatiently. "Yes, but whole thing was in *newspaper*," he complained. "They put my name in *newspaper*. I see it in the *Times* and the *Post* Monday, and my youngest son call me and ask me about it."

"Well," I said, "he was probably concerned about you. Of course he'd call; wouldn't you call him if you saw in the newspaper that he'd been assaulted?"

Pavelka continued to look unhappy. I decided to take a different tack; "Did you get a good look at your assailant?" I asked. "Could you describe him to the police?"

"He was wearing a cloth on his face. I couldn't see

what he looks like. He was very tall; tall like a tree. And I grab his arm when I fell: very strong, this one." Pavelka waved a hand over his own biceps. "But tell me, Doctor, I have a heart attack?"

"No, not that I can see," I said. "Dr. Kaplowitz took your cardiogram and that was normal, and we sent your blood to the lab and I have the results here; they're normal too. I think maybe you're a little upset about the burglary. When people get upset, they get chest pains sometimes. It's nothing to be embarrassed about."

Pavelka looked embarrassed anyway.

"Now, c'mon, Mr. Pavelka. I had a patient last week who had a bad fight with his wife and he got chest pains. I think maybe he just wanted to get his wife off his back."

There was a pause; then we both laughed.

"O.K.," Pavelka said.

I took the cardiogram leads off his chest, then turned his head toward the light. "Let's see your stitches. You're keeping them dry, like I told you?"

"Yes, of course. I have my wife to yell at me."

"She's just taking care of you," I teased. "That's her job, right?"

Pavelka grinned. "You have a husband, Doctor?"

"No . . . but I have a friend."

"Ah," he said, nodding his approval. "So you marry him?"

"I don't know . . . he's very busy, you know." I laughed, and hoped my laughter was light enough for Pavelka's ears.

"Maybe you haven't meet the right man yet," he suggested pointedly. "The right man, he want to marry you and have babies."

Not necessarily, I thought. But I could see I wasn't going to derail Pavelka from this line of thought. I could also see I was cheering him up, letting him cajole me about marriage as if he were my uncle or godparent. Let it pass, I thought. I patted his hand. "Well. Maybe."

"I think so. When you meet the right man, you will have babies. They will grow up tall like trees, I think."

I laughed. "Yes, and with my luck, they would grow up and ether museum guards. I'll see you Friday to take those stitches out, O.K.?"

I smiled about this for the next twenty minutes. When I signed Pavelka out, handing him over to his clucking wife, it was all I could do not to write in the chart, "Uncle Vanya states physician should have babies as tall as trees."

It was a good feeling. I liked patients who brought out the mother in me and made me feel affectionate.

The rest of the day went downhill from there.

When the call from the medical examiner's office came through, Whizkid Larson, one of the medical students, was suturing the hand of a patient who had stuck her hand in food processor. I was standing over him, gloved, watching his progress.

"Dr. Sutcliffe, call for you on three!" the clerk shouted out.

"I'm suturing!" I yelled back. "Can I get back to them?"

"She says to tell you it's Dr. Bayard."

I got a lightning bolt to the breastbone. Beck Bayard. Calling about Shelley's postmortem. "I'll be right back," I said to Whizkid. Removing my gloves, I made my way slowly through the ER to the nurses' station.

I didn't want to talk to Beck about Shelley's post. I made a detour to the water fountain and ran cold water in my mouth without drinking any of it.

While I was bending over the icy stream of water, Drs. Julie and Barry Steinberg came in the ambulance-bay door, stomping snow off their feet.

" 'Over the meadow and through the woods,' " Barry sang out cheerily when he saw me, " 'to grandmother's house we go.' You're outta here, Sutcliffe. We owe you for covering for us the other night."

I wondered if anyone had told Barry and Julie about Shelley's death. "I'm on the phone," I said, straightening up. "Be with you in a minute."

I sat down in a chair at the nurses' station. Put my feet on the chair's feet, adjusting my posture. Aligned the chair with the desktop. Pulled the phone over, then pushed it away a little bit. Took my stethoscope off my neck and laid it on the desktop. Pushed my glasses up on my nose. Combed my hair out of my eyes with my fingers. Picked up the receiver and depressed the blinking button on the console. "Yeah, Beck," I said.

I could hear the adrenaline in my voice.

"Ev. Post on Shelley Reinish."

"Yeah."

"You got salicylate overdose on the form here?" Beck asked.

"Yeah."

"You got any other ideas? Any other possible agents, something you might have forgotten to test for? I'm not sure what I'm looking at here."

I put my feet on the floor.

"Something intravenous," Beck prompted when I didn't say anything.

"Beck, she had a serum salicylate of eighty-five milligrams. That's enough to kill a horse. What are you telling me?"

"Her stomach was empty," Beck said.

My heart threw itself up against my sternum. Then it worked its way up into my head, pounding wildly in my ears.

"Christ," I said. "I'll come down."

I hung up the phone and put my head on the desk.

The only think I could think was this: *Who takes aspirin intravenously, and then sticks Band-Aids on the injection sites?*

CHAPTER

20

The sign over the security desk at the medical examiner's office read:

VISITORS MAKING IDENTIFICATION PLEASE SIGN SHEET ON RECEPTION DESK AND BE SEATED—ALL OTHER VISITORS PLEASE SIGN LOGBOOK INDICATING TIME OF ARRIVAL AND DEPARTURE—THANK YOU—ALL LAW-ENFORCEMENT PERSONNEL ARE REQUIRED TO SHOW THEIR SHIELD

"I'm Dr. Sutcliffe from University Hospital," I announced. "I have a case here and I want to talk to Dr. Bayard about it."

The security guard, a portly, heavy-breasted black woman, nodded and held out her hand for my hospital ID badge. I gave it to her. While she wrote in her log I looked through the door behind her to the room where people waiting to identify the dead sat until the bodies were ready for viewing. I noticed two little old ladies, accompanied by a woman I guessed to be a social worker, and I wondered whom the little old ladies were there to identify. A relative? A person who lived down the hall from them in their apartment building? I didn't much like being at the medical examiner's office and I could feel my emotions going into the Off mode. I wondered if the little old ladies had emotional

Off modes. I hoped so, for their sakes. I hoped too that they hadn't known the dead person very well, and that the dead person wasn't in awful condition.

Over the heads of the little old ladies a large poster took up most of one wall; it showed a hand growing out of the ground like a tree, its upstretched fingers unfurling in a tangle of green leaves.

"Stick this on yourself in a prominent position," the guard said, peeling the back off a visitor's badge. I unzipped my ski jacket and pasted the badge mid-chest on my sweater, then clipped my hospital badge on the front pocket of my jeans.

The caption of the tree-hand poster read: "CREATIVITY THE HUMAN RESOURCE."

"Sign this, please." The guard turned the log around for me to sign. I signed, my eyes still on the poster. For some reason, I found the poster profoundly disturbing.

"You know where you're going?"

"Yes, thank you."

I went through a large, heavy door into a dimly lit space with cinder-block walls. I paused for a moment to let my eyes adjust to the dimness, then began to descend a steep spiral staircase. A chilling place. As I made my way down, I remembered Shelley raising a schoolmarmish finger and asking with theatrical sobriety, "To what can this be compared?" Shelley had been imitating her husband imitating a world-renowned Talmud scholar; cocking her body stiffly, one finger poised heavenward, she began to bob rigidly back and forth, repeating the question in Hebrew, Yiddish, and Yiddish-accented English, bobbing herself into a trance of somber concentration. The other doctors in the ER had taken this question up as a litany, occasioning great hilarity, and for days afterward fingers had been raised in the doctors' lounge, on rounds, at case presentations: *To vhat can dis be compared?*

I got to the bottom of the metal stairs and pushed my way through another heavy door.

The long, wide hallway was completely deserted except for a stretcher parked next to the door of the autopsy room. There were refrigerated body lockers the entire length of one wall, their metal doors dull in the funny greenish lighting from the overhead fluorescents. As I came abreast of the stretcher, I looked at the dead woman lying on it. She was completely naked, parked in the hall without so much as a sheet to cover her, her forearms up in the air as if she were about to do press-ups with an invisible set of weights. Her face was screaming in its rigor mortis and her eyes were open, glazed to the land of the living. I resisted the urge to close her eyes.

Multiple stab wound, I noted.

To vhat can dis be compared?

Another heavy door. I passed from the deserted quiet of the hallway into the beehive activity of the autopsy room, pausing for a moment as the door swung shut behind me.

There were eight autopsy tables in the brightly lit room. Each was a kind of stainless-steel box with a grate to lay the body on; underneath the grate the box was filled with water that could be flushed away, much the same way water in a toilet can be flushed. All of the tables were occupied with the previous night's dead, and about a dozen pathologists were milling about in white or green surgical scrubs, white plastic aprons, and rubber dishwashing gloves. Two of the pathologists were yelling at one another from opposite ends of the room, exchanging a kind of rapid-fire riposte, full of innuendo and gallows humor. I was always amazed at what pathologists joked about; I listened to the two voices bouncing playfully off one another and tried to stifle my uneasiness as I looked around for Beck Bayard.

I didn't want to see Shelley gutted in the gore of her

own autopsy; I didn't even want to see her cleaned up after having been gutted, wrapped in a shroud, waiting for transport by whatever funeral home the Reinish family had chosen. I knew the autopsy had already been performed and that they had very likely put Shelley wherever they put the bodies waiting for the morticians, but I didn't know where that was and I didn't want to know where they had put her.

I also wasn't too sure how to deal with Beck. She had been my best friend in medical school. We had fallen out sometime during our last year of school and I still wasn't able to articulate to myself exactly how or why we had fallen out; the only thing I was clear about was how much the falling-out had hurt me. I still missed her, the way I sometimes still missed my old lover Richard. I felt the same when I saw either of them occasionally at parties given by mutual friends. If I had to be in a room with either Beck or Richard, I became anxious and distracted, and if I had to talk to either of them, I didn't recognize myself, somehow. I didn't seem to recognize them either. I was overwhelmed with a feeling of strangeness, of not being able to connect with the fact that Beck and I had once been the closest of friends and Richard and I had once been lovers and apartment mates. It didn't help to know that Richard and Beck had been lovers briefly after their separate fallings-out with me; I always wondered if they had talked about me, and, if so, what had been said.

And now I had to talk to Beck about Shelley, with whom I had never really connected, about the sorry fact of Shelley's suicide, which I had not been present to prevent. In a room full of death and gore, in which Shelley's own gory gutting had very likely been perpetrated.

When I found Beck, she was cutting someone's chest open with a circular saw at a table midway between the two yelling pathologsts. She was standing with one foot on a riser and the other on the foot bar, which ran around the bottom of the autopsy table about eight inches off the floor like a brass rail in a saloon. I stood apart from her a moment and watched her: a woman about my age, ramrod posture, gold wire-rimmed glasses, shoulder-length salt-and-pepper hair held off her face with twin barrettes, very businesslike, cutting open a corpse as if she were a hired gardener trowelling in the earth of a client's rose garden.

She felt me watching her and looked up. When she saw me she smiled tentatively and scratched her nose with her forearm. "Hey, Sutcliffe," she called.

I miss you, I thought.

"Hey," I greeted her back, walking up to the table.

"I'm sorry about Reinish," Beck said. "Did you know her well?"

"Yeah."

Beck nodded self-consciously, put her saw down, and picked up a scalpel. She tore open a blade packet and fitted the blade into the scalpel. She was around death so much she never knew what to say about anybody's.

"What's this?" I asked, to distract her.

"Guy went under a bus on a bicycle. Hospital says he died of a double hemothorax." She paused, thought about something for a moment, then went back to work with swooping broad sweeps of the scalpel. Swoop: half of one lung came loose. Swoop swoop: lung came out. ("Here's where the rib went through the lung," she pointed out to me.) Swoop swoop swoop: she tossed the organs onto the grate willy-nilly. When the scalpel was too bloodied, she wiped it on the thigh of the corpse: swipe swipe. When she had all the organs piled up and there was nothing left in the body cavity except a lake of black blood, she went to some industrial shelves along the wall and collected an armful of bottles with color-coded labels, arranged them in no particular order next to the body, and started collecting specimens. She filled a bottle labeled "Blood" by scooping it through the black lake the way you scoop a glass in a sink to fill it with water, screwed on the lid, and set it down. Then she did something with the body to get the blood out of the body cavity. I watched the water in the table cloud with red like you see in those movies about sharks when the camera pans away from the person being eaten.

I said, swallowing, "You do the post on Reinish yourself?"

Beck nodded. She was rummaging in the pelvic region. "Got a fracture here; you can feel the crepitus."

"Did you do it here?"

"What?" She looked up, met my eyes briefly. "No, in Special Cases." Special Cases was the ME's equivalent of a private room. "Give me a little credit, Ev."

"Sorry."

Beck was examining the heart, holding it up in front of her face. "Look at this!" she exclaimed. "There's no blood in the heart, the guy bled out completely, he bled dry!" She made a few cuts with her scalpel. "This is an incredibly normal heart, I'm going to save this. Not much artherosclerosis . . . about forty percent, maybe. Probably asymptomatic. A little calcification . . ." She put the heart on a scale; it weighed in at 243 grams. Then she picked it up again, marveling over it, and made a sudden stab with her scalpel. Some gunk squirted out and splattered on her glasses.

"That was stupid," she said, blinking. She took her gloves off and wiped her glasses on the shirttail of her scrubs. "Good I had my glasses on. Besides, he looks healthy, probably didn't have AIDS. You get any?"

I shook my head. "No."

"I try to get people in here to wear eye protection, and they don't do it." She put her gloves and glasses back on and went about weighing the rest of the organs, writing the results with a black Flair pen on a piece of brown paper toweling. The toweling was held by a clipboard that Beck had set across the body's thighs; there was as much blood on the paper towel as there was ink.

"Beck," I said.

"I'm almost through; five minutes."

"You gonna open the head?"

"No; don't need to. Not a mark on his face. Look at this kidney, it's pulverized. Spleen's ruptured too. What a mess. Never go under a bus."

"I wasn't planning on it," I said dryly.

I waited until she finished what she was doing, took off her dishwashing gloves, and untied her apron and slung it over a stool.

"Come down to the office," Beck said.

I followed her out of the autopsy room and down the wide hallway. The dead woman about to do press-ups was gone, and at the end of the hall there were wood screens set up; one of them had a sign which said "VIEWING IN PROGRESS PLEASE GO AROUND." I thought of the little old ladies and wished them well.

We went around. Beck pushed open a glass-windowed door which said "NO GLOVES IN MORTUARY OFFICE."

"What's that for?" I asked.

"What's what for?"

"The no-gloves-in-the-office."

"Oh," Beck said. "We try to keep the blood off the paperwork. You want coffee?"

I shook my head and watched Beck pour coffee into a mug with a profile of Winston Churchill on it. I said, "Beck, do guys on dates ever throw up when you tell them what you do?"

"All the time," Beck said cheerily. "Right now I'm going out with an assistant D.A. who used to be a cop. So far he's only thrown up once, but I think he drank too much that one time. How about you? You seeing anyone?"

"A psychiatric attending at University."

"Yeah? You like him?"

"Yeah, I do. A lot."

"He throw up ever?"

I laughed. "Not the last time I looked."

"Gotta watch the ones who throw up too much."

A young man stuck his head in the office. "Dr. Bayard, can you take a call from a Detective Russell from the One-nine?"

"Yeah, sure," Beck said. She punched a button on her phone and sat down behind the desk. "Bayard. What can I do for you, Detective?"

I listened to Beck's voice as she spoke with the detective and I marveled at the difference between it and her mother's voice; Beck's mother spoke high-society Kentucky and Beck spoke something which approximated *ABC Eyewitness News:* clipped, brassy, and devoid of regional accent. I once overheard someone ask Beck where she had learned to talk like that and she said she had hired a speech teacher after she decided to go work for the medical examiner ("I mean, can you just see me walking in a courtroom to testify on a murder case and saying, 'Wha, how kin Ah be of help to y'all, Counselor, l'il ol *me?*' "). But Beck had talked the same way as long as I'd known her, and we had met the first day of med school—long before Beck had decided to go into pathology.

I wondered if I had really ever known her.

Beck got off the phone.

I took a big breath. "So what can you tell me about Shelley's post?"

"Well, here's the chart," Beck said, tossing it across her cluttered desk to me.

I picked it up gingerly and laid it across my lap without opening it.

"Her stomach was empty," Beck said. "That strikes me as pretty damned unusual for salicylate overdose."

"We got a serum salicylate of eighty-five milligrams."

"So you say. But to get a serum level that high you'd have to swallow a family-size bottle of aspirin, and autopsy should show at least half of it still unabsorbed in the stomach. My guess is she took it IV."

I lit a cigarette. "Yeah, that's obvious. But her husband is a sharp cookie and he didn't mention any IV equipment in the apartment, and he's the one who found her."

Beck thought about this and gave me an odd look. "How was she found?"

"Unconscious in her own living room. On the couch. Feet on the floor, like she passed out. That's what her husband said."

"She didn't pull the line out and throw it under the couch?"

"I don't know. That's a good question."

"Huh. I'd like to see the police report. You talk to the cops?"

"Yeah, but they don't tell you what they know."

"That's true." Beck picked up the phone and dialed. "Who are the cops?"

"Ost and Kelly."

"Let's find out." She waited, and when someone answered she said, "Detectives, please. This is Dr. Rebecca Bayard at the ME's office." Pause. "Yes, this is Dr. Bayard at the ME's office. I have a case here, Shelley Reinish, I'll spell it: R-e-i-n-i-s-h. Detectives Ost and Kelly." She reached for Shelley's chart and read off a few particulars to the person at the other end. "Can you tell me what I'm looking at here?" She listened for a while, looking at me, said, "Uh-huh," and, "Yeah, O.K.," a couple of times, then, "Can you tell me if any intravenous equipment was found in the apartment? Intra-ve-nous. Right." A longer pause. "They're looking," she said to me. "Excuse me? No intravenous equipment. All right."

"Did they find a note?" I asked.

Beck glanced at me. "Do you see anything about a suicide note?"

"And amphetamines," I said.

"How about any drugs in the apartment?" She put her hand over the receiver. "No note," she said to me. She listened to what the person on the other end was saying. "Motrin. Right. Anything else?"

"Large aspirin bottle," I said.

Beck waved a hand at me. "Aspirin? I'm looking for a large bottle of it, or an empty one. . . . No aspirin. O.K. Can you tell me what you like for this one?" She nodded. "Thank you. Please make a note that I called, and I'll have a report for you this afternoon. I'm here until six this evening." She hung up the phone. "No IV equipment. They have Motrin—Ibuprofen—and the usual stuff, antihistamines, some Valium, and a muscle-relaxant—Robaxin. No aspirin or aspirin bottle. They like suicide."

"They *like* suicide?"

"Cops talk funny, what can I tell you? They 'like' suicide. They don't 'like' homicide. They're closing it as suicide pending autopsy."

"Jesus," I said. I took a last drag of my cigarette, dropped it on the floor, and put my foot on it. "What are you saying?"

"Suicide. No foul play. Not homicide."

My mind took a 360-degree turn, and I felt a chilly fizz go out in my chest as if someone had upended a bottle of root beer in there. "Was homicide a consideration?"

Beck looked puzzled. "Of course. It's always a consideration; you don't know until you investigate."

My scalp pulled back, drawing the skin on my face tight. "Beck, what if someone ran the aspirin into her IV and then went away with the IV equipment?"

"She had access to IV equipment; she knew how to start a line on herself," Beck said, shrugging. "How fast does an IV line run? She could run it in, get up and throw the stuff down the garbage chute, then go back into the apartment and sit down again. The cops would look in the garbage for it, but if it's already been bagged at the bottom they're not going to go through all that stuff. She was emotionally disturbed, right? They've got statements to that effect."

"But who would do something like that? Why would she take an OD of aspirin IV in the first place, and then why would she throw the IV equipment out? And even if she wanted to do that, don't you think she'd be *unconscious* by the time she ran enough into herself to get a serum level of eighty-five milligrams? To say nothing of the Band-Aids on the injection sites!"

"She had a recent abortion," Beck said. "They must have started a line for that. And they give you a Band-Aid." She put her coffee mug on the desk.

My mind was buzzing. "Listen. Let's say they took her blood, routine, at the abortion. That's the injection site at the elbow, right? And then they give her an IV, that's the injection site on the back of the hand. Then someone comes along and runs *another* IV into her, and puts the needle in one of these injection sites—Monday morning, to kill her, in her apartment. Or to help her kill herself, whatever." I listened to my thoughts tumbling out, jumbled, as if they were someone else's and not mine. "And then that person throws the IV equipment out. Beck! How is she going to get up and throw the stuff out herself? She's *unconscious!*"

"Ev," Beck said.

"And who the hell has an abortion and then kills herself? Why bother? Just kill yourself, the kid dies with you!"

"Look," Beck said gently. "Somebody committing suicide is not exactly going to exhibit rational behavior. Killing yourself is not rational. You wouldn't believe what I see here. I get a lot crazier than injecting yourself with something and sticking Band-Aids on the injection sites, if that's what she did. Or sticking yourself in one of the injection sites you already have from tests or IV's or whatever at the abortion, and putting the Band-Aid back over the injection site. Anybody talk to her before she did this? Was she coherent? You've got statements here that she wasn't, that she was emotionally disturbed. Maybe *you* wouldn't have an abortion and then kill yourself, but that's logical thinking, and an emotionally disturbed person is not going to be capable of that kind of logical thinking. Maybe she killed herself because she had the abortion and she had remorse."

"No," I said. "There's something here I'm just not buying. Do we have salicylate at the injection sites?"

"We're looking. I sent tissue to the lab. She must have taken it IV."

I stood up abruptly. I reached for my jacket; I had a sense of not knowing what I was doing. And a very pressing sense of having to get out of the ME's office right *now*. "I gotta go. You got my paperwork?"

Beck riffled through Shelley's file and handed me the copy of the autopsy report for the hospital. "Hey," she said, standing up. "You want to have dinner sometime?"

I paused. "Yes," I said. "I'd like that." I swallowed. "Very much."

"I'll call you."

"O.K." I knew she wouldn't, and that I wouldn't call her either.

I got out of there as fast as possible, clattering up the spiral staircase and ducking out past the tree-hand poster that said "CREATIVITY THE HUMAN RESOURCE." When I was outside in the cold snowy air I realized what it was I didn't like about that poster.

It was a hand coming out of the ground, from the grave.

CHAPTER
21

Rabbi Steve Reinish greeted me with a sad smile when he opened the door to his apartment.

I knew from my grandfather's funeral that I was not supposed to greet the mourner verbally in any way, nor ask him how he was, nor speak before he spoke. On the subway coming back uptown from the medical examiner's office I had done my best to remember what I could of the traditional Jewish mourning practices. My grandfather's funeral had been the most stringently observed in my family, out of deference to my grandmother, so that was the one I was focusing on.

"Dr. Sutcliffe," the rabbi said as he closed the door behind me, careful not to greet me either. "Listen, do you have a first name? I don't think I ever heard her call you anything but your last name."

The *"her"* went through me like a blast of birdshot. "Evelyn," I said after a pause. "Ev for short." I touched his elbow, at a loss for words. "I'm so sorry, Steve," I said eventually. "I don't know what to say."

"Nobody knows what to say, except the people who don't know you well enough to share the loss. . . . And they always wind up saying the *wrong* thing." He shook his head slowly and took my ski jacket. While he was hanging it in the foyer closet, I studied the funny little collage on the wall that Shelley had made of Steve. She had fashioned the body and head of a plump, cuddly bear out of black construction paper, and carefully cut out a space for Steve's photo so that his face looked out. Then I looked at their wedding picture hanging next to it, and at a huge Chinese calligraphy on the same wall. The calligraphy was about four feet long and two feet wide, and had been a wedding present from Shelley's parents. My heart ached for them.

Steve turned around, saw me examining the things on the wall, and abruptly walked into the living room. I had been about to say something about the wonderful little bear collage, and realized with a pang what a bad idea that might be.

"Thank you for coming," he said over his shoulder. "Come sit down."

I followed him into the living room.

Shelley and Steve's apartment had a southern exposure and the afternoon sun was spilling in through the windows, warming the room pleasantly. Outside, the snow was melting on the fire escape. The apartment smelled of oranges, books, and old furniture, as if it had recently been inhabited by a dozen wonderful old ladies serving tea and reading classical literature aloud to one another. There was a large contemporary sectional couch, which looked like it could seat about nine people, around a coffee table; other than that, all the furniture seemed to be family hand-me-downs, wonderful old stuff that exuded a sense of continuity and comfort. The sunshiny atmosphere contrasted to and underscored the signs of a death: the cushions had been removed from the back of the couch and scattered on the floor—sitting on the floor being a practice of mourning—and the mirror on one wall had been smeared with shaving cream. When my grandfather died, my grandmother hung black scarves over the mirrors; nowadays many Jewish people smeared their mirrors with shaving cream so you couldn't see your reflection in them. It achieved the same end—to avoid the self-serving vanity of looking at yourself in a mirror during the time of mourning—and it seemed less morbid than the black scarves.

Steve sat cross-legged on one of the couch cushions and I sat down across from him on another, on the other side of the coffee table. There were so many books on the coffee table I could hardly see Steve over them. When I had come to go over Shelley's manuscript with her, she had always piled the books on the floor so we could use the table, and then, when we finished, piled them all back on the table again.

I wanted Shelley to be there to move the books, and since she wasn't there, I wanted to move them myself.

I got up and moved to another cushion, where I could see Steve better.

"You know," Steve was saying, his voice an odd mixture of chatty and subdued, "in the Book of Job when Job's friends come to comfort him, they just sit there on the ground with him and nobody says anything for seven days. And in the Talmud somewhere there's a pithy remark I've been trying to find, something about how the person who gets the true reward is the one who shuts up in the house of mourning and talks loudly at weddings. My brother-in-law repeated this to me this morning, but he doesn't know where it's cited either. I think my favorite, though, is in a book I read once, I can't remember the title, where this English doctor's wife gets run over by a bus and killed, and the doctor's best friend takes him to Scotland to the moors. For about five weeks the friend gets the doctor up every morning and makes him walk across the moors all day, for hours and hours, and then gets him drunk on Scotch each night so he sleeps. I remember reading that and thinking: what a helpful thing to do for someone whose wife died. I wish I could do that. I don't know what to do with myself."

He laughed self-consciously, a pitiful sound that sliced through me.

"I'm not allowed to *daven* until after the burial" —"*daven*" means "pray"—"and it's spooky as hell, really unnerving. I started *davening* every morning when I was in the army, so that's about eighteen years now that I haven't missed putting on *tefillin* every morning. These last two days it's taken me halfway through the afternoon to wake up; I don't know what's going on around me in the morning until I've got through *davening*. And normally I run at the gym every morning I'm here—I'm usually in Philadelphia at my congregation on weekends, and I run there too, if the weather's O.K., except on Shabbes. Now, I'm climbing the walls not running."

I nodded, looking at the books and blinking back tears of a profound sadness.

"Do you have to stay inside?" I asked, when I heard him pausing, waiting for me to say something. I looked up at his broad chest and massive, muscular arms, remembering that Steve lifted weights too—with Jay Hollander. I tried to picture the two of them together, working out: the short, squarely built rabbi with his boxer's body, and the tall, angular physician with the physique of a swimmer more than a weight lifter. I tried to put together in my mind what I thought the two men had in common, and then realized that I knew, intuitively, but couldn't articulate it.

"I should," he said, smiling a little. "I guess I could go for a walk around the block for some air, but then I wouldn't be here if someone came to see me. Maybe I'll go out later after my parents get here."

"Where are they coming from?"

"Israel. They'll be here this evening. We moved there when I was in high school."

"Oh," I said. He was surprising me in some way I couldn't put my finger on. "I knew you were in the army there; I didn't realize you had lived there so long."

He nodded, running the fingers of one hand through his uncombed, tousled hair. I remembered my father's not shaving or combing his hair when my grandfather died. "I didn't like it. I figured I ought to do my bit for Israel and go in the army, so I did that. But as soon as I got out I came back to the States."

I wondered if he didn't want to talk about Shelley, and if that were what was surprising me. I was mindful of the fact that I wasn't supposed to mention her until he did. I nodded.

He was fishing for something among the books on the coffee table. "There's an ashtray here somewhere," he said. "I know you smoke. I don't mind. But when my brother-in-law comes back, maybe you'd better not. He's very *fromm*—observant—and he'd probably think it was very disrespectful of you. He's a typical *Baal T'shuvah*—someone who didn't grow up observant, but became observant as an adult. He's so observant he drives us all nuts. But in the meantime, please."

He handed me a small ashtray of brightly painted Israeli pottery, which Shelley had handed me on countless occasions. "My first wife, Daniela, smoked like a chimney. Israelis smoke a lot. It's a very stressful society."

"I didn't realize you'd been married before," I said, fishing my cigarettes out of my shirt pocket and gratefully lighting up. I was beginning to feel as if I were steeling myself for an ambush.

"For five years. I think Dani wanted to marry an American. We came here and she left me as soon as she got her green card."

He began to weep.

His weeping was so sudden and such a different tack from his idle chatter that I became disoriented. I put my cigarette in the ashtray and made a move toward him, but he waved a hand at me, so I sat back again. I spotted a box of Kleenex on the couch behind him and reached over and handed it to him. He wept quietly for a little bit, unselfconsciously, the tears rolling down his face into his black beard. Then he nodded as if I had said something, and blew his nose.

"I cry a lot," he said.

"It's O.K. So do my patients and their family members."

He wiped his eyes. "When I got married again, I knew marriage was a difficult proposition. You learn that when you get divorced, you're not so naive the second time around. You know you have to *work* at it, you know? God knows Shelley was difficult. *I'm* difficult. But you find ways to work at it, and you just kind of fight your way through the bad times, dig in your heels. Have you been married?"

I shook my head. "But I lived with a man named Richard for three years; Richard and I were just starting to talk about marriage when we split up. I guess we got to that point where you have to either get married or split up. And I know it's made me think about working things through better this time around."

"With Phil," Steve said, nodding. "Does he talk to you?"

I blinked; the question seemed odd to me. I took a long drag of my cigarette. "Yes, actually. . . . I guess I would have to say that he's very verbal, and he challenges me to be verbal too, to talk things out when there's a problem. But he does that for a living."

"Shelley wouldn't talk to me," Steve said, talking to himself as much as to me. "She could never tell me why she was mad at me. She'd just get into this terrible sulk and slam doors and stomp around, or yell at me about fifty things she *wasn't* mad about. Or things she was mad about three weeks ago. I'd do something to upset her, and she'd start yelling about my library books. 'Take some of these books back to the library! You can't possibly read all these books all at once!

How can you read more than five books at the same time?' She had a point: I usually have about eighty library books out at one time, and I have a couple of projects going at once. Right now I'm writing my doctoral dissertation, trying to do the footnotes, and I'm also working on my lectures for next semester—I teach a course in history at the seminary here—and I'm also trying to finish an article. Shelley had *one* project, her book, and that's about five audiocassettes— the tapes of her interviews—which she erases as soon as the typist types them, and you can keep the whole project in one typing-paper box. And she doesn't read books; she reads the newspaper. She's fanatical about that . . ." He trailed off sadly, then went on, correcting himself, his voice clutching in the back of his throat, "She *was* fanatical about reading the paper every day. . . . She used to read it every morning and throw it out every evening. So she's yelling about there being more than five library books here, like it's a criminal act." He was beginning to speak more quickly, his words tumbling over themselves: "You know what I found this morning? Xerox copies of letters she wrote to librarians about my library books. Totally incoherent, something about how books were 'bad for the body'—whatever that means—and the *Yezer Ha-ra*, the Evil Influence." He stopped abruptly, and I watched him trying to put this together in his mind, make sense out of it.

"She's been yelling about the library books for years. Maybe it's the mess; she was such a neat person, and I'm so . . . disorganized. I always let her read the newspaper first, because she used to complain I didn't fold it up right again after I'd read it." He rubbed his eyes. "I'm sorry, I'm not talking very coherently right now."

"It's O.K.," I said quickly. "Talk whatever way you want."

He absented himself briefly, went inside himself,

and then came back again. "But one day—this was a while ago—I got the idea that if she wouldn't tell me why she was mad, I'd just read her journal and find out—she wrote this journal every day, *religiously"*—he blew his nose again—"and there it was, right there on paper, what she was *really* mad about. So I got into the habit of reading her journal every couple of days, to see what was going on with her. Then one day she came home while I was reading it. You know what she did? She just grinned and grinned, from ear to ear. She was *pleased* that I was reading it. I'll never figure it out. So you know what I did? I started writing in it too. She began leaving me space to write—she'd write only on the one side of the page, then if I had anything to say, I would write on the other side. Things were a lot easier after we started doing that."

I stubbed my cigarette out and considered this startling revelation. "You read her journal?" I asked. *"Do you have the journal now?"*

"No, the detectives took it. But I looked before they came, and she hadn't written anything for at least a week. Not since last Thursday."

I felt my heartbeat filling up my ears. "Did she say anything . . . ? I mean . . ."

"About killing herself," he said flatly. He looked down at his hands, which were folded in his lap, and his mouth twitched. "No . . . And I find that odd. I mean, she wrote *everything* in there. When the detectives wanted it, I said I didn't want them to take it. I said there was . . ." He trailed of, looking embarrassed. "Our sex life. Very graphic."

I fell into a stunned silence. I was astonished that he was telling me all this.

"I'm sorry, I'm embarrassing you," he said, as if he could hear my thoughts. "But I can't . . . talk to my brother-in-law about this. I don't know *who* to talk to about it. I called Phil several times yesterday and I couldn't find him. Shelley and I were seeing him for marriage counseling, you know." He coughed, then went on, "There was some stuff in the journal that seemed strange to me. Some stuff that looked like . . . Well, I don't know *what* it looked like. Something for her book maybe. She's writing about some surgeon, a woman named Sasha I never heard her mention, and these conversations Sasha is having with someone— the someone is never identified—about systemic lupus erythematosus. Sasha's having an abortion. Sasha didn't know whether to have the abortion or not, but she had lupus, which was making it sort of imperative. All this medical stuff, too—stuff like you'd see in patients' charts." He stopped talking and regarded me very intently.

I thought: He knows. He's asking me to confirm what he already knows. "Steve," I said quietly, "what is Shelley's Hebrew name?"

"Shoshana," he said. And then his eyes widened. "Oh, my *God!* Shelley's named after her grandmother Sasha!" He threw himself to his feet. "Did she have *lupus?* Did Shelley have *lupus?* Is that what all the aspirin was for? And the Ibuprofen?" He stood over me, his arms hanging at his sides, the muscles bunching up. "Why didn't she *tell* me?"

"Maybe she did tell you. Maybe that's the best she *could* tell you: in the journal. In her own indirect way."

He began to walk around the room aimlessly, running his hands through his hair.

"If she had lupus, she couldn't have children," I said. "Maybe she didn't know how to tell you that."

He made a strangled sound. His back was to me, and I couldn't see his face.

After a long time he said dully, "I know about lupus. My cousin's sister-in-law had it. Her kidneys failed, and she went on dialysis. Then she got chronic heart failure, and she died. She was thirty-four. But I thought you got a rash, like measles." He sank down on his couch cushion again and leaned his back against the couch.

"Not everybody gets the rash," I said. I could hear my own voice, equally dull. My heart had gone out of me. I lit another cigarette. I saw Steve looking at the pack. "Do you want one?" I asked. "Are you allowed to smoke?"

He shook his head, but then took one anyway. "Shelley made a *geshrei* until I quit," he said.

I handed him my lighter. He lit up and said, completely switching tacks, "My brother-in-law hit the ceiling over the autopsy. He's not only observant, he's Orthodox. My in-laws are observant, but they're not Orthodox. I said, 'Shmuli' —his name is Samuel, but he uses the Hebrew now— 'even Lamm says you have to permit an autopsy if the civil authorities order it.' "

"Lamm?"

"The Orthodox authority. He wrote a book about Jewish practices in death and mourning. It's a book rabbis consult when they have questions with their congregants about funerals and so forth. I read Klein. Klein is Conservative. He's not as strict as Lamm." He took a long drag of his cigarette and grimaced. "God, this tastes *awful*. Aach! Excuse me." He ground it out.

I said, "I don't know much about this, but it seems to me I'm always reading in the paper about observant Jewish families opposing an autopsy. I assumed that an autopsy wouldn't be allowed, either."

"Well, yes and no. Maybe you're talking about the article recently, about the Lubovitchers—the one in the *Times*, Shelley showed it to me. An autopsy is technically *Nivul Hamet*—desecration of the dead, mutilation of the corpse. The contention of the Lubovitchers in this particular case was that the man was killed by an automobile in front of about fifteen witnesses, I think, and the family said there was no reason to do an autopsy because all these people saw it and the cause of death was already known. So why do an autopsy to find out what killed him? But it was a hit-and-run, so of course there had to be an autopsy. Because it was a criminal case. Otherwise the authorities might have given in to the Lubovitchers. This is New York, after all, the authorities are used to the religious sensibilities of groups like Lubovitch. A Conservative rabbi would not have argued with the authorities on that one. The Conservatives don't do all that European bugaboo, refusing autopsies and burying suicides next to the cemetery wall and embarrassing the family. Klein is very clear on this . . ." He trailed off, blinking back tears. Then he said, "Why didn't she *talk* to me? Did I push her too much about the baby?"

Then he let go, and sobbed openly.

I felt my own face pull, and my throat close down. I put my cigarette out, and when I moved toward Steve he threw himself on my shoulder.

I held him a long time, stroking his hair while he cried, my fingers running up against the bobby pins that held his yarmulke. I thought about my mother and the ambulance-driving in London during the war, and of the intimacy of grief among strangers.

Sometime later, Steve made us tea in the kitchen, while I sat at the table watching him, trying not to think about Shelley peeling oranges for Alex McCabe and ranting about Steve's library books and the letters she'd written to the librarians about the *Yezer Ha-ra*, the Evil Influence.

"We can bury her tomorrow," Steve said. "They released the body." He was talking and moving in slow motion, as if every gesture exhausted him. I thought: It probably *is* exhausting him. But I didn't know how the kitchen worked, what was what in the kosher scheme of things, and when I had offered him help with the tea he had refused politely. "I need to do something," he said.

I watched him put loose tea into a teapot and pour boiling water over it. He put the pot on the table with two cups and set out a tin of *rugelach*.

"My grandmother used to make these," I said, taking one of the flaky cookies.

He nodded, sitting down. He took one of the cookies, looked at it, and put it on the table. "They fingerprinted me," he said, showing me his hands, which had traces of the ink. "They took everything out of the bathroom cabinet and put it in little plastic bags, except my shaving cream, which I don't need now anyway, since I can't shave until after *shloshim*." He was referring to the first thirty days of the year-long mourning period. "They took my Robaxin—I have trouble with my back sometimes—and now I have to call up the pharmacy and get them to renew my prescription for it. I don't know why they took all that stuff. Presumably they were looking for what she . . . what she took. But I didn't see the big bottle of aspirin I bought last week. I told them that. Then they looked through her desk and took her journal and her manuscript. There were wineglasses on the kitchen table and they put those in little plastic bags too." He shook his head and poured the tea. "They crawled around on the living-room floor and looked in the rug—you know, combed the pile with their fingers, looked under the couch. Asked me very carefully about everything, how I found her." He mimicked the detectives: " 'How *exactly* was she when you found her? Were her feet on the floor? Was she wearing shoes? Have you moved anything? Is this how the room was *exactly?*' "

Listlessly he picked up his cookie and put it back in the tin.

"How *did* you find her?" I asked carefully, fearful of upsetting him.

"Sitting on the couch. With her feet on the floor.

Like she'd sat down and passed out. With the windows wide open. Snow was coming in on the floor. That's why I came home early—because of the snow—they canceled my class in Philadelphia, the one I teach there on Monday nights. Otherwise . . . otherwise I probably would have come home late the way I usually do and found her . . . dead already." A shiver went through him.

I let him sit quietly for a beat, then said carefully, "Steve, was there any IV equipment anywhere?"

He looked puzzled. "IV equipment?"

I took a deep breath. "The autopsy showed that she took the aspirin IV."

Steve put his teacup down with a clunk. *"What?"*

"Her stomach was empty. If she'd swallowed it, there would have been unabsorbed aspirin in her stomach."

His astonishment was palpable; it filled the room. "How is that possible?" he asked incredulously. "Why would she do that? What's the point?" He put a hand over his mouth, then let his hand fall to the table. "How *could* she do that?" He blinked rapidly, his face working with the implications. "What did she do with the IV equipment? Throw it out the window? What . . . ? What . . . ? *Did somebody help her do it?"*

"I don't know," I said.

CHAPTER

22

Fast forward to late Wednesday evening, a little after eleven P.M. I'd come home from the rabbi's around four in the afternoon, had slept for seven hours, and had just got up again. I was scrambling eggs in a frying pan, squinting, doing things with my eyes to see if I could get them to open and shut properly.

My brain wasn't working either. Somebody was in there driving all over the road, through this thought and that thought, with the radio blaring. Pieces of conversations I'd had with people over the preceding forty-eight hours were being broadcast willy-nilly like a series of interview highlights spliced together by a demented editor:

The rabbi: *Did somebody help her do it?*

Beck Bayard, at the ME's office: *They 'like' suicide. They don't 'like' homicide.*

I saw myself examining Mrs. Neville, carefully explaining things to the med students as I went along: *O.K., you see this tremor?*

I heard Mr. Pavelka, with his huge handlebar mustache: *He was very tall; tall like a tree.*

And: *The right man, he want to marry you and have babies.*

I took an English muffin out of the toaster oven, buttered it, and made myself a sandwich with the scrambled eggs. Getting orange juice from the fridge,

I took a swig out of the carton and sat down at the kitchen table.

I remembered McCabe sitting there opposite me, telling me about Shelley peeling oranges and ranting about Steve's library books and Jay Hollander's porcelains and Tony Firenze's surgical scissors.

I wondered what Tony Firenze thought about having thrown his scissors at Shelley now that she was dead. Or if he was sorry for having thrown me up against the wall.

I wondered if I called Phil if he would come downstairs and sleep with me, but then I remembered he was on call.

I saw Hollander's shoulders lunging over mine.

I saw Hollander showing me his porcelains: *Have you ever seen a Bunraku troupe?*

I heard Phil, saying about Hollander: *Jay doesn't like people, Ev. Jay likes things*.

I ate my sandwich and polished off what was left in the orange-juice container. Then I made a cup of tea. I thought about the black Chinese tea Hollander had in his kitchen; I'd liked that tea a lot. I made a mental note to ask Hollander where he'd bought it.

I saw myself rummaging in the drawer in Hollander's kitchen where he threw all his medical junk, looking for a spoon.

Hollander: *I've got chopsticks here someplace. How about some double-aught suture? I've got that too.*

I thought about Steve Reinish, and I thought again about the first time I'd met him, the time Phil and I had gone to the New York Philharmonic to hear *Carmina Burana* and had bumped into Steve and Shelley and her parents in the bar. I remembered Shelley's father and the distinguished-looking Oriental gentleman bowing when introduced to me and Phil.

My mind blanked as I remembered that.

And then it filled again, and I sat bolt upright in my chair.

Jesus Christ, I thought. I threw myself to my feet and ran into the living room and dived on my pile of newspapers, throwing papers every which way until I found Monday morning's.

There it was, a one-column article beginning on the front page of the New York *Times* and continuing on the third page of the second section, spelling it all out for me in black and white.

My heart began to slam against my breastbone as I read.

It continued to slam as I hurriedly dressed and dashed out the front door, downstairs to see Hollander.

Hollander was glad to see me. When he opened the door he threw his good arm around me and held me tightly against him, nuzzling my hair and running his hand over my back. I was conscious again of how tall he was; the top of my head was about level with his nose. And how strong; I imagined him lifting weights with Steve Reinish.

It took every ounce of concentration I possessed to stifle a gasp of terror as he folded me into his one-armed embrace. The plaster cast on his left arm came up hard against my ribs.

"I can feel your heart," he said into my ear, his mouth against my throat.

"I ran down the stairs," I said. "I smoke too much." I pushed him away as gently and naturally as I could. My voice rang peculiarly high in my ears, as if I had been inhaling helium. I coughed.

"You want a drink?" he asked.

"Yes," I breathed.

I watched him turn away. When his back was to me I picked up the porcelain horse in the bookcase next to the door, the one that had been sitting on the twenty-dollar bill I'd used to pay the deliveryman for the Chinese takeout. I turned it over and looked at the bottom of it. There was a seven-digit cataloging number in black marking pen, beginning with the letters NH.

The little horse fell out of my hands and I caught it against my thigh just before it hit the floor. Replacing it as quietly as I could in the bookcase, I followed Hollander into his kitchen, tripped over the threshold of the kitchen doorway, and fell up against his back.

He turned around and gave me a bemused look.

I made an attempt to laugh. The sound that came out of me was more on the order of a shriek. *Get a grip on yourself, Sutcliffe.* I scurried to one of the kitchen chairs and slid into it, groping in my shirt pocket for my cigarettes.

"I'll get you the ashtray," Jay said, disappearing back into the living room.

By the time he returned with the ashtray I had calmed myself considerably. I hoped. The adrenaline was buzzing in my chest but I was in second gear with it, past the initial paniclike rush. My head was clear and my hands were steady.

"I went to see Steve Reinish," I said. "The ME's office released Shelley's body after the autopsy this morning, so he can bury her tomorrow."

Jay turned his back to me to take two glasses down from the cupboard over the sink. "Yeah, he explained the autopsy business to me when I went to see him last night," he said over his shoulder. "I didn't know you could *have* an autopsy when you're Orthodox Jewish."

Turn around, I commanded him in my head. *I want to see your face when you're talking to me.*

I said, "They're not Orthodox. They're observant Conservative. Shelley's brother is Orthodox, but he only converted when he was in rabbinical school. If 'convert' is the right word. He's a *Baal T'shuvah*. He *became* Orthodox."

"Whatever," Hollander said. He put his good hand on the kitchen counter, fingers splayed, then bunched his hand into a fist. "I have vodka here; what do you want in it? Orange juice, tomato juice, tonic water?"

"Tonic water." I watched his hand relax and wondered if he were consciously relaxing it. Then I watched him very carefully as he got ice out of the fridge and made the drinks.

He set the drinks on the table and sat down.

"The autopsy results come back?" he asked, poking with his finger at the ice cubes in his glass. His brown eyes came up to mine and locked in.

I pushed my glasses up on my nose. "I don't know," I said. "I was only at the hospital until about noon. Barry and Julie Steinberg came in, and they owed me for covering Monday night, so I left."

He nodded, lifting his glass and taking a long pull of the vodka and orange juice he had poured for himself.

I smoked my cigarette. I couldn't take my eyes off him. My mind was busy disbelieving everything I had ever known about him, starting with all the playful things he had ever done or said to flirt with me, get my attention, bid for my admiration. What was most incredible to me at the moment was the fact that I had actually gone to bed with him. And what a caring, intimate, and passionate lover he'd been. I'd been to bed with a number of men over the years and it had been my experience that most men don't open up fully in bed the first time, or even the second or third time. But Jay had opened up immediately. I'd been able to feel him opening himself to me totally, brilliantly, even before I'd got him out of his sling and his shirt.

My hand went involuntarily to the purple spot on my throat. I was wearing an open-necked shirt under Phil's old sweater, and I pulled at the collar of it.

Jay poked at the ice cubes in his drink with his finger again. He put his finger in his mouth and sucked on it. "I've been thinking about you all day," he said. "I was afraid you wouldn't come see me again."

I stubbed my cigarette out.

"You going to tell Carchiollo?" he asked.

"I did tell him."

He stiffened.

"I'm sorry about yesterday, Jay," I heard myself say, and was astonished. Astonished that I could talk about sex with him, astonished that I had ever even *had* sex with him, astonished that he could possibly believe that this was the reason I was sitting with him in his apartment at this moment: to talk about the fact that we'd had sex.

I found my eyes on Hollander's kitchen drawer, the drawer with the cache of medical junk, and I willed my eyes to look anywhere but there.

"*I'm* not sorry about yesterday," he said bitterly. He stood up. "I'm going to the john. I'll be right back." He turned on his heel. "Unless you want to leave right now," he said as he went out of the room.

I sat frozen at the kitchen table until I heard the bathroom door close, then slowly I got to my feet. I moved silently across the kitchen to the drawer and carefully opened it. I had the sense of moving underwater, and of watching myself with an uncanny attention to detail and an extended sense of time.

When I opened the drawer, the faint but instantly recognizable odor wafted out into the kitchen.

After a moment of search I held in my hand a disposable plastic oxygen mask. Taped across the inside of the mask, so that it would not come directly into contact with the skin of the face, was a gauze pad. The pad had been soaked with ether. Judging from the smell of it, it had been used at least several days ago. The smell was very faint.

But it was there.

Pavelka: *He took china statues.*

I would not have lost, I am strong myself, but he put the plastic thing over my face, with the smell.

"Jesus Christ." My voice came out in a low hiss. I dropped the oxygen mask back in the drawer and rummaged around in the rest of the contents: freebie ball-point pens from the drug companies, a couple of syringes still in their sterile wrappings, a few rolls of adhesive tape, and a box of burette IV tubing.

I shook the box.

It was empty.

I held the box in my hands for several beats, frozen with horror. I was still holding it, in fact, when I heard Hollander come into the kitchen behind me.

"Well, well," he said.

CHAPTER

23

My attention to detail became overwhelming. I looked at Jay Hollander standing in the doorway to the kitchen, wearing a pair of faded jeans and a red silk kimono robe with a gold-and-green dragon stitched over the left breast. He had taken his shirt and sling off and pulled the left sleeve of the robe over his cast. The robe was open, baring his dark-haired chest in all its muscular splendor.

I was dumbfounded by the kimono. I could not for the life of me figure out why he had gone into the bathroom, taken off his shirt and sling, and put on the robe. I was dumbfounded by Jay's bare chest; I could not imagine ever going to bed with him, then, now, or ever again. In fact, I could not imagine sharing any other moment of my life with him, or anyone else for that matter. I was stuck in this moment. It was endless.

Without taking my eyes from his I slowly replaced the empty box of IV tubing in the drawer and closed it by backing up against it. A few ludicrous thoughts sailed across my mind. If I have to hit him, I thought, I'll get something heavy and go for the collarbone of his good arm. The collarbone is easy to break and without it the whole carriage of the shoulder blade collapses. I tried to assess in my mind how far it was to Hollander's front door from where I was standing, and what my chances were of getting to the door and getting it open without offering him the opportunity to jump me. I remembered two things Detective Kelly liked to tell the nurses while regaling them with hairy recitations of his police escapades: *Never turn your back on them* and *You can't run and fight at the same time.*

Every nerve I owned went on full alert.

"I saw Steve this afternoon after you'd been there," Jay said quietly. "You're not the only one around here who knows how to hold your cards to your chest."

His voice scared the shit out of me. It had a quality I couldn't quite grasp, an evenly modulated rationality that belied the situation.

I searched in my throat and found my own voice.

"Shelley's parents are dealers in Oriental art," I said. "She knew the real stuff when she saw it, and she knew you had stolen pieces. You saw her this weekend after Friday night, didn't you? You saw her and she told you she was going to write letters to the police and museum curators about your stolen pieces, didn't she? The robbery at the museum was in the Monday morning *Times*, for Chrissake—with *pictures*. The horse in the bookcase in the foyer and the other one you showed me—the one you said had been to the kitchen and was coming to tell the other pieces on their way to the kitchen to forget it." I took a deep breath. "What in the world did you *show* me those pieces for? Are you out of your mind? Pictures of them were in the fucking *paper*." With horror I heard the words spilling out of my mouth, but I couldn't seem to stop myself.

"Did you show them to Shelley too? And then kill her because she knew what they were, where you'd got them? Was she threatening to go to the police with what she knew? You figured no one would realize she hadn't taken the aspirin herself, because there wouldn't be an autopsy because she was religious? And that

Steve wouldn't come home and find her until late Monday night because he teaches Monday nights? Except that they canceled his course because of the snow and he *did* come home and find her. Lucky for you she was too far gone to save!"

None of this seemed to make a dent in Jay's even, coldly bland expression.

"And you put the IV line into one of the puncture marks she already had from tests or the abortion?"

Hollander put his good hand into the pocket of his robe.

Everything in my chest—heart, lungs, trachea, esophagus, the lot—flew up into the back of my throat. *What does he have in his pocket? His gun? Is he going to shoot me?* The fear mixed with a sense of the ludicrous; there was Dr. James J. Hollander, an intern at University Hospital in New York City, a graduate of Mexico's Universidad Autónoma de Guadalajara, fluent in Japanese and Spanish, standing in his kitchen on a cold February night, wearing a brilliantly embroidered Chinese kimono and looking like a supporting actor for the latest James Bond thriller. With his hand in his pocket. Where there just might be a gun. That he just might shoot me with.

Alex McCabe's voice, in the back of my brain, summed it all up with classic understatement: This is a little hard to assimilate. My heart beat in my ears and it seemed as if my pulse had accelerated to at least a hundred and fifty. Incongruously I remembered that your pulse supposedly hits a hundred and fifty when you go into orgasm. I wondered if death were like orgasm.

He's going to shoot me.

"I'm going to give you a shot of morphine," Jay said, producing from his pocket a syringe and a small vial. "It will put you out for about eight hours, and when you get up in the morning you can tell anyone you want whatever you like."

I watched him uncap the needle and fill the syringe from the vial. The motion was so familiar to me it enabled me to collect my wits somewhat. How many syringes had I myself filled? Thousands. I was sure of it. This silly realization gave me courage, and I started thinking about getting out of there. Front door in the living room. If I could get to it.

Never turn your back on them.

He was advancing toward me with the syringe like a veterinarian toward a skittish horse. My mind was racing through contingency plans. The fire escape was out the window in the bedroom. But I didn't know if Jay had the window nailed shut or barred with safety gates or any of those other things New Yorkers bolt up their windows with. I didn't have time to fuck around with safety gates. Besides, he had those shoji screens on the windows.

It would have to be the front door.

I wondered if Tony Firenze, who lived down the hall, would hear me if I screamed.

"What makes you think I'm going to let you stick me with that?" I asked. "Is that how you got Shelley to let you run the aspirin into her IV? Or did you ether her? You ethered her and left the windows open to get the smell out?"

"I'm not going to kill you, Ev."

"You sweet-talked her into it? Told her you just wanted her to sleep for eight hours, then she could get up and tell anyone she wanted whatever she wanted to?"

The man was invincible. He did not even flinch. He kept coming toward me with the syringe, his body bent into a half-crouch, his good arm held loosely away from his ribs. He looked as if he expected me to leap into the air and execute a series of hits and kicks karate-style; his posture was ready for anything.

Step. Pause. Step. Pause. He knew he would get to

me eventually. What he didn't know was whether or not I would let him stick me, or whether or not he could manage to stick me if I resisted.

I made a quick decision. "All right. Stop. I agree. I'll lie down and you can give me the morphine." Like hell, I thought. "But you can't inject me while I'm standing up. It makes me faint. Seriously. I always faint when I get a needle." I began to pull up my sleeve, making a half-motion in the direction of the doorway, the way one moves when there is a large dog of dubious friendliness present.

"No," he said. "I want to hold your arm. Give me your arm and we'll go into the bedroom together."

He had only one good arm. What could he do to me with the other one while he was holding on to me with the good one? I held out my elbow.

Jay moved his mouth into a smile that wasn't a smile. "That's my girl," he said. He lodged the syringe between the thumb and forefinger of his casted hand. Then, quick as a swooping hawk, he clamped down on my biceps with his good hand and snapped his casted left arm up under my chin. The plaster connected with the force of a tire iron. I went down immediately, smacking my head on the tile floor when I landed.

For a moment, I was very far away. I seemed to come back with extraordinary slowness. He was bending over me. The syringe was in his good hand again. He was going to solve the problem of how to hold me down by throwing himself on top of me; he aimed his weight at me like a wrestler descending on his opponent.

That was his mistake: like a wrestler. I could wrestle too. In a flash I got my feet up into his stomach, just in time to take advantage of his forward thrust and steer him so he landed not on top of me but two or three feet beyond me. I heard one of the kitchen chairs go over, and I was up and running.

Or trying. I ran smack into the doorjamb and fell

down again; hitting my head on the floor had knocked my equilibrium out of whack. I struggled to my feet. The room tilted precariously as I tried to aim myself in the direction of the front door. I pitched headlong over the back of one of the futon sofas.

He was there again.

"Get away from me with that fucking syringe!" I shrieked.

He stood over me, panting slightly. His robe was all askew, the little dragon sagging down near the bottom of his rib cage.

"Tony!" I screamed. *"Firenze! Help!"*

"Yell all you want," Jay said. "There's no one on the floor. They're all on call except me and Firenze, and he went out with his girlfriend. No one will hear you."

He was right. Jay lived on the fourth floor of the doctors' residence. The third and fifth floors were office suites. It was doubtful whether anyone on the second or sixth floor would be able to hear me yelling. But I decided to give it a try. *"Firenze!"* I screamed as loudly as I could, forgiving him for ever having thrown me up against the wall. *"He's trying to kill me!"*

Jay lunged for me. I kicked him in the kneecap, buying enough time to scramble to my feet again. My head was clearing. We grappled with one another, falling against the bookcase next to the front door. The little porcelain horse in the bookcase toppled over and the Oriental vase next to it shook. With his good hand Jay pawed at my neck, trying to get me in a carotid hold and cut off the blood supply to my brain.

With his casted hand he was groping with some difficulty for something in the bookcase. Out of the corner of my eye I caught a glimpse of something black and metallic.

I heard a door opening and closing down the hall and Tony Firenze's tenuous voice: "Hello?"

I hit Jay over the head with his goddamned vase,

museum piece or no museum piece, shattering the vase, and made it out the front door. *"Tony! He's trying to kill me! He has a gun!"*

Tony Firenze stood in the hallway, watching me fly at him like a bat out of hell. He was wearing pajamas and a plaid wool bathrobe and was in his bare feet, making me wonder if I were the only full-dressed person in the world.

Jay came out of his apartment.

Things happened very quickly then. Tony had obviously been sleeping and was a little slow in the thinking department. With my adrenaline-sharpened mind I could see him trying to put together what the hell the commotion was all about, and the conclusions he was coming to might as well have been displayed across his forehead by digital readout: that Jay and I must be having an affair of sorts, that we were obviously having a fight of some kind, a lovers' spat that probably didn't need his intervention, and that my mention of a gun was probably a hysterical exaggeration. Tony could see the wild-eyed expression on my face and I guess he wanted to get a look at Jay, but I was in the way, so Tony stepped sideways to get a clear line of vision.

Jay shot him.

I screamed. Tony's body slammed back against the door of his apartment and slid to the floor. I couldn't see where he'd been shot and I didn't know if he was alive or dead, but I wasn't about to stand there and find out. I threw myself through the fire door into the stairwell and catapulted down the stairs. I was so scattered I ran right past the second-floor landing and down into the tunnel to the hospital, remembering only too late that the first-floor door had been locked when McCabe had wheeled Shelley home on the stretcher the previous Friday night.

Upstairs I heard the fire door bang open, the metallic sound echoing up and down the stairwell. Then footsteps clattering down.

Gasping for breath, I bolted through the tunnel toward the hospital. I still had part of the broken vase in my hand and I was clenching it so hard I cut my palm. I put it in my back pocket as I ran. Behind me the running footsteps got to the bottom of the stairs in no time at all and came after me. I remembered with near-panic what an athlete Jay was, always out running with the rabbi or going to the gym. My breath began to wheeze in and out in whimpers.

In another fifty yards or so I would make it to the hospital basement. This presented several immediate problems, all of which boiled down to where I wanted to go. The underground tunnel came out in a warren of laboratories occupied by the Nuclear Medicine Department. It was after midnight and no one was ever in the labs after eight or nine P.M. The staircase that went upstairs from Nuclear Medicine went up two flights before it opened into the hospital proper, and it opened onto a corridor containing the gift shop and the volunteers' office—another area of the hospital that was deserted after eight P.M. Around the other side of the gift shop there was a hall which would bring me into a patient area where I knew there were nurses awake and on duty. The problem was getting to the nurses before Hollander got to me. I could hear his footsteps echoing down the tunnel behind me and I was sure I could not run up two flights of stairs without being overtaken.

I went around a corner in the tunnel and burst through the doors by Nuclear Medicine. As I had feared, all the glass doors to the lab were dark. My chest was beginning to ache; each breath felt like fire as it went in and out. I tore down the hall to the stairs. There was no place else to go.

The door swung open behind me with a crack as it hit the wall.

The noise the gun made when it discharged was

deafening. The glass of a door at the end of the hall shattered, throwing glass in all directions. I scrambled around the last corner, took one look at the stairs, and realized I would never make it, and threw myself out through the heavy fire-escape door.

For a split second I didn't know where I was. It was snowing again and there were no lights in the courtyard. But to my left I saw a gateway to the street beyond, a gate that was open, and I made for it. Hollander came out behind me and shouted something that I didn't understand. I kept on running until I was through the gate and onto the street, hunching my shoulders down, in an absolute panic that he was going to take another shot at me.

Then I saw where I was and how stupid I had been.

I had come out on the east side of the hospital, the side that faces Morningside Park. South of me was the Jefferson Pavilion, a building of laboratories deserted at night, and below that, the back wall of the huge Episcopal cathedral complex that stretched for several blocks south of the hospital. North of me was a Catholic church, and beyond that, buildings that belonged to the university. I was at least four blocks in either direction from civilization and other people. If I wanted to get back into the hospital I would have to run clear around to the Amsterdam Avenue side.

My legs were giving out, and my feet were sliding this way and that in the snow. The snow that had fallen the other night had melted and refrozen and was now covered with a layer of new snow, and I was wearing running shoes.

Like a complete fool, I ran straight into a mountain of snow the snowplows had plowed up, thinking I would climb over it to the other side and go over the wall into the park.

The gun went off again and I went down.

I remember getting unsteadily to my feet. Everything was in slow motion. Then I went down again, and I went down further than the sidewalk under me. I went down and down and down into unconsciousness.

CHAPTER

24

I was asleep. In a place I had never slept in before. It was very far away from anyplace I had ever been. I struggled to open my eyes.

I was lying facedown in the snow, sprawled in a drift piled up by the snowplows. As my mind came back I reached into my back pocket for the rim of the vase I had broken over Jay's head. It was the only weapon I had.

But I was moving too slowly.

Silk fluttered against my cheek. An apparition was looming over me, in a flowing red robe. Hands turned me over onto my back.

"I'm sorry, Ev," Hollander said. He fumbled with the sleeve of my sweater, bunching it up over my elbow.

I felt the prick and then the burn of the needle.

I opened my eyes and focused on Jay Hollander's face.

"You son of a bitch," I mumbled. The words didn't come out quite clearly—"You sumbish" or something like that. But I managed to lift my arm up and I raked the shard of pottery across Jay's jaw making a deep cut. His face, which was already bleeding from where I'd hit him before, poured blood. As he cried out and jerked his head back, the blood from his wounds spattered from his face to mine.

He hit me, a resounding blow to the side of the head with his fist. At the same time his fist connected, the morphine hit my brain like clouds rolling in. My eyes went out of focus and I could no longer see him, or anything else for that matter.

Then he was gone, without another word, and I was lying in the snow, drifting pleasantly.

I knew I would have to stay awake. If I let myself go to sleep I would freeze to death before anyone found me. Very, very slowly I began to go about the business of sitting up. I pulled my elbows in against my ribs, then engineered my arms so my hands were where my elbows had been, and I pushed up. It didn't work at first, but on the third or fourth try I managed it. I had the impression that it took me a very long time to sit up and that I had forgotten what I was doing and what I was trying to do at least five times while I was trying to do it. The whole task was very confusing. When I was finally sitting up I remembered hazily that I had been shot, and I worked my hands up under my shirt and sweater and ran them over my back, searching with my fingertips for the bullet wound. I didn't find one. All right, no bullet hole. Not shot viscerally or in the lungs. So where was I shot? Or hadn't I been hit? Had I slipped and fallen at the moment Hollander fired, and had he missed me? This series of questions seemed to have large philosophical implications for my muddled mind, none of which I could even begin to deal with at the present time. Not shot. That was the important part.

I spent a while thinking about my feet and where they were. In order to find them, I had to go on a mental reconnaissance tour down my legs and past my knees to my ankles. I was halfway up on one leg. Then I was halfway up on the other. Then I seemed to be on my feet, God knows how, slanting sideways at a rakish angle.

I realized I was giggling, or crying, or maybe both. I

took an unsteady step forward and fell headlong into the snowbank.

Maybe you want to walk the other way the next time, toward the hospital, I told myself. Now, let's see if we can get up again. One . . . two . . . *three* . . .

Take two: face the hospital. Pick up one foot . . .

I was flat on my face again. It began to dawn on me that there might be something wrong with one of my legs. I sat up again—I was getting good at this—and carefully ran my fingers down my left leg from thigh to ankle. Left leg seemed intact. I repeated the process on my right leg. When I got to the knee I discovered there was a small hole in my pants leg. Hollander had shot me in the back of the knee.

The discovery didn't upset me. It is probable that *nothing* would have been capable of upsetting me at the time, I was so blissed out on the morphine. Nor did I have any pain; the morphine took care of that, as well. But it did occur to me that this might be why I had fallen down the two times I had stood up, and that maybe I shouldn't try to stand up anymore. I got to my hands and one knee and crawled across the street in the direction of the hospital, dragging my wounded leg.

Bury me at Wounded Knee, I thought blearily. No. Scratch that. Let's not get morbid.

I crawled through the gate to the hospital courtyard, and then I crawled up to the door. I had to stand to open the door—or I thought I did, at any rate—the door was actually ajar, and when I pushed against it, it swung in, and I fell in after it. Then I started crawling again. One hand forward. The other hand forward. Good knee forward. I began to repeat this sequence in my mind, like the refrain of a very long song, that song and dance you do at weddings, what was it called? *"The Hokey-pokey";* Put your right hand forward, then put your left hand forward . . .

I found this so funny I collapsed and laughed about it for a while.

I decided being on morphine was like being very, very drunk. Smashed. Stoned out of your gourd. I got up on my hands and knee and somehow made it to the stairs. Then I somehow made it to the *top* of the stairs, much to my astonishment. I think I did this by sitting on the stairs and backing my ass up one step at a time. I wasn't sure. I could have flown, for all I knew, I certainly seemed to be flying. Flying high.

Eventually I seemed to be looking a teddy bear straight in the eyes. And what the hell was that? A turkey? Jesus Christ, where was I? I realized very slowly that I was looking at a row of stuffed animals in the gift-shop window. I found this very funny too. It began to dawn on me that the unusual gasping noise I was listening to was the sound of my own hysterical laughter ricocheting off the walls of the deserted hospital corridor.

It was a lifetime before I came out into the patient area. It took the last of my drunken energy to fall through the swinging doors, and I think I went to sleep. I seemed to have been lying there for a while by the time they started shaking me.

"They" was, of all people, Phil. I opened my mouth and said, "Hello, sweetheart," and dissolved into giggles. The giggling wasn't all morphine. Most of it was the sweetest, most refreshing sense of relief I had ever experienced in my entire life.

Phil, of course, was not giggling. He was trying to get me to tell him what was going on, what had happened. "Ev! What happened to you? Are you *bleeding?*" He wiped at my face with his hands, at Hollander's caked blood on my cheek.

I pushed his hands away. "Give me some Narcan," I said. I had trouble getting my mouth around the word. "Narcan."

"Narcan?" Phil asked. "Ev, what's going on? Are you hurt? Have you been drinking?"

This was too much for me. I started to cry. *"Narcan,"* I pleaded. "Please. Phil."

"Get me an amp of Narcan," Phil said to one of the nurses. By this time there were lots of nurses' feet, all seemingly right in front of my nose. One pair of feet left and returned.

I felt the needle go in, and all the clouds blew away.

And then my right leg screamed, all by itself. The scream went up my body and out of my mouth.

The last of my strength went out of me with the scream. I felt myself began to drift into unconsciousness, and there didn't seem to be too much I could do about it. I heard Phil talking to me, but I no longer knew what he was saying. I did hear someone calling, very clearly, for a stretcher. I felt hands going over me, up and down my chest and back, under my shirt, over my arms. I said, "I'm shot in the leg." My voice was slurred, but they seemed to understand. They were taking me out of my pants, and I was drifting.

Phil said, "For God's sake, Ev, *who did this to you?"*

I tried to talk. "Holl'm'r," I managed to get out.

"Who?"

Someone said, "It's the right knee."

"Exit wound?"

"No, posterior entry only."

I wanted to go to sleep. When they lifted me to the stretcher, my leg screamed again, and screamed and screamed. Sleep was impossible. I did the next best thing.

I fainted.

There were a lot of lights, all of them too bright. I wanted to sleep forever. I did not have a sensation of being cold, but how cold I was caused a sensation in the emergency room; there were conversations about my body temperature and I was wrapped in blankets to raise it. I debated whether to try to wake up or sleep through it all. It was hard to tell if I was thinking about sleeping or dreaming about waking up; it was hard to tell about a lot of things. I think I eventually chose sleep. Or maybe I didn't choose it. But that's what I did.

They wanted me to wake up; they were afraid I had concussed myself. They kept asking me, "Ev, do you remember hitting your head? You have marked contusions around your left eye. Did someone hit you?"

I couldn't remember.

I imagined the faces of detectives looming in front of my own face and eventually I imagined them clearly enough to discern Detectives Ost and Kelly, but I couldn't quite get my mind out of the realm of imagination to reality. I floated off again.

When I was warmer, I found it easier to be conscious. I also found it easier to remember. "Firenze," I said. "How's Firenze?"

"He's O.K. He took one shot in the lower-right quadrant. He's up in the OR."

"Who's cutting?"

"Attenborough."

I wanted to ask who found him, but I didn't have the energy. "Hollander," I said.

Phil was holding my hand. He leaned over and kissed me on the forehead.

"Later," he said.

Eventually they operated my leg, when they had decided I probably wasn't concussed. They shook me out of the anesthesia afterward and I sat up and vomited into a basin they held for me. Then I was awake. I felt as if it were the first time I had been awake in days.

Phil and Alex McCabe were there. I was in a room,

not in Recovery as I thought I was. I realized that they had already moved me from Recovery.

"What time is it?" I asked.

"A little past noon. How do you feel?"

"More or less."

They smiled. A nurse came in and gave me a cup of hot tea with lemon and sugar. I sipped at it. It was wonderful.

"Is Firenze O.K.?"

"He's in Recovery. They resected his ascending colon. He'll be fine."

I nodded and sipped my tea.

"Hollander?"

"A long story," Alex said. "But maybe I can make it short. Kelly and Ost talked to Firenze. Luckily, Firenze's girlfriend was with him at the time, and she called the cops. A whole battalion of them responded to the scene, and they nabbed Hollander outside the hospital, running around in his bathrobe with blood all over himself. Kelly and Ost wanted us to call them as soon as you were awake."

"They got him?"

"They got him." Alex took my hand and kissed it, then held it against his cheek.

" 'Oh that I were a glove upon that hand, that I might touch that cheek,' " I quoted, trying to find myself. I put a hand to my own cheek, wondering if I still had Hollander's blood on it. Probably not; one of the nurses undoubtedly had swabbed it off with an alcohol wipe. I shuddered.

Both men groaned at the Shakespeare. "She's awake," Alex said. He let go of my hand.

"Tell me," I said.

The two men looked at one another.

"There's no deterring her when her mind is focused," Phil said. "O.K., here it is. You know that officer who's always in the ER with the looniest of the loonies? The one who always, for some reason, happens along when some guy is exposing himself to little old ladies on Riverside Drive or taking a crap right in the middle of the floor in the supermarket or some such thing?"

"Officer Haddad," Alex added helpfully, appropriating the narrative. "The one who doesn't say much but rolls his eyes a lot." He paused dramatically, then launched himself. "It is a dark and snowy night. Along comes Officer Haddad, our fearless representative of NYPD. He's walking past the hospital on a Hundred Fourteenth Street, mosying along over to Morningside Drive, and here comes Hollander from the opposite direction, out for a stroll in his bathrobe. With the snow coming down. And blood pouring out of about five different places on his face. Haddad says, 'Why, Dr. Hollander! What happened? You're bleeding! Let me help you into the ER here!' And Hollander punches him in the face."

"You're forgetting the part where Haddad rolls his eyes," Phil said drolly.

"That comes later," Alex countered. "A little patience on your part, Phil, might help the story along a bit. You're spoiling the mood."

"C'mon, Alex. Ev is just coming out of the anesthesia here."

Alex peered at me. "You don't have to throw up again, do you?"

"I don't think so," I said.

Phil made an annoyed sound in his throat.

I patted Phil's hand, which was next to mine on the bed. He jumped at my touch, and I realized how upset he was. I became strangely wide-awake in an instant, and I wondered why I wasn't more upset myself. I knew McCabe well enough to know that a flip attitude and sharp wit were his usual cover-up for tension. He was upset; Phil was upset; and I was not. It hasn't sunk in with me yet, I thought.

"Carry on," I said.

"Well, the punch in the face raises Officer Haddad's suspicions," Alex continued. "It in fact makes him *very* suspicious. Haddad considers his own personal history of encounters with code-P-type individuals, persons in need of psychiatric evaluation, and he resigns himself to the idea that Hollander, too, needs psychiatric evaluation. Haddad might have let it pass except for the fact that Hollander was bleeding buckets all over himself. Haddad decides that the situation requires him, Haddad, to bodily remove the obviously distraught Dr. Hollander to the ER for surgical attention to his wounds and psychiatric evaluation of the stressful results of an apparent mugging."

"*I'm* going to throw up," Phil said, "even if Ev doesn't."

"I assure you, you will not throw up. The first time you heard all this, you didn't throw up."

"The first time I heard all this was without your editorializing." Phil waved his hand in the air. "Knock it off, McCabe. Hollander shot Firenze and Ev, and if I understand the detectives right, he probably *killed* Shelley. This is nothing to joke about."

"Phil, he's letting off steam," I said. I was still curiously divorced from my emotions. But I did have the sense of growing tired, and I wanted to finish my tea and go back to sleep, Hollander or no Hollander. And maybe when I woke up again I'd feel something. "Let's get to the end of the story."

McCabe went on, "So Haddad hauls Hollander's ass into the hospital, and there's Firenze and his girlfriend and the rest of the cops. And Firenze's girlfriend gets up and starts screaming like it's the *Perry Mason* show: 'It's him! It's him! That's the man who shot him!' "

There was a brief silence while I tried to digest this.

Then Alex coughed and said, "Phil's right. It's nothing to joke about. I apologize. But Haddad did say he sees crazies all the time, and Hollander seemed like another crazy, one who was bleeding, and so he brought him in."

I shook my head at the apology. "It's O.K.," I said. I was remembering something. "I have one question," I said. "Where the hell did you go after you defrosted my fridge, Phil? The night Shelley died."

Phil blinked. Then he laughed, despite the sobriety of the moment. "God, what a mind you have." He tilted his head to the side, smiled, and sat there looking at me for a moment. His longish blond hair fell across his forehead and he reached up a hand and pushed it back. "This is going to sound like a real anticlimax. Bear with me. You went to the hospital and I was going to go upstairs and call Beth, remember?"

"Lordy, Lordy," Alex said, making an attempt to regain his customary glibness. He was not altogether successful; I could see him blinking back tears, which I imagined were tears of friendship and relief, and I was touched. "Shall I leave?" he asked. "I think I will leave. I'll go call the detectives." He leaned over and kissed me on the forehead. " 'Parting is such sweet sorrow, that I shall say good night, till it be morrow.' "

"I think I will throw up after all," Phil said. "That's the balcony scene in *Romeo and Juliet,* right? Do me a favor and don't start with the rest of it."

Alex leaned over and gave me a kiss. Then he got up from his chair and went out the door.

"Move over," Phil said to me when Alex had gone.

"Jesus, Phil, what will people think?" I teased as he lay down next to me, sliding his arm under my neck. "Watch the IV."

"Yes, Doctor." He held me a moment, nestling my head against his shoulder. "So you want to know where I went Monday night."

"It would be nice."

"I decided I would call Beth at two A.M. our time, about the time she should be getting up in London. I defrosted your fridge. Ev. I can't believe what you had in there; do you know there was leftover beef burgundy from the Saturday night in December you cooked that for your brother Craig and his girlfriend? Not in the freezer part, either. Jesus. Anyway, then I went up to my apartment and called Beth. Her roommate was surprised to hear it was me. Turns out Beth is in New York. I should have known something was up then, but I didn't. Classical case of denial, I guess. So I called Beth's sister and got a grand reception of dead silence. She said Beth wasn't there, but she would have Beth call me. I'm making this story way too long. The upshot is that Beth called me back, we met at my office—there's a fucking blizzard out, but she wants to see me at my office—and it turns out she's getting married to Nicko. So . . ." He trailed off.

"Oh," I said. I didn't know what else to say. I drank the rest of my tea and put the empty Styrofoam cup on the bedstand.

"Well, it was a shock," he went on. He took his glasses off, held the lenses up to the light and peered at them, then put them back on again. "I decided I needed to take the day off and think things through. I should say, take the night off. The electricity went off and I lit Gina's candelabrum and I sat there at my desk all night, thinking. I made a pot of coffee on the coffeemaker and looked out the window at the snow coming down." Phil began to talk more slowly. "I decided that I had been using Beth as a wedge to not make a commitment to you and I had been using you as a wedge to not make a commitment to Beth, and that I had to start thinking about commitment and why it was so threatening to me." He stopped. "We can talk about this later," he said. He looked embarrassed and waved a hand at my leg. "You're hurt, and you've just come out of the OR, and you've had this terrible experience. God. I can't believe he *shot* you." He put his other arm around me and held me against himself. "I could have lost you. The bastard could have *killed* you."

I didn't say anything. I could feel him being there for me, and I was so relieved to have him next to me, have his arms around me, that nothing else seemed to matter.

After a while he said, "I'm terrified, Ev. I do love you, but I'm not very good at this relationship business."

"You're fine," I said.

I went to sleep on his shoulder. When I woke he was gone, and there were a half-dozen red roses in a vase on the table next to the bed.

CHAPTER

25

It was Saturday morning.

Phil was talking to one of his shrink friends on the telephone and I was lying on his couch, dozing under one of Phil's soft Mexican blankets, my injured knee propped up on a pillow.

The shrink friend was having a problem with her boyfriend.

Phil said, "I don't think you can work this conflict out intellectually. He needs the emotional experience that you are not going to make those demands on him. He needs to experience it *emotionally* that there's a woman he can trust about that." Pause. "No, the emotional experience of resolving the conflict, not intellectual discussion *about* the conflict." Pause. "Yes, but that's *your* need. That's not *his* need. Don't let yourself get into the position of being the mommy-analyst. That's destructive and addictive behavior for you. Besides which, that kind of thing interferes with the sex."

I thought: Shrinks make everything very complicated.

But I smiled affectionately at Phil from underneath the Mexican blanket. I had the blanket pulled up to my nose, and I felt warm and secure and cuddled by the blanket. I felt warm and secure and cuddled by Phil too, listening to his voice on the phone with his friend.

Then Phil said, "You're telling me. It's been pretty damn hectic here. The guy—Jay Hollander, one of the interns here—has apparently been burgling museums and Madison Avenue art shops for years. They found a whole cache of stolen porcelains in his apartment." Pause. "No, little figurines, mostly Chinese stuff from the seventeenth century or something, I forget. Anyway, he hid in the Museum of Natural History after it closed and stole three pieces on Saturday night. He whopped the guard over the head and ethered him, then went down two flights on a rope out the window. They found the rope still hanging there the next morning. It was in the *Times* on Monday." Pause. "Yeah, can you believe this?" Longer pause. "Well, the cops aren't talking to us. We're reading it all in the newspaper like everyone else. Shelley Reinish—the surgeon he murdered—apparently threatened to turn him in to the police. Her parents are dealers in Oriental antiquities, and she saw something he'd stolen and confronted him, and he killed her. He went over to the emergency room at the hospital and got a couple of bags of intravenous solution, then knocked her out with ether, dissolved enough aspirin to kill a horse, and ran it into her IV."

I pulled the blanket over my head.

Phil went on, "Well, you know Ev—she's very action-oriented and confrontational, and she calls a spade a spade. When they found the museum guard Hollander ethered, they brought him into the ER at University, and Ev saw him, and Ev knows Hollander"—slight change in vocal tone here—"and she put it all together, and on Wednesday night she went to see Hollander and confronted him."

I took the blanket off my face. "How about some theme music in the background?" I asked testily. "Maybe the music from *Dragnet*."

Phil looked up, met my eyes. "Yeah, he *shot* her. Can you believe it? He shot her in the leg. Luckily it was only .22-caliber. They think she'll be back on her feet in another week or so. He shot another one of the surgeons too—Tony Firenze. Tony took the bullet in the gut and had to have his colon resected, and he's going to have a colostomy bag for a while, but he'll be O.K. We've been very lucky here, all things considered. Except for Shelley."

"Phil," I said.

"Ev's getting restless," he said. "I gotta go."

"I don't think 'restless,' is the word," I said with some annoyance after Phil had hung up. "It bothers me to hear you talk about all that like this."

"I'm sorry. Am I being insensitive?"

There was a pause, then both of us said in unison, "Can you say more about that?"

The laughter that followed was nice. Phil got up from his chair and came over and knelt on the floor next to the couch, putting his arms around me. "I know you're working through all this, Ev," he said. "And I'm sorry if I'm being insensitive. It's hard for me to know what you're thinking and feeling about it if you don't tell me." He nuzzled my hair.

I moved my leg, swathed in bandages and propped up on the pillow. "Working through" seemed inadequate to the task. Too organized; too deliberate; too intellectually oriented. ' 'Working through" did not, for example, encompass the rubbery smell. Every time I put a hand up to my face to push the hair out of my eyes or fix my glasses on my nose, my head filled up with the rubbery smell of the handgrips on my crutches. The smell displaced me somehow, sent me into a vacuum of thought where I didn't know where I was. "Working through" did not help me when I woke up in the middle of the night, frightened because I didn't know why I had awakened. Only when I turned over to go back to sleep and moved my leg the wrong way and the pain throbbed out of my mangled kneecap would I realize that the pain had awakened me in the first place.

There didn't seem to be much I could do to "work through" these things; they just happened, they were *there*. The rubbery smell. The pain in the night. The visions of Shelley that stopped and started and stopped again like movie film breaking in the middle of scenes and being spliced back together again. The nightmares about Hollander; Hollander making love to me and then strangling me while he did it; Hollander chasing me, Hollander shooting at me.

I would get up in the morning and say to Phil, "I had another dream about Hollander last night, and Shelley was in it, and he was chasing us, but then I got lost and didn't know where either of them was anymore," and Phil would hold me and say kindly, "Yes, you're working through all that." And I would think: No, I'm not, you're missing the point. But then I could never figure out exactly what he was missing, and after a while I began to think that he was right.

Alex McCabe called it "rehashing."

"It's hard for me to talk about it," I said to Phil at length.

"Move over so I can lie next to you," he said.

I moved and he lay down, holding my head against his chest.

"I feel . . ." I said slowly, "I feel as if the whole experience has opened up this tremendous gulf between me and other people, and . . . that people are fascinated with the sensationalism of it. Everyone seems to want to participate vicariously, they want to have been me running down the corridor to the hospital with Hollander chasing me. I feel, when I talk about it, as if I feed something in them, a kind of lust for violence or something. And I don't want to feed them that. And I don't want you to be proud of me and feed it to them on the phone on my behalf. I can't listen to you talk to your friends about it if I think that's what's going on." This last bit came out in a rush.

I could hear Phil thinking. Then he began to kiss me, and take us gently out of our clothes. We made love very quietly on the couch, and when I held him to me after his last thrusting had stopped, I began to cry.

"Cry all you want," he said.

And I did. I cried for what seemed to me to be a long time. Phil readjusted his position on the couch so he could lie next to me, and he held me while I cried.

When I was able to talk again I said, "There's something I have to ask you."

"Ask me anything you want." He pulled the Mexican blanket up and tucked it around us, snuggling up.

"Did you ever sleep with Shelley?"

He stiffened. His arm was under my neck and cheek, and I could feel the muscles bunch up in it.

"I have to know," I said.

"I can't believe you're asking me this, Ev," he said at length. "No. I have never slept with a patient. It's unprofessional." He leaned over me to reach for his glasses on the floor, then disentangled himself from my embrace and sat up. "I couldn't bring myself to do it, no matter how I felt about the woman, if she was my patient."

This was a good answer, and I believed him. I believed him and I was relieved. But somehow just that moment believing him wasn't enough; I wanted an explanation for his behavior. "Well, what were you doing taking her to have an abortion?" I asked. "That's not exactly within the realm of a professional relationship, is it?"

He shook his head.

"I'm trying to understand," I said. "I need to understand what was going on between the two of you, why you were in her on-call room smoking cigarettes and washing your face in the bathroom. And why there was all this secrecy."

"Of course there was secrecy," he said. He was looking off into the middle distance, at something I couldn't see, his eyes unfocused. "She didn't want her husband to know she was having an abortion. But you're right. My behavior was unprofessional. And I saw that at the time. But I didn't know what else to do, Ev. There was no one else she wanted to tell, and she was incredibly stressed. And I was her friend.

"Maybe that was the problem," he said, reaching for his cigarettes. "I was her friend. I never should have agreed to see her professionally in a therapeutic setting when I knew her and she was my friend and we had to work together." He lit up and laughed ironically. "I'm never going to do that again—see a friend as a patient. I'll tell you that right now."

I waited.

"I admit that I had those feelings for her," he went on. "Sexual feelings. But that's part of the counter-transference. The patient initiates a drama about sex in order to pick a fight with the therapist. Almost any therapy eventually reaches the point where the patient says, 'Admit it! You don't find me attractive!' Or 'Admit it! You don't like me!' Well, of course the therapist doesn't say, 'Of course I like you!' or 'Of course I find you attractive!' The therapist may have the hots for the patient so bad he can barely contain himself, but that's something the therapist has to work through."

"So what are you telling me? That going with Shelley to have her abortion was a way for you to work through your attraction to her? Phil, if I hear 'work through' one more time from you, I'm going to throw up!"

"Well, I'm sorry," he said defensively. "That *is* what I'm going to say about it. Maybe it wasn't a good judgment call on my part, but the issue is intimacy, and the resistance the patient has to intimacy mixed up with the drive *for* intimacy—"

"What kind of way is that to work through intimacy, taking a patient to have an abortion?"

"Well, you asked!" he shouted. He leapt up from the couch and stomped across the room, stark naked, stubbing his cigarette out in the ashtray on the coffee table. He stomped around for a while, then turned to face me, waving his arms and looking like all hell was about to break loose with him.

Then he got a grip on himself. I could see him doing it, bending his emotions back so he could get a good look at them. It was, after all, what I was asking him to do: look at his emotions and tell me what they were and what he thought of them.

I hated his ability to do it, but I loved him for it.

He squared himself in front of me and said quietly, "O.K. It wasn't a good idea for me to go with her to have her abortion. I was trying to work the counter-transference through. And I botched it. I didn't work it through. I acted it out.

"But she was my friend and she asked me to go with her and I went. I never slept with her. I never even kissed her."

He looked me directly in the eye. "And I want you to know that," he said.

Sometime later Alex McCabe came in. "Hey, Peg-leg," he greeted me, ruffling my hair.

Phil and I were dressed again by then, and I had washed my face, and Phil had calmed down. We were sitting on the couch having tea and coffee.

"I bring you tidings," Alex said, sitting down on the hassock. "The latest from Detectives Kelly and Ost."

"They talked to you?" Phil marveled. "They won't talk to *us.*"

"They talked to Steve Reinish and Reinish talked to me. Shelley has made you executor of her book, Ev."

I put my teacup down on the coffee table.

"The cops went round to talk to Shelley's typist,"

Alex went on. "The typist says she had a letter from Shelley saying that if anything happens to Shelley before the book is completely finished, you're to work with the typist and the editors at the publisher's to see that it comes out all right."

I didn't say anything. I had the same vision of Shelley I'd had in the ER when she died: I saw myself reaching out an arm to help her in the locker room after we'd gone swimming together. I thought about sitting with Shelley in her apartment, going over the manuscript together, our feet on the coffee table. I thought about walking in the snow and wondering how to mourn for her. I had the funny sensation that Shelley was in the room with me, her feet on the coffee table, and that Phil and Alex were not.

And then I knew.

Working through.

I knew at last how to mourn for her.

About the Author

LEAH RUTH ROBINSON was an Emergency Medical Technician and has served at St. Luke's Hospital. She lives in New York City.